PRAISE FOR *TH*

"Pane writes with such energy and wit ... gets blown away, zapped, caught up in a zany, madcap adventure full of nuclear experiments... This book reminded me of Connie Willis, Charles Yu, or Douglas Adams: sci-fi with heart and smarts—and humor."

—AMBER SPARKS, AUTHOR OF *THE UNFINISHED WORLD* AND *MAY WE SHED THESE HUMAN BODIES*

"Wading in the territories where quantum physics meets the human predicament, Salvatore Pane has created a multiverse where every parallel reality in which he has written this novel will make you laugh and cry. The remaining universes are probably evil or apocalyptic and aren't worth visiting. *The Theory of Almost Everything* hooked the sci-fi fanboy in me with wormholes and secret labs but pulled me through its pages by my heart. Told with wit and insight, this novel will have you embracing all of the possibilities of who you are and who you could have been."

—SEQUOIA NAGAMATSU, AUTHOR OF *WHERE WE GO WHEN ALL WE WERE IS GONE*

PRAISE FOR *LAST CALL IN THE CITY OF BRIDGES*:

"Quite obviously, Salvatore Pane's mind has been dunked in video games, social media, comic books, the WebNet, and everything else our august literary authorities believe promote illiteracy. I'd like to hand the authorities Pane's novel—a funny, moving, melancholy, sad, and immensely literate book about what being young and confused feels like these days—and tell them, 'See? Things are going to be fine!' "

—TOM BISSELL,
AUTHOR OF *EXTRA LIVES: WHY VIDEO GAMES MATTER*

"Like the comic book heroes he obsesses over, Michael Bishop has an origin story, the story of the first wound that makes his powers necessary—and in *Last Call in the City of Bridges*, Michael at last faces into that tragedy, resurfacing suddenly at the mid-point of his twenties, those years of snark and expectation spent proofreading DVD subtitles, drinking literature-themed cocktails, and pining over preacher's daughters and college crushes. In this witty and charming debut, Salvatore Pane reminds us that while you can't retcon your past, you can perhaps learn to live up to its responsibilities, by using your powers not necessarily to save the ones you love from loss, but to care for those left behind in its wake."

—MATT BELL, AUTHOR OF *IN THE HOUSE UPON THE DIRT BETWEEN THE LAKE AND THE WOODS* AND *SCRAPPER*

The Theory of Almost Everything

THE THEORY OF ALMOST EVERYTHING

A NOVEL BY

SALVATORE PANE

Printed in the United States of America
10 9 8 7 6 5 4 3 2 1

FIRST EDITION, December 2018

ISBN 10: 1-7328956-1-4
ISBN 13: 978-1-7328956-1-4

Book design by Savannah Adams
Cover photo by Patryk Grądys, Unsplash

Braddock Avenue Books
P.O. Box 502
Braddock, PA 15104

www.braddockavenuebooks.com

Braddock Avenue Books is distributed by Small Press Distribution.

To Theresa

“The mind reels when we realize that, according to this interpretation of quantum mechanics, all possible worlds coexist with us. Although wormholes might be necessary to reach such alternate worlds, these quantum realities exist in the very same room that we live in. They coexist with us wherever we go.”

Michio Kaku

Parallel Worlds: A Journey Through Creation, Higher Dimensions, and the Future of the Cosmos

“The shortest space between us is a cooperative heaven. And I will dare reaching into the universe and its sly belly as long as you are on the other side. ”

Jason McCall

“Wormhole”

THE THEORY OF ALMOST EVERYTHING

A NOVEL

THE NOSTALGIC, THE FUTURIST, AND THE GHOST

My journey to parallel realities, a secret laboratory hidden beneath the red mountains of New Mexico, and even the end of the world itself, began with a lonely glass of bourbon in the saddest bar in Indianapolis. I'd ventured to that glittering city rising up from the cornfields to hustle and glad-hand at the ASA, the most prestigious gathering of scientists in the academic and corporate research worlds. Yet how odd it was to sit at the hotel bar and gaze upon the glum faces of our aging luminaries. Gaggles of graybeard professors laughed with Young Turk colleagues over rounds of scotch.

Women in tailored pantsuits checked and rechecked their notes for the final hour of presentations. These were my supposed kinsmen, the anointed champions of knowledge, but I felt a curious detachment in my heart. I was a scant two weeks away from the end of my postdoc, an endeavor slightly removed from my chosen field of cosmology, a rogue and esoteric strand of theoretical physics. The conference should have been a final hurrah, a last ditch effort to decide what new course my life would take when my self-imposed Alaskan exile at last drew to a close. I sipped my Eagle Rare and reassured myself that I had really tried, that I'd attended panel after panel about transitioning into the professoriate, pure research, corporate research, and felt no tingling of excitement, no stirrings of joy. I couldn't envision myself in any kind of future, and the truth gaining shape and weight in my bones was that I didn't care about the practical uses of my degree or talents. I yearned to slip back into the embarrassing sci-fi novels of my youth, the terrible covers and overwrought prose that made me feel as if my life was barreling toward some strange and futuristic destiny, that one fine day I'd wake up in a subterranean landscape overflowing with peculiar geniuses and infinite possibilities. It was a boyish impulse I should have long outgrown, but what I really wanted was to continue my impractical research on Einstein-Rosen bridges and the cosmological Multiverse, the scattershot chance that somewhere, beyond our stars and sour reality, there existed an alternate version of me, a better Teddy Copeland, truer, kinder, unburdened by his multitude failings and tragedies, a Teddy Copeland Prime.

As I ordered my second bourbon, a woman sat down two stools over. She was young and black, and she too sported the ASA badge branding us as the only conference attendees who had opted for the bar over the humming web of networking scientists beyond. I was comforted by her youth, that we were contemporaries amid a sea of the middle-aged. Her glasses were too large for her face—her bangs grazed the upper rim of plastic—and forgive me for noting this, but beneath her blazer and t-shirt my contemporary was slightly plump, joyously so. Her cheeks were warm and as inviting as the cherry Air Force Ones on her feet, and she reminded me of a woman I'd been infatuated with as a raw and intense Binghamtonian high schooler. Lane Orrington from my Advanced Physics class shared a similar build and demeanor: curvy, short dark hair, an ever-present smile, a face grim with overbearing optimism. I remembered extolling Lane's virtues to a pal during Chess Club, how I wanted to drink her up like a sunny glass of OJ. Metaphor had not been one of my strengths.

I turned the glass in my hands. It had been so long since I'd been curious about another human being, about something beyond the dense calculations behind wormholes and the parallel worlds waiting just out of reach. But the conference, not to mention my unfulfilling postdoc, was ending, and a new and unknown chapter in my life was set to begin. I felt strange and open to possibility, and for the first time in my life, I struck up a conversation with a stranger at a bar.

"Enjoying the conference?" I asked.

She searched my eyes before her lips curved into a hesitant smile, the kind you might reserve for a puppy with a cone around its neck outside your favorite Sunday brunch spot. "I've enjoyed parts of it. But some of it's been disappointing, you know? Everything's been a tad on the conservative side, like people are really interested in dealing with problems coming one, two, maybe five years down the pike, but nobody's projecting what issues we're going to face as a scientific community twenty years from now, fifty, a hundred." She sipped a vodka Red Bull. "What's your name? What's your deal?"

I dug through my pockets for the lousy business card gifted to me by the fine folks at the University of Alaska print shop. "My name's Dr. Theodore Copeland. My deal? I don't know. I'm really into wormholes. Cosmology?"

She nodded skeptically and handed me her card, a quirky little number that obliterated mine before I even read the text. It felt thicker in my hand, substantial, and the back was powder blue and embossed with the familiar Google logo which was conveniently just the word "Google" laid out in a pastel rainbow. The front read: "Dr. Nessa Newmar, Chaos Mathematician/Googler/Futurist." I resisted a smirk. People obsessed with the future confused me. The past was a comforting balm against the perils of modern life. The future was vast, terrifying, and unknowable, a blank slate harbinger of humiliation, suffering, and inevitably, death.

"Wormholes?" she asked.

"Yeah. My research is about the differences between wormholes and black holes. We could never differentiate between them before. Now we can. It's called The Copeland Principle. It was published last year?" It was the sad elevator pitch I'd memorized before leaving Alaska, but the part I always left out was my desire to link my obscure work to the much more famous and still unproven Many Worlds Interpretation of Quantum Mechanics, a theory positing that our reality is merely a membrane within an endless web of similar membranes, parallel worlds, a grandiose and interlocking Multiverse. A handful of us—the quacks and mainline believers—believed that perhaps wormholes were the strings that might lead us to these other universes.

What a beautiful idea, the sparkling hope that somewhere, beyond all the grime and hurt and human messiness of our world, there might exist a place that was better, forever unbroken. A second key element I conveniently failed to mention was that The Copeland Principle originated from work I'd completed in grad school, and since finishing my PhD a year earlier, I'd been trapped in a postdoc at my alma mater assisting a geriatric physicist blindly search quantum heterostructures for colossal magnetoresistance and nanoscale electron self-organization, esoterica far removed from my beloved wormholes.

"Cool." But from the way her voice dipped, it didn't sound cool at all. "I like how you named it after yourself. Very original. Must have taken you a long time to come up with that name, huh?"

I smiled. All my life, I'd secretly enjoyed being joked with, the same kind of masturbatory impulse of people who relished the smell of their farts. "So what's Google doing at the ASA? I thought they stuck to their trade shows in Mountain View?"

"I'm not here in a Google-related capacity. I'm more futurist than Googler this week."

"What do you do there?"

"I work on prediction software. Google Now? It analyzes your history to predict exactly what you'll want to do next on the web. It's kind of like this personalized page with links to cool stuff our algorithm thinks you'll want to know. Instead of having to type in CNET, we boot it up in a nice little card because we've predicted that's what you really want. Isn't that something?" When Dr. Newmar grew excited, she spoke even faster than her already quicker-than-average clip, and I was rather charmed by her enthusiasm. When she signaled the bartender for another drink, I followed her lead and did the same. "But I'm not saying it's perfect. I'm not saying it's my life's work or anything. It's problematic. I get that."

"So if you're not here as a Googler, what are you here for?"

She grinned. There was something knowing about our conversation, a meta-awareness that we were dutifully playing our roles as ASA attendees, that we were almost required to probe new acquaintances about their work. But her delivery and wry excitement intrigued me, and I realized that my conversation with Dr. Newmar was the first I'd enjoyed since stepping off the plane. "A few months back," she said, "I started working on an extracurricular project with three engineers from Data Visualization and a biologist from Google Forever. We've been trying to figure out how to take the core algorithms of Google Now and apply them to larger problems with more variables. What if we were trying to accurately predict where and when the next genocide would happen, the next famine, the next rape? What if we were able to harness those results and actually prevent said catastrophes to make the planet—and not just for first worlders—a better place? What if we could solve everything?"

Maybe it was the Eagle Rare. Maybe it was the phony chatter of hundreds of scientists who somehow bought into the fallacy that kissing up to the right person at an academic conference might lead to a cushy research position or tenure-track job. Maybe it was the speedy delivery of Dr. Newmar's impassioned plea. But something about her tone and demeanor subconsciously signaled that Dr. Newmar and I might be likeminded, that she too had reservations about the narrowly defined paths set in front of the world's most curious scientific minds.

"Why not go straight to the venture capitalists for funding?" I asked.

At the mere suggestion of VCs, notorious for how they'd pump outrageous sums of money into fresh-faced Silicon Valley startups only to dismantle any weirdness two clicks left of the mainstream, Nessa's face soured. "No VCs. No corporate interests or anyone else motivated by money. We've been pitching universities."

I then understood something new and intriguing about Dr. Nessa Newmar. This was a woman with world-saving aspirations, but also the kind of woman who refused to dirty her hands with capital. This went far beyond optimistic Lane Orrington from high school who left Binghamton to become a hedge fund manager in DC. Dr. Nessa Newmar was a towering monolith of human idealism, and although I related to her desire to remain above the fray, I was intimidated by her unwavering faith. It was obvious from her tone and drinking that she hadn't found funding in Indianapolis and that the ASA had ground us both up in the mortar and pestle of a larger scientific world chained by the limited ideas and conceptions of the previous century. Yet there she was, smiling as though the answers to all her problems waited just beyond the revolving doors of the convention center. I nodded at my new friend. I felt kind of drunk and a little cool, like anything might happen, like the convention doors might swing open and the sci-fi ambassador scientists I'd always imagined might appear and lead us into a better life.

"Let me ask you a question," I said. "This is going to sound weird, but I think it says a lot about a person. It's a game we used to play in grad school. If you had a time machine, where would you go?"

The answer was printed in bright, bold letters on her business card, but I wanted her to say it, to hear those reasons articulated.

"A thousand years into the future."

"But the future's so unknown. What if you go too far ahead and the entire planet's dead? What if it's worse than the present?"

"Are you saying you'd go to the past?" she asked.

"Absolutely. Isn't that what everybody fantasizes about? Isn't that why whenever there's a flashback in a movie it's sepia-toned? Doesn't everyone want to see their missing loved ones again? Don't we all want to go back and do things right this time?"

"Not everyone." Dr. Newmar set a handful of twenties on the bar for our drinks. "I've got a plane to catch, but let me guess. You're a nostalgic, right?"

"You might say that."

She pushed in her stool. "Here's what I think, and I'm not trying to offend you. Honest." She smiled wide. "Nostalgia is nihilism. Everyone here—" she gestured to the crowd— "is a scientist. We're all working toward a better tomorrow even if it is in our own hyper-specialized ways, even if I don't think they're really doing enough. But that's what scientists do. That's what we've always done. Leave the past to the historians and the bitter. It ruins people." She stuck out her hand for a professional shake. "Pleasure meeting you, Dr. Copeland."

I watched her slip past the sea of scientists and was stunned to discover that I'd miss her. There was something about her proclamation—*nostalgia is nihilism*—that made me want to prove her wrong *and* finally give up the ghost of my troubled past. I was silent, and the buzz of the chattering scientists seemed to grow and grow until all I could hear was mechanized static. I pushed my hands against my ears and stared at my shoes. They were Italian loafers I'd ordered off the internet. They didn't fit well, and I couldn't really afford them, but I'd purchased them as my postdoc drew to a close with the naïve notion that these totems of maturity would safely steer me from the world of childhood into the land of adults. I was twenty-eight-years-old and my toes burned.

#

A half hour later, I found myself expelled into the wilds of downtown Indianapolis, a vista of jagged buildings that reminded me of the algorithms comprising The Copeland Principle. I walked past the line of cabs waiting to take conference attendees to the airport where they could return to whatever identical college towns they hailed from. My hotel—the charmingly rundown StayRomp—waited for me twenty blocks north, and all my grad student and post-doc colleagues were at that precise moment high above me, hurtling through clouds en route home to Anchorage. I'd chosen a redeye to save money. Unlike them, I hadn't shored up post-Alaska plans and could scarcely believe they had agreed to teach freshmen in strange places like the Pacific Northwest or Florida swamplands. I felt a sharp sadness coming on, but before it could really settle, my phone buzzed thrice in my pocket. It's hard to express how strange this was. I wasn't the type of man who regularly received calls and only continued to pay my phone bill out of some sentimental attachment to my life pre-Alaska.

"Mr. Copeland? Hi. This is the front desk from the StayRomp? In Indianapolis? On 16th Street? There's this man here. His name is—what did you say your name is? He says it doesn't matter. Now he's saying it's Jin. His name is Jin apparently. He says he needs to take a meeting with you immediately. Maybe you should get over here?"

I'd only crossed one street since leaving the conference center, and I watched the steady stream of scientists spilling out. We were divided by twenty yards max, but I felt that separation humming in my chest. One side was full of well-adjusted adults heading toward jobs and promising futures. The other was populated by a sour malcontent harassed by hotel clerks and mysterious unknowns named Jin.

"This has to be a mistake," I said. "I don't know any Jin."

"Jin?" the clerk shouted. "Copeland says this is some kind of mistake. Oh? Oh, it's not a mistake? Well, all right then. He says it's about science stuff, Dr. Copeland. I think you better get over here."

I hung up and returned the phone to my pocket. It was a tiny gesture, the kind most people make multiple times a day. But something about it felt significant, like my life was drifting into new and unknown territory. I decided that before confronting Jin, I would embark on the kind of academic walk my many heroes wrote about. Carl Sagan. Anita Borg. Niels Bohr. What connected those great men and women? They all professed a belief in the soul-cleansing powers of a mid-afternoon walk. I would eschew a cab and walk right into the thriving center of my new kind of life.

I walked on and discovered that downtown was ringed by abandoned houses. I should have shied away from those places, but I found the decay rather comforting. I'd grown up in the industrial morass of Binghamton, and the dilapidated houses of Indiana reminded me of my east coast homeland. What stuck out to me was how different I appeared from that long ago teenager sulking in his bedroom memorizing *A Brief History of Time*. I'd traded my baggy jeans and ill-fitting tees for slim cut dress shirts and silk knit ties. I wanted to inherit the legacies of Einstein and Feynman and even

Oppenheimer, the long line of dapper genius fops. I believed becoming a dandy was somehow connected to intelligence, but surrounded by the empty buildings of Indy, it became obvious just how far my adult life had strayed from my working class origins. Was I on the right track? Would my collection of choices accumulate into something meaningful? I fingered my badge and zigzagged through town as the sun set in the west, casting everything in the red-orange glow of personal crisis. I was so fantastically buzzed that I almost didn't realize when I chanced across the StayRomp. Without even intending to, I had arrived.

The StayRomp was flanked by boarded up houses fallen into disrepair, their lawns as shaggy as my parents' living room carpet. It was more boarding house than hotel, complete with rickety porch and white paint peeling off the walls in uneven flakes. I nervously climbed the stairs and entered, half-terrified that some instigator named Jin might pop out from behind the front desk and bludgeon me into submission until I had no choice but to relinquish my Italian loafers. But there was no Jin, not even the frazzled clerk who'd phoned me earlier. The small lobby was empty save for the elderly bellhop in a purple uniform and matching fez catnapping in an armchair. His chest rose and fell, and I wondered what it would feel like to disappear amidst the abandoned esoterica of Indianapolis and become a wandering nomad performing gentle feats of scientific whimsy for children and the elderly.

Instead, I rode the shuddering elevator to the third floor and unlocked my hotel room. It wasn't a special door in any way, shape, or form. Constructed of wood, maybe particle board, with a handle that needed its screws tightened. It wasn't until later when I realized that door was the one I'd been searching for my entire life, the portal that would shuttle me away from the painful commonplace. I opened it and was drunk enough that I briefly believed what I saw was normal. There was a stranger on my bed. A buff-looking man in a suit—presumably the Jin I'd heard so very much about—sat rigid trying to look as mean as possible while awkwardly positioned on a hotel mattress. I looked into his unblinking eyes and turned to his partner, finally realizing that some fundamental law of the real had broken down during my walking tour of Indianapolis. A translucent blue man stood beside Jin. A smiling ghoul repurposed from every olde-time horror flick I'd consumed as a boy. The ghost's cheeks were sunken in, his nose long and prominent, an unlit clove cigarette perched precariously between his lips. He was skinny and raised both hands in gentle supplication. "Don't be frightened, Dr. Copeland, but I'm awfully delighted to meet you."

I stood very rigid and swiveled from Jin to the ghost back to Jin again. The street tough appeared nonplussed—perhaps he palled around with ghostly visions all the time. I understood that the rational course of action was to turn on my heels and sprint all the way to the airport, but I had half a pint of bourbon in my belly, zero future prospects, and an all-consuming desire to contribute something meaningful to the world. Perhaps all great thinkers were befriended by grinning apparitions.

"Everyone calls me Oppie," the blue stranger explained, "but you probably know me as Dr. J. Robert Oppenheimer."

I steadied myself against the door. I had long understood that the world was a very strange and unpredictable place, that a true understanding of existence would remain forever beyond our simian grasp. But this, the appearance of Robert Oppenheimer—the father of the atomic bomb!—in my

StayRomp room decades removed from his death, this I was in no way prepared for. I had been raised by the internet and television and farce, and I looked around the room for hidden cameras half-expecting a reality TV crew to leap out and guffaw at my expense. "Are you a ghost?" I asked.

"Har har, Copeland! Don't be ridiculous." He futzed in his pockets for a lighter. "I'm a hologram. Hey. Do you mind if I smoke? I won't do it if it bothers you, but it'd be really neat if it didn't bother you. Love that nicotine. Just love it." The newly lit cigarette emitted a tiny cloud of smoke. "Smoking's good for a physicist. We're high-strung individuals, and sometimes we need a little something extra to calm us down." He tapped the outline of a flask behind his shirt pocket.

"That cigarette's a real cigarette," I said. "I don't—I don't understand."

"Jesus Christ, relax, Poindexter. There will be time for all the details later." He walked the length of the room and punched me hard in the shoulder. "I've applied a Physicality Algorithm to my hologram. Don't worry about it. Science and discovery are supposed to be fun, madcap even. Stop worrying about the details, all right? They don't matter." He blew a cloud of smoke in my face. "Hey, how familiar are you with my work exactly?"

"I've read your biography."

Oppie again socked me on the shoulder. "Now I know why we picked you." He pointed his embers at me. "If you know my bio, then you know that after my role in the Manhattan Project I headed up the Princeton Institute for Advanced Study and tried to transform it into a utopia for thinkers and artists. It didn't exactly pan out, but guess what, Cope, old pal? There exists a laboratory I've constructed near Los

Alamos by my old Perro Caliente ranch in New Mexico. You know about Los Alamos, I'm sure?"

As a tender young physics major, I'd devoured the biographies of all the great scientific wunderkinds—Max Born, Max Planck, J. Robert Oppenheimer. I'd read long ago how he visited the New Mexico mesa as a perennially sick youth and shouted "hot dog!" upon seeing the Pecos Valley after a long and grueling donkey ride. As a newly minted college professor, he built a ranch there and christened it "Perro Caliente." As a middle-aged physicist, he oversaw the construction of the Los Alamos National Lab an hour's drive away, the birth site of the atomic bomb, a place where the American government still sentenced scientists to develop weapons in their never-ending war against everyone.

"I amassed a great fortune in my day, and at the Perro Caliente Research Laboratory, I've built a place where the greatest thinkers in the world can tackle man's problems without interference from the misguided governments of man. It's Princeton's Advanced Institute on steroids. Dr. Copeland," Oppie announced joyously, "the end of the world approaches, and we believe our salvation may lie in wormholes and, you guessed it, parallel worlds! I'm sure very few people read The Copeland Principle, but I did. For real! Now, because of your expertise, I'd like to personally extend an invitation for you to join our little whiz bang collective." Oppie's expression turned solemn. "But I'm only going to ask you this once. Either pack up your things and go with my man Jin here to the airport or decline and return to your dusty old life. The choice is yours. I can only show you the door and all that jazz. You have to step through it."

There was something superior in Oppenheimer's tone, something untrustworthy in his faux-jokey demeanor, like a cackling hangman. The variables didn't add up. If he wanted a leading voice in the field of wormholes, there were at least a hundred other living scientists—each far older and more accomplished than me—that Oppenheimer might've turned to. But had the phantom Oppenheimer actually discovered a way to squeeze inside parallel universes, something I assumed wouldn't be possible for a century or more? And hadn't I already observed phenomena stranger than this? A corporation from Silicon Valley named Google was working on immortality and artificial intelligence. Swiss scientists toiled underground at the Large Hadron Collider searching for the answers behind creation. The universe wasn't slowing down as originally thought, but expanding at an exponential rate. Was the appearance of a hologram really so much more shocking?

Maybe I was drunker than I realized. Maybe I'd been hit by a car on my walk home, and this was the gonzo afterlife I'd never truly bought into. Either way, this felt like the moment I'd been striving toward my entire life, all those years in academic laboratories crunching numbers, the language of celestial gods. I suddenly thought of my father, the man who first inspired my love for science. He was a mechanic with an endless curiosity for machines. He was the one who sat with me in our basement building elaborate electromagnets and Erector Sets. He was the one who drove me into Manhattan for physics conferences when I was just twelve-years-old. I remembered his favorite Bible story, the one about dastardly Saul on the road to Damascus, how Christ appeared and transformed him instantly into Paul the Apostle. Perhaps Oppenheimer's laboratory was a place where I might stage my own evolution into a legendary scientist, the kind of man who could look in the mirror and not feel ashamed.

Who better to mentor me than one of the greatest physicists history had ever known?

"I'll do it," I said. "I'll go to New Mexico."

"Neato. Glad to have you aboard," the Hologram of J. Robert Oppenheimer said. "Jin will bring the auto around outside. See you in the desert!"

Just like that, the hologram vanished, a teleportation accompanied by a slow churning like a church organ gone sour. Jin nodded before leaving, and I was suddenly left alone with the meager suitcase of possessions I'd dragged to the conference. I only had a few moments to collect my belongings and join Jin outside, but I knew that wouldn't be an issue. If I was truly abandoning my old life, there were only two talismans I couldn't live without, and I brought them with me on every trip. I lifted the suitcase to the bed and unzipped it. I slid my hand past my dirty underwear and hit the miniature safe I'd purchased mere days before graduating college. I entered the four-digit code and held my breath, even though I knew what I'd find: my golden wedding band and a picture of my once stunning wife looking desperately sad on the shores of the Atlantic, the crimson scarf atop her head flailing in the ocean breeze. I tried not to look directly in her eyes and carefully, oh so carefully, held those holy relics to the sky like sacraments, proof of a better age, proof that I had once been an unbroken human being, proof that with due diligence and time I might become whole once again.

THE GOD LASER

By sunrise the next morning, I was zooming down the highways of the New Mexico desert in an unmarked black sedan. I'd never been to New Mexico before, but I'd read about it in Oppenheimer's biography. It was startling to suddenly appear in this landscape I'd read about for so long, no less disorienting than if I'd magically found myself teleported to Middle Earth for a stroll with those incessantly singing dwarves. Jin had accompanied me from the very moment I'd walked out of the StayRomp. He drove me to the airport and flew our private plane. Yet he'd barely spoken a word the entire trip. Every time I tried to draw him into conversation, Jin murmured under his breath and turned in the opposite direction. And so I was left alone with my thoughts, my feeble attempts at processing the bizarre events of the previous evening. Perhaps Dr. Newmar had laced my drink with some powerful Google narcotic, and everything that had transpired was simply a dream. Perhaps at that very moment, I was spread eagle in the convention center screaming about Mexican hot dogs and atomic ghosts.

We exited the highway and took a winding two lane road surrounded by brush and ramshackle houses into Pecos, a small town with an intact main street populated with mom-and-pop bars, mom-and-pop drug stores, mom-and-pop churches, mom-and-pop everything, before slicing north along the brutal edge of the Pecos Valley. Outside of Alaska and Binghamton and recently Indiana, I'd barely been anywhere in my life and was rather moved by this sweeping vista of small town desert Americana.

"Nice town," I shouted through the open divider of the sedan.

Jin nodded.

"You been doing this a long time?" I asked.

Jin nodded.

"What's it like working for Oppenheimer?" I asked.

He met my eyes in the rearview before the divider rolled shut. We continued up a jagged orange mountain, and on my right, I was granted a view of the Valley proper, hilly and crisscrossed by river, vast and eternal, the sky above a neon blue dome. On my left, I could make out the buildings of Santa Fe shining against the horizon, and as we climbed higher, I fooled myself into believing I could even see the fenced edges of Los Alamos beyond. But surely this was an impulse of whimsy, a childhood inclination reactivated in the mysterious desert I'd read about as a wide-eyed undergraduate desperate to believe in the inherent goodness of the world.

Eventually, we reached the summit of the mountain and our true destination: a simple log cabin, just two floors tall, barely bigger than the taco hut off the Port of Anchorage I often frequented after work. Perro Caliente overlooked the entirety of the Pecos Valley, and even though this was an impressive sight, I was taken aback. This tiny ranch couldn't be the mythical laboratory the Hologram of Oppenheimer told me about. This couldn't be where he intended to prevent the end of the world.

Jin pointed at the cabin, and I flashed him an awkward peace sign as I retrieved my suitcase and exited the sedan. He didn't wave goodbye, and I watched from the dusty trail as he made a three-point turn and left the way we came. I was all alone atop a mountain in New Mexico. No one outside of Jin and Oppenheimer knew where I was. There was nothing to do but enter Perro Caliente and begin the alternate path I'd set out upon.

The interior of the ranch was no more reassuring than the exterior. It was a cabin built in the '30s, no more, no less. Velvet couches and mahogany chairs had been arranged around a fireplace. I blinked at the kitchen with its modern refrigerator and felt engulfed by panic, beads of sweat prominent under my armpits. I needed a haircut. What if there were no stylists nearby? What if I'd been tricked? What if the hologram had all been some ruse to lure me here with nothing but the clothes on my back and my suitcase of wifely relics? Perhaps this was how the story of the one and only Dr. Theodore Copeland reached its tragic conclusion: bamboozled, left to starve and perish atop a New Mexico mountain, his early potential forever snuffed out by starvation. I imagined a wolf howling in the distance, its tummy rumbling with murderous glee.

But then, a middle-aged black woman climbed down the stairs, her eyes the deepest blue, her face more than pretty. "Are you Theodore Copeland?"

"Everyone calls me Cope."

"All right, 'Cope.'" She drew quote symbols in the air. "Oppie told me you were coming. Name's Barb. I work in Human Resources, and it's my job to bring you down. Oppie's waiting by the monorail. Was your trip pleasant?"

I narrowed my eyes at the phrases "bring you down" and "monorail" and asked, "Is this really Oppenheimer's laboratory?"

"Oh, my gosh, no. Aren't you supposed to be a scientist? You really that dumb?" She slipped her hand on the small of my back. "Follow me, 'Cope.'"

Barb yanked on a candlestick above the fireplace, and just like in a hundred black and white mysteries, the dusty bookshelf slid away revealing a futuristic glass elevator reminiscent of those in only the best and most elegant malls. I followed Barb inside, and we shot down into the earth at near stomach wrenching speeds. I involuntarily reached for Barb's shoulders and she whispered in my ear not to worry, that everybody got nervous their first time. I thought about replying with a crude, yet amusing, joke but had the wherewithal to refrain.

We plunged deeper and deeper until the glass elevator emerged at the top of a massive underground snow globe surrounded on all sides by the hard orange sediment of the Pecos Valley. The tube slowed as it neared the tail of its descent, and I was finally able to unclench Barb and take in my new surroundings. Oppenheimer had erected a city underground, complete with dazzling skyscrapers tinted the light blue of his hologram and sidewalks populated with hundreds upon hundreds of people scurrying in lab coats and suits and dresses, a mish mash of races and ages. I pressed my hands to the glass and tried to reconcile what I was seeing with what I'd previously accepted as my known reality. I'd arrived in a small, thriving city a mile beneath the harsh conditions of the American desert, and there were still so many tunnels at the far edges of the dome extending ever outward into more mysterious chambers and antechambers, presumably secret laboratories. Monorail tracks hugged the curves of the buildings, and trains zoomed by at fantastic speeds over the populace's heads. The roof of the dome was a giant scooped screen that simulated the sky and sun. I was stunned and did not speak until the elevator kissed the ground and Barb once again reached for my shoulders. "Welcome to the Perro Caliente Research Laboratory, Dr. Copeland."

I followed Barb onto the powder blue streets. When the Hologram of Robert Oppenheimer invited me to join his collective, I imagined something similar to the World War II-era setup of Los Alamos: a few fenced-in buildings where we could quietly focus on our experiments surrounded by a makeshift town of amenities covered in sand. What I was not expecting was this. Barb and I passed a tapas restaurant, a feminist book store, an '80s theme bar, and a row of posh apartment buildings. We saw scientists, food workers, bartenders, janitors, even a roving band of jubilant mimes. Perro Caliente reminded me less of a traditional laboratory and more of the University of Alaska's campus, a cross-section of students, professors, administration, and blue collar workers, an earnest stab at modern utopia. This was Princeton's Institute for Advanced Study taken to its improbable zenith.

"We call this main dome the Mezzanine," Barb said.

"You work in HR?" I managed.

"The last ten years."

"How many people live down here?"

"Three thousand. There's a lot more at the Large Hadron Collider."

"Can they leave whenever they want?"

Barb nodded. "Sure, but Oppenheimer frowns upon it. We can't have that many people coming and going without arousing suspicion. You'll sign your non-disclosure agreement later today. It's a near-replica to the one used during The Manhattan Project. Besides, most people don't want to leave. We've got a lot of activities. Intramural sports. Community theatre. Potluck dinners. Book clubs. Dynamite curling club. Just dynamite."

"What about food? Clothes?"

"We have access to acres upon acres of farmland on the western edge of the facilities, and there's a service elevator beneath a cave at the base of Round Mountain. We use that to bring down anything too large for the cabin elevator."

I shook my head. "Are all these people working on what I'm going to be working on?"

"Most of the scientists. They make up 80% of the population. The rest are like me or your driver: support staff hand-selected by Oppenheimer." Barb led me up the metal stairs of a monorail platform, and waiting for me at the top was none other than the Hologram of Dr. Oppenheimer beaming in front of a subway-sized tram.

"Welcome, Dr. Copeland," Oppie shouted happily. "It's time to save the world! Chop, chop!"

I bade farewell to Barb and followed Oppenheimer aboard the monorail. It zipped through the Mezzanine level of Perro Caliente, jutting around building after building where I could spy portly scientists huffing on treadmills or chuckling in front of their flatscreens. Our train disappeared into one of the many tunnels along the northern edge of the dome, and what I first thought was a wall running along our right side turned out to be something very different indeed. It was an enormous pipe, gold in color, as large as the Integrated Science Building where I'd toiled for so long back in Anchorage. I had long known about synchrotrons: massive, circular particle colliders capable of generating impossibly powerful particle beams constructed of pure kinetic energy. But never before had I seen one up close. They had evolved from cyclotrons, and no physics department in the country—not even those fund rich jerkwads from Harvard—had been able to convince their snub-nosed provosts to pony up and build one.

I pointed out the window. "Is that a particle accelerator?"

"I can see why we've brought you on, Copeland. You're nobody's fool. You're aboard the trolley, all right."

"How big is it?"

"One hundred." Oppie smiled wide, his gaunt cheeks trembling with manic pleasure.

"One hundred what?"

"One hundred miles long. We call it The God Laser. It's the biggest on earth. Pretty superior, huh?"

The monorail glided by the collider at a fantastic clip, and I openly gawked through my window, keenly aware that I was one of a small handful of people on the entire planet who had ever and would ever bear witness to a scientific spectacle as stunning as Oppenheimer's God Laser. Soon, we came to a stop in front of a giant stone cylinder seemingly lifted from ancient Greece. The two pipes of the particle accelerator entered the cylinder from opposing sides and almost touched in the building's hollow center. Dr. Oppenheimer grinned like a madman as we disembarked and hurried over to what he dubbed The Control Center, and I was again left to wonder if this was really my life and what else the father of the atomic bomb had hidden beneath his summer getaway home from the prehistoric 1930s.

We entered The Control Center, and the raw, beating heart of Perro Caliente was at last laid bare. Inside the hollow Control Center, the particle accelerator culminated in two superconducting quadrupole electromagnets, their laser gun ends pointed at each other in the center. A curved stone walkway reached up to the hollow space between. The interior wall of the stone cylinder was constructed of glass, and inside I could see six levels of computer terminals one after another, NASA-esque control rooms, each facing the electromagnet lasers. If it wasn't already abundantly clear, I finally realized how far removed I was from quantum heterostructures and my tepid postdoc.

"This is where we're going to save humanity from itself," Oppenheimer announced. "Every government in the world would weaponize us if they knew what we were doing, son. During the atomic bomb project, I was under the impression that after the war we'd turn our findings to the other governments of the world, that we'd isolate every plutonium mine on the planet and declare them under international control. As you know, that wasn't the case. Can you imagine what would happen if The God Laser fell into the wrong hands?"

I nervously fiddled with my tie. A week earlier, I was eating croutons straight from the bag in my messy catastrophe of an apartment. Now I was rubbing elbows with the hologram of a legend speaking wistfully of particle accelerators. "What's the purpose of this place, Doctor?"

Oppenheimer led me up the stone walkway. "Teddy, three months ago we cracked The Theory of Almost Everything."

The Theory of Everything was something every scientist learned about in college. A final scientific theory that would accurately link everything, a perfectly sculpted mathematic sestina that could explain every known phenomenon in the entire universe and Multiverse beyond. Everyone from the ancient Greeks to Einstein himself had failed to grasp The Theory of Everything in their lifetimes, but all of them believed it existed, that it was only a matter of time before humans ascended from mere mammals chained to the rock of the earth and took their rightful places as all-knowing gods.

"All the research says a Theory of Everything's a century away at least," I said.

"We're splitting hairs here, but it's a Theory of *Almost* Everything, and trust me, our research is at least a century ahead of everything aboveground. In our Theory of Almost Everything we've been able to use mathematic equations to explain 99.9999999999999999999999999999999999999 9999999999% of everything. What we've discovered is that existence is nothing more than a living, breathing, constantly evolving mathematical equation. There's an equation for literally everything in the universe." Oppie pointed toward the computer terminals within the Control Center. "You see where one of our scientists left a mug on his desk? There's an equation that explains that precise mug's position in the universe. It's a hundred pages long, but it exists. There's even an equation for that scientist's choice to leave his mug there instead of, say, taking it to the break room. The more complex something is, the longer the equation is. Your existence is thousands of pages of equations long, the sun millions. Your soul is a math problem, Dr. Copeland, and we've solved it."

He stubbed out the husk of his clove on the stone walkway. "We've been able to solve a lot of quantum riddles using the theory, but the one that pertains to you is The Copeland Principle. We've actually been able to test it underground. I don't want to lecture you on your own your work, but let me sum it up. We've known for years that the universe is analogous to a two-dimensional plane, and the Many Worlds Interpretation of Quantum Mechanics tells us that wormholes are strings that lead to other planes of existence, other universes, the grand web of the Multiverse. Black holes share all the same properties as wormholes but lead nowhere. That's one of the reasons we could never harvest wormholes in the past. We couldn't tell them apart from black holes. But your principle solved the Black Hole Information Paradox, how to tell a wormhole portal from a black hole dead end. Black holes give off tiny bits of Hawking radiation. Wormholes do not."

Dr. Oppenheimer fished his flask out of his breast pocket and took a long, thoughtful sip. As flattering as it was that some far-fetched theory I'd cooked up as a depressed graduate student might prove useful in saving the world, there was something troubling lurking just behind Oppenheimer's hologram eyes. It was clear there was potential for him to mentor me, for Oppie to shepherd me from the ranks of the thousands of cosmologists across this country and into the hallowed pantheon of the all-time greats. But I couldn't shake the feeling he was withholding vital pieces of information, a sensation that perhaps Oppenheimer wasn't as altruistic as he seemed. I remembered a documentary I'd seen in a college history course taught by a middle-aged leftist complete with jangly Vietnam POW bracelets running up and down her arms. The film showed the human effects of the atomic bombings of Hiroshima and Nagasaki, images of newly radiated doctors peeling burned flesh off children's faces. Oppenheimer was directly responsible for the lone uses of atom bombs against humans. I told myself to remember that.

"Think of our universe as a giant, floating membrane with wormhole strings that lead to other membranes," Oppie continued. "Each membrane is a new universe birthed from the different results of an event no matter how important or seemingly unimportant. Because you've taken this job, an alternate reality must exist where you didn't take it. If you get a cold here, there must be a universe where you don't get a cold." He started pacing. "Now, remember that we have the formula for our universe. The God Laser here is a giant antenna, and all those other parallel realities out there are radio waves. We knew they were there before, but we couldn't reach them. Now we have our frequency, and if we modify that—say you change the equation in the Theory of Almost of Everything for a rainy day in Idaho and turn it into a nice one—we can find the frequencies for these other realities. The God Laser generates a miniature wormhole here underground, and blammo, we have a portal into a parallel universe where it's sunny in Idaho instead of raining." He handed me the flask, his face all smiles. "It's a giant, magical car radio, Copeland! Huzzah!"

I sat down, grateful for the sensation of something real against my body. I couldn't wrap my mind around what Oppenheimer was saying and was reminded of when my parents first explained the concept of Halloween to me as a child—you get to dress up as something you love and everyone you know gives you candy? It was all too big, too massive, and in response, I took a long pull from Oppenheimer's outreached flask. "So what are we supposed to do with this... magical car radio exactly?"

Oppenheimer sat next to me and reclaimed his whiskey. Our legs dangled over the edge and, in a strange sort of way, reminded me of two childhood pals sitting atop the monkey bars happily discussing baseball players or superhero power levels. "Ever since we built the atomic bomb a few miles west, it was clear humans would find a way to off ourselves. No news there, right, kiddo? I've developed a formula that takes into account every conceivable threat to our continued existence as a species—global warming, water shortages, nuclear winter, overpopulation, dysgenic mutations, global pandemics, ecological collapse, meteors, large scale volcanism, all of the super scary stuff basically. I've run the numbers, and my Apocalypse Hypothesis accurately predicts how much time we have left as a species unless we make radical changes to the way we live. You know what the range is, Copeland? Sixty-to-seventy years before one of the aforementioned crises, or probably a combination of them, eliminate all human life on this planet. That's within your lifetime. Grim stuff.

"What we're able to do is modify our universe's equation in small ways, then go inside these parallel universes and scan them for environmental data we can bring back into our own equations. Each scan will hopefully bring us one step closer to a universe free from apocalypse, and once we learn how they achieved such a feat, we can apply their solution to our own world. In a way, we're looking for better versions of ourselves, a world where humans have already solved the riddle of eradication. You and the rest of our team will attempt to code equations for better worlds, universes where we're kinder, universes where Kennedy never died, where the electric car became popular, where we were all better people. The God Laser here will generate miniature wormholes that lead into these other realities, and then, Dr. Copeland, writer of The Copeland Principle, we'll send you inside to complete the data scan."

And so, my role in this spectacle was at last made clear. I, a not-so-humble Binghamtonian cosmologist, was to bravely explore parallel realities for a solution to global warming and all the other self-inflicted wounds that might steer the long Titanic cruise of humanity into its final inevitability: iceberg. I would have the freedom to search for any type of reality I wanted, worlds where I never existed, realities where the League of Nations thrived or where Vietnam turned out differently. This was the kind of opportunity I had dreamt of my entire life, maybe even since I strode confidently into the registrar's office and declared physics as my major field of study, a proud declaration that my life was to be memorable, important, and infinitely weird. But I still felt that gnawing anxiety: why me?

"Well, Copeland, I think that's just about enough for your first day. We'll really get started tomorrow morning, but I do have a bit of homework for you tonight." Oppie hoisted himself up from the ground. "We won't be sending you into these parallel worlds alone. You'll have a partner. We need a specialist in chaos math who can accurately trace how the changes we make to The Theory of Almost Everything affect reality. They'll co-lead the project with you. There's a computer in your apartment with files on all the specialists we've deemed worthy of the job. Scan them, make a decision, then I'll go recruit the lucky bastard tonight. Comprende?"

"Apartment?" I asked.

"Sure." He threw his arm around my back and led me down the stone walkway. "Housing Unit Seven. I'll drop you off there on my way home. It's a kickass apartment, Copeland. Real top notch shower heads. Fantastic pressure!"

Housing Unit Seven, although not "kickass," was perfectly suitable for my purposes. It reminded me of the ruddy places I'd lived during my seemingly endless education—the same brick walls and lumpy community furniture clustered around vending machines and televisions—only this time the halls were populated not by dopey teenagers preoccupied with sex and books and ideas but with middle-aged scientists from all across the globe preoccupied with sex and books and ideas. My room was a tiny yet functional studio, a stark contrast from my Alaskan abode in the Templewood Apartments. I'd lived in the same four-room suite since arriving in Anchorage seven years earlier, and there were still a few unopened moving boxes piled in the corner of the dining room, heaps of ancient, yellowed mail on top of that. That apartment was overrun with old takeout boxes, splayed DVD cases, empty bottles of beer. I hadn't made my bed in years. I hadn't washed my sheets maybe ever. I never had people over and in many ways felt that squalor was the physical manifestation of mourning. I was bound to clutter, filth. My Perro Caliente apartment, on the other hand, featured a clean double bed and a spotless mahogany desk, and I hoped I was up to the task of maintaining my fastidious living quarters. From the window, I could spy the neon blue Mezzanine and its so-called SimuSky. The SimuMoon was beautifully full that evening, showering we denizens of science in its tranquil SimuMoonlight.

I was exhausted from my long journey, my mind fried by how totally my life had changed over the course of thirty hours, but I knew I had to complete Oppenheimer's task of finding a partner before retiring to bed. I poured myself a drink—how kind Oppie was to provide me a small liquor cabinet filled with three fine bottles of bourbon—loosened my tie, and sat down to read the files for Oppenheimer's worthy candidates. The first thing that surprised me was how few there were: only twelve. Were these gifted souls the only people on earth qualified to join my adventure into parallel worlds? Surely there were at least a hundred genius chaos mathematicians scattered across the globe. Another oddity was that no one was older than thirty. Wouldn't Oppie want a graybeard? Wouldn't Oppie want a long beloved luminary in the field? I was about to call him and ask, when I came across the name of the final candidate, none other than Dr. Nessa Newmar, chaos mathematician, Googler, futurist.

I scanned her CV—her various accomplishments were certainly comparable, if not superior, to the others, and I learned of her childhood near UC Berkeley and how she later attended the beach-adjacent campus for undergrad and grad school. It turned out that the spirited Nessa was the daughter of none other than Dr. Elgin Newmar, a British physicist made mildly famous for his many contributions to the field in the '50s and '60s. I remembered learning about him as an undergraduate but couldn't for the life of me recall hearing about a daughter, or for that matter, anything he had accomplished in the post-Watergate world. I clicked open my browser—the Wi-Fi signal in Perro Caliente was as robust as the one on campus, and I wondered how much it cost to supply an underground city with unlimited internet—and searched for Nessa's father discovering two important factoids: 1) he died six months earlier after spending the previous fifty years as a professor at UC Berkeley, and 2) he worked alongside Oppenheimer on The Manhattan Project as part of an exchange program with Britain and was one of the very few people of color to do so. I tried imagining what it might feel like to be the direct inheritor of the legacies of Hiroshima and Nagasaki, how that would affect Oppie or Elgin or even the insistently optimistic Nessa Newmar. I stood, bourbon in hand, and wandered over to my window overlooking the great blue glory of the Mezzanine. Oppenheimer hadn't asked me to research Nessa's father. He'd asked me to decide whether or not Nessa was a suitable choice for a partner. If our mission was to save the earth, then I couldn't imagine anyone better suited for the task than Dr. Nessa Newmar. Forward thinking and obsessed with bettering the planet, it felt like she'd been forged explicitly for this underground opportunity. If I was the cautious nostalgic who maybe overvalued the past, then who better to have by my side in parallel realities than an overconfident futurist specializing in prediction? I returned to my computer and forwarded Dr. Newmar's file to Oppenheimer with a glowing recommendation. Not a moment later, he replied: *I'll go recruit her right this very second.*

I kicked off my Italian loafers and plopped on the bed in my khakis and dress shirt. I was exhausted and buzzed—only then did I realize Oppie hadn't mentioned where to grab dinner—and for the first time since Oppenheimer revealed the scope of his underground project, I allowed myself to acknowledge the forbidden possibility I'd glimpsed the moment he explained his inter-dimensional scheme, the impossible scenario I'd dreamt up during my self-imposed Alaskan exile.

I closed my eyes and whispered an incantation, a sentimental plea to the universe to make my semi-drunk words real. "If I explore parallel worlds, I might see my secret wife again."

The Copeland Principle: An Examination of Parallel Worlds in Three Parts (Part One of Three)

By Dr. Theodore Copeland

ABSTRACT

Cosmologists who subscribe to The Many Worlds Interpretation of Quantum Mechanics have long understood that wormholes can function as gateways to parallel worlds while black holes—their cosmic cousins—are dead ends. The problem—known more widely as The Black Hole Information Paradox—is that we have yet to discover a way to differentiate between wormhole portals and black hole dead ends. I posit that the only difference between the two is that black holes emit miniscule amounts of Hawking Radiation while wormholes do not. Theoretically, we can use my Principle to isolate wormholes and enter the aforementioned parallel worlds.

I wish I could tell you this is a noble endeavor on par with Edward Witten's fanciful forays into the glorious mysticism of M-Theory, but unfortunately, my motivations are slipshod at best and damning at worst. If we solve The Black Hole Information Paradox and pry open wormholes leading to parallel worlds, I might at last be reunited with my wife. I might at last be remade whole.

INTRODUCTION

I met the woman who would eventually become my wife on an otherwise ordinary autumn day my freshman year of college, an afternoon ablaze with orange and red in the final throes of warmth before winter would come and transform the entire campus white, students trading their sneakers and flats for snow boots, their hoodies and pullovers for parkas. It was early enough in my collegiate career that I still walked everywhere with a goofy smile spread across my lips. It was still so unbelievable. At last, I had traded my friendless life in Binghamton for this: North Hall on the edge of Susquehanna University in central Pennsylvania, a tranquil utopia where I discovered similarly nerdy teenagers content to meet in my dorm after a vigorous day of higher education to eat microwaved food and engage in long bull sessions about life and the universe and butts. On this particular October night, my roommate—a plump, pimply fellow from Philadelphia who, for reasons to-this-day unknown, demanded everyone call him The Bull—and I put our conversation about microprocessors on hold and huffed over to the student center for a much-hyped Battle of the Bands. You must understand that this was central Pennsylvania. Outside of our tiny university campus there was nothing but miles upon miles of farmland dotted with the occasional Wal-Mart or townie bar we were not yet permitted access to. So The Bull and I joined the majority of our underage classmates in the cafeteria and endured a full hour of bands with practically zero musical ability and even less stage presence. There were white boy harmonica players and amateur rappers who lifted their rhymes wholesale from Dr. Seuss. There were music sorority dropouts pounding accordions and sandal-wearing burnouts banging Dave Matthews on bongos. The Bull and I almost left—he'd sniffed the possibility of a Nintendo tournament in a dorm across campus—before her band took the stage. Seven short women—none taller than five feet, none older than nineteen, their pimply faces caked with makeup—snarled their way up a ladder and onto the makeshift stage erected in the center of our cafeteria. They sported the fishnet-cum-scissored-t-shirt uniform of punk queens past, but their hair and makeup were positively Stepford, an alluring, yet puzzling concoction that made me think of bohemians raised in the prison-fortress malls of New Jersey. They brandished tubas and horns and basses like weapons, and the lead singer approached the microphone and announced in a shockingly deep voice, "We are the Femme Furies, you Christian motherfuckers!" Severe, black bangs kissed the edges of her cartoonishly thick eyebrows. She was petite, but I sensed she could leap down into the quivering audience and bash in my skull with a folding chair if she really wanted to.

This was Wren Wells.

This was the woman I would marry in only three short years.

But that unthinkable future was still far ahead of us, and on that first night, I, an aggressively nerdy teenager who spent more time discussing Olbers' paradox in chat rooms than listening to bands my peers enjoyed, was stunned that this woman and her music existed. The audience grew smaller and smaller as the Femme Furies launched into one screeching tirade after another about politics or religion or identity, and I was moved that through all of it they still maintained their sense of playfulness and would occasionally play a song about Cheez Whiz or Go Karts. Before I knew it, I was among the handful of people clustered around the stage, banging our heads wildly as Wren—her name then unknown to me—leaned her head toward the undulating scrum and shouted, "Fuck you! Fuck you! Fuck you!"

When their six song set ended, I assumed the merry members of the Femme Furies would hang out at least until the final three bands played and the results were announced—The Bull had long ago defected for that fabled Nintendo tournament. But the moment their set ended, those fierce ladies made a beeline for the cafeteria exit, and I was presented with a fateful choice. As a high schooler, I had been the classic wallflower, content enough to avoid scorn and perhaps make the occasional sarcastic remark in class to my peers' mild delight. The old me would have forlornly watched the band disappear and chalked up the whole experience to the confusing Bildungsroman of my final teenage years. But I recognized that at Susquehanna, far away from Binghamton, I could be reborn into a newer, better Teddy under the mothering shadow of country forests and leather-elbowed professor-cum-physicists, the aging prototypes for what I one day might become. I followed the Femme Furies out of the cafeteria and into the student lobby where I finally called after them.

"Hey," I shouted.

They turned to look, their faces deadpan.

"I really like your band," I managed. "I mean set. I really liked your set? I mean I like your band, but that set was awesome. The songs were really good. I liked them. It was cool." I nervously furled and unfurled my tie. In high school, I'd traded the prototypical uniform of all Binghamtonian males—oversized t-shirt, oversized jeans, Wolverine shit kickers—for the slim shirts and ties of my beloved scientists. My style of dress was an ongoing proclamation that I wanted to stand out from my peers and take my place amongst the scientific pantheon of men and women like Richard Feynman and Rosalind Franklin. But I wondered how I looked to the Furies then, if this was why six of them appeared ready to hurry off. Wren Wells was the only one who met my eyes. There was a momentary flash behind her glasses that even then I recognized, some moment of mutual understanding that this exchange was meaningful even if we weren't exactly sure why. Later, she told me it was because of how earnest I looked, how unlike our peers I seemed, co-eds locked in an endless arms race to see who might become the most detached and ironic and therefore cool and deserving of love and praise.

"Yeah?" Wren asked.

"Yeah." I took a step closer. Her face glistened, and I still can't imagine anyone more beautiful than sweaty Wren Wells that night in the student center.

She cocked her head. "You want to come hang out with us?"

I followed Wren Wells to the Femme Furies' suite in one of the upperclassmen dorms on the other side of campus. Wren was a sophomore, and her brood of punk/ska renegades had transformed their suite from a sterile holding cell into a Technicolor dream factory lifted wholesale from the pastel mind of Andy Warhol. They'd papered the walls with Polaroids of their grandest adventures—grainy images of basement shows in nearby Harrisburg or State College, cave painting-quality photos of the ladies starting camp fires in mysterious Centralia, an old mining town permanently evacuated because the underground tunnels had caught on fire. Blinking Christmas lights hung from every surface, and a massive boombox blasted out the menacing thud-thud-thud bass line of a band I didn't recognize. The Femme Furies' drummer—a svelte woman in pig tails and a neon green tank top—broke out two bottles of peppermint schnapps from the kitchen, and before long, more and more people filled the tiny suite. Men and women in ratty sports coats, Chuck Taylors with lyrics Sharpied on their sides, ironic t-shirts with images of beardo Hemingway. To say I was out of my element—if only The Bull could see me!—would have been the greatest understatement of my collegiate career. But I bravely accepted a red Solo of schnapps, and after thirteen silent and terrifying minutes—during which I considered evacuating no less than a hundred times—Wren Wells approached and introduced herself.

"That was cool back there," she said.

"What?"

"What you said about our band. Most people don't have the balls to come talk to us after shows. It's weird."

I took my very first sip of alcohol. It reminded me of when I tried coffee for the first time. I didn't much care for it in the moment, but understood how, over time, with a great deal of patience and study, one might learn to appreciate its adult splendors. "You guys just have all this energy. It's inspiring really. I thought everyone our age was so unenthusiastic about everything. You guys have passion. I admire that."

She smiled in a condescending way that made obvious she was holding back a laugh. "You're a weird dude, Cope."

No one had ever called me Cope before. No one had ever described me that way before, and I could suddenly envision a future where I became weird and joined ranks with this awkward crew gathered in the Furies' suite. I *wanted* to be weird. "Thank you," I told her. "Who are all these people anyway? I haven't seen them around."

She finished her drink and bopped her head to the music. "What's your major?"

"Physics."

"That's why." She jerked her head toward the crowd. "These are mostly English majors. Some design people. Those buildings are on the other side of the tracks."

"Are you an English major?"

"Creative writing. Poetry."

"I love poetry." I'd never read a poem outside of school a day in my life.

"Cool. Patti Smith's my favorite." She grabbed two drinks out of the drummer's hands with a conspiratorial grin and handed me one. "I wish I could write like her, sing like her, be like her."

"You want to be a poet?"

"I don't know if people are still allowed to be poets in the 21st century. It's like wanting to be a Knight of the Round Table, right? But, sure, I'd like to. Sounds dandy."

I chugged what remained of my first drink and moved onto my second. "I'd love to read your poetry someday."

"Play your cards right. What about you? Physics? What does that mean exactly?"

I steadied myself against the wall even as I spotted the drummer returning with more drinks. My tongue was loosened, and I was ready to tell Wren the truth. "Ok, so this is going to sound kind of weird, but I went to Catholic school, and what I like about science is that by studying it, mere human beings have been able to explain and order the chaos of the world. Curie. Oppenheimer. Einstein. Bohr. Those brochachos are the solvers of mysteries. When others saw a world of shadows, they marched forward erasing the darkness of ignorance with the light of knowledge. They're torchbearers." I finished my second Solo of schnapps and called to the drummer for another. "I want to become one, I think. I want to be a torchbearer, maybe."

Wren nodded, and this time there was no look of condescension in her eyes. "Cool."

"Yeah."

Our flirtatious, boozy banter continued for another hour or two, and at last, when the party begun to wind down and the English majors and punk fans started to disperse, Wren touched my virgin hands and asked that question that will forever be seared into my brain: "Do you want to go upstairs?" Oh, how I did. She led me by the hand and did not break her fierce gaze even when her bandmates jokingly cooed at us. She locked her bedroom door behind her—I could scarcely even believe that some of the upperclassmen were allowed singles—and started undressing, not in a quick and sexual way, but slow and luxurious, as if Wren Wells and I had all the time in the world—a naïve notion that would soon be disproved. She took off her shirt with her back to me, and it was, without a doubt, the sexiest image I'd ever borne witness to in my life—the pure white of her back divided by the neon orange of her bra, her butt still concealed by denim skirt and fishnets. I tore my clothes off with wanton abandon and had half a mind to leap headfirst atop the laundry-cluttered mattress when Wren faced me, peeled off her underwear, and shook her head. "Make me feel good first."

I approached, unsure exactly what she wanted. Perhaps a back rub or a piece of cake? Cake always made me feel good. But Wren knowingly placed her hands on my head and guided me down until my face was even with her beautifully fragrant womanhood. That first taste of Wren was so wonderfully delicious—I was stunned to discover it warm—that my insides felt newly electrified. I happily knelt before her for a half-hour, so deliriously thrilled by the taste of her that I came all over the floor without even being touched. When it was over, we sat back stunned, panting, blinking, mildly confused by what had transpired like people who gorge themselves on Thanksgiving dinner and can barely bring themselves to collapse in front of the Cowboys game. I lay next to Wren in her dorm room bed, our smells mingling, and reached out for her hand.

"We'll definitely have to do that again," I whispered.

"Yes. Definitely."

Of course, what we didn't know was that even then the seeds of leukemia lay dormant in Wren's blood only waiting for their chance to mutate and bloom. We were supposed to have our whole lives in front of us.

We were supposed to have time.

THE FINAL FATE OF DR. ELGIN NEWMAR

The morning after my arrival in Perro Caliente, I awoke to the wind chime sound effect of The Communications Center, a steel tower rising from the heart of the Mezzanine. The noise was pleasant and endlessly preferable to the high pitched alarm of my cell phone, and I was comforted by the officers in The Communications Center who kept our humble community abreast of any major developments. I opened my window to the SimuSun as one of the officers' voices bellowed throughout all of Perro Caliente. "Good morning, everyone. Exciting news. Cafeteria 17 will be serving two kinds of bacon today. You heard that right, folks. Two kinds of bacon! Two kinds of bacon!"

I dressed and hopped a monorail en route to The God Laser. The train was filled with scientists in lab coats, their faces buried in glowing tablets or newspapers delivered from all corners of the world. It wasn't that different from how I imagined the mass transit systems of Chicago or Manhattan, modes of transportation I'd envied my entire life. In Alaska, it had only been a brief walk from the Templewood Apartments to the Integrated Science Building, and just riding the monorail through the sweet blue skyline of the Mezzanine was enough to make me feel sophisticated and cool, a worthy candidate for the task Oppenheimer had laid before me.

I met the Hologram of Robert Oppenheimer outside The Control Center, his patented clove cigarette pursed between his lips. "Moshi, moshi, Dr. Copeland. Are you ready to put that old schnoz of yours to the grindstone?" I told him my nostrils were more than up to the task, and Oppie replied by flexing open his pocket watch. "Bully! And your partner should be here—right now."

Another monorail pulled into the station, and we watched a second set of scientists stream past into The Control Center. One, however, made a beeline in our direction. Despite only arriving underground a few hours earlier, Dr. Nessa Newmar strode as confidently as Barb or Oppie, workers who'd toiled away in Perro Caliente for a decade or more. I wasn't the least bit surprised. This was a Googler, a self-identifying futurist, and surely her entry into an underground wonderland of technological miracles must have felt foretold and inevitable, the bright reality she'd been cruising toward since birth. The SimuSun lit up her face, and beneath her lab coat I could see a blue v-neck and red Air Force Ones, the uniform of the modern startup wizard.

"Hey! Hey!" She waved at Oppenheimer who'd recruited her the night before, then cocked her head at me. "Oh, you're here too? Weird. Ropeland was it?"

"Copeland."

"Was our conversation at the ASA a setup? Were you recruiting me? Are you a Perro Caliente spy?"

Oppenheimer puffed a cloud of smoke and narrowed his eyes. "You knew her before I gave you the files?"

I flashed my most confident smile. I could understand Oppenheimer's sudden paranoia. He'd warned me yesterday about what might happen if the governments of the world learned of our extraordinarily powerful underground particle accelerator.

"I met her at the ASA right before you and Jin ambushed me at the StayRomp. I went through all the files and thought Dr. Newmar was right for the job."

Dr. Newmar slid her glasses over her forehead and dramatically waggled her eyebrows. "I'm watching you, Ropeland."

Oppenheimer cleared his throat. "Shall we go inside, children?" He led us inside The Control Center lobby where we were approached by a Middle Eastern scientist carrying two tablets. She dressed not like Dr. Newmar and the legions of post-grad tech gurus she'd left behind in Silicon Valley, but like the professional powerhouses I only saw on reality TV shows about business women devouring every last available resource throughout corporate America and the wider earth beyond. She wore what I can only describe as a skirt suit in that the bottom half was a dark skirt and the top half—beneath her lab coat no less—was a matching suit coat. Her dark hair fell to her shoulders and not a single strand was out of place. Her makeup too was perfection, the kind of sheen that alerted you to the fact that she was wearing it, but in a way that no man could accurately say where or how. Her most striking feature, however, was the pronounced cleft on her chin. It gave her a handsome strength, like a '50s matinée hunk, someone deserving of power and riches. Oppenheimer clapped his arm around her and said, "This is Dr. Delbar Javari, our lead engineer. She's been here two weeks finishing up The God Laser and spearheading the development of everything you'll need in parallel worlds. Keep this on the low, but she's the seventh smartest person on earth."

"It's not a perfect ranking system," Dr. Javari said with a roll of her eyes, her voice sun-kissed with the final remnants of a foreign accent. "Great to meet you both, and please, call me Del. Delbar is kind of lame." Del handed us two tablets, and I was surprised by how lightweight and unassuming they were. The hipper professors at Alaska—those clad-in-black forty-somethings desperate to prove they were up-to-date on youth tech—had jettisoned their laptops for tablets a year prior, and I enjoyed watching them struggle during class to run PowerPoints, their greasy fingers awkwardly swiping at virtual keyboards like monkeys attempting to work a typewriter. Dr. Javari's tablet resembled those, except her screens were hyper HD, as realistic as nature.

"Neat," Nessa said. "What do they do? How much RAM do they have? Are you using internal memory or cloud computing? Are there cases? Are there color options for the cases? I want mine to look really awesome."

"Uh, no, there aren't colored cases. These aren't consumer tablets," Del said. "They just look that way to keep things kosher in parallel worlds. These are state-of-the-art Calabi-Yau Computation Tablets. They'll accomplish anything you need in parallel worlds. They provide information, allow you to teleport to another location, load the internet, complete the environmental scans we're sending you to gather. And most importantly, they return you to our world when you're done. You lose or break these, and you're trapped in another universe which might potentially suck. So my advice is keep them safe."

A rawness in her voice revealed a vast reservoir of strength beneath the sophisticated cool of Del's exterior. Oppie beamed proudly—this is not a term of literary extravagance in that he was literally a beam of neon blue light affixed with physicality from his so-called Physicality Algorithm—and ushered us up the stairs to the bank of computers I'd spied the day previous. "Seventh smartest person on the planet! What did I tell you? I'm so happy to have you here, my ambitious prodigies!" He smacked his forehead. "That's truly what you are, isn't it? Ambitious prodigies! My trio of ambitious prodigies!"

We followed Oppenheimer to the top floor and its perfect view of the stone walkway below bending up into the empty space between the dual electromagnets of The God Laser. Unlike my first visit, every computer save for three was occupied by engrossed scientists, their fingers dancing over keyboards with the flair and authority of classical pianists. Dr. Javari steered us to two empty terminals and powered up our humming machines.

"We have The Theory of Almost Everything loaded on every single one of these devices. This is where we spend most of our days, at least until our live test next week when we begin sending you into parallel worlds," Dr. Javari explained. "Every physicist here is working on slight modifications to the equation. Each modification gives us the correct signal to enter a parallel world. The bigger the modification, the longer it takes to code. If you want to change the equation to open up a universe that has one grain less of dirt than our Earth has, that'll only take you an hour. But if you want to change the equation to enter a world without global warming, that could take a century. The more data we have, the easier it is to know where to make the modifications. That's why your inter-dimensional trips are so important. That's where there's the most opportunity to gather new data and shorten the time it'll take us to find a solution to extinction."

I raised my hand. When no one called on me, I cleared my throat and pontificated. "Dr. Oppenheimer insinuated that The Theory of Almost Everything is a trillion-page plus equation. That true?"

Del flashed another smile, and this time I noticed her bottom middle teeth overlapped just slightly, a tell that she'd never endured braces as a child, and perhaps, was the product of a working class upbringing like myself. "The master equation is 3,691,480,191,272 pages long, but it's made up of an extremely high number of smaller equations that account for everything in our universe." She bent over the keyboard and entered a few, quick keystrokes. Then she held up a pencil. "This equation represents this pencil."

I leaned into the screen and gasped. What waited there was a ghastly concoction of unholy algorithms droning on for nearly a hundred pages. Each line represented the type of mathematical equation that would have stumped my colleagues and me for twenty minutes minimum in Alaska. "That's just one pencil?" I took a precautionary step back from the computer. The enormity of our undertaking suddenly dawned on me, and I wondered if I, a cosmologist who'd spent the last seven years hibernating in Alaska, was truly up to the task of saving the world. I glanced over at Nessa to see if she was as panicked as I was, but there wasn't even the slightest hint of trepidation on her face. She was Google made flesh.

"This is all just totally great and super amazing," Nessa said before hardening her face and aiming a death stare at Oppenheimer. "But I've still got a lot of difficult questions specifically for you."

Oppie furrowed his brow in innocent confusion. "Go on, child."

"Why do you even need a chaos mathematician for all this? We're not exactly world savers."

He laughed. "That's easy. We need one to figure out why the changes we make in The Theory of Almost Everything result in certain parallel worlds. You know the old saying, if a butterfly flaps its wings, it can cause a hurricane a world away? Well, if we go into the Theory and code a world where that pencil was never manufactured, what effect will it have on reality? Chaos math can trace the steps."

"Ok, and correct me if I'm wrong, Dr. Oppenheimer, but the three of us— myself, Dr. Javari, and Ropeland—we're leading this project? Is that correct?"

He nodded. "Under my supervision of course, but if you're asking if you have to report to anyone other than me, you don't. Children! I'm giving you free rein down here. Go nuts."

"Copeland," I said.

They all stared at me.

"It's Copeland. You said Ropeland again."

Nessa pointed at Del. "How old are you?"

"29."

She pointed at me. "Ropeland?"

"28," I said sheepishly. "Copeland."

She turned back to Oppenheimer. "And I'm 29 too. You're telling me that I'm supposed to believe that J. Robert

Oppenheimer is entrusting a trillion dollar particle accelerator and the fate of the entire world to a trio of unproven twenty-somethings? There are people with decades more experience than us."

Oppenheimer was silent, and we all sensed it was because he didn't want to reveal his true motivation. As thrilling as it was to see Dr. Newmar get the drop on our more-than-a-century-old boss—the equivalent of watching a classmate pull one over an especially pompous fifth grade teacher—I felt pretty dumb for not asking Nessa's questions myself.

"Your precious Google or whatever it is you kids call it was started by two PhD students, was it not?" Oppenheimer asked. "My understanding is kids are running the show up there now."

Nessa shook her head and came face-to-face with the hologram. I was impressed and a tad scared. Oppenheimer was an anointed saint of physics. He'd not only constructed the atomic bomb, but had found some means of enduring—even in this reduced form—beyond death. And here was Nessa, admittedly only twenty-nine-years-old, staring him down like they were equals. She possessed a charismatic magnetism as alluring as it was frightening. "That's true, but Google isn't run by a hundred-year-old hologram."

Dr. Oppenheimer finally dropped the friendly façade. Lines appeared in his blue forehead, and it was obvious he'd now take a different approach to mollify the good futurist Newmar. He was slightly taller than Nessa, and as he dipped his head, the beak of his hat almost poked her forehead. "You want to know exactly why you're here, Dr. Newmar? Tell your new pals what happened to your father."

Nessa folded her arms, clearly taken aback. But still she would not back down. "What do you mean?"

"I'm talking about Dr. Elgin Newmar, a pupil of mine on the Manhattan Project. I'm talking about his death."

"I don't see what *he* has to do with anything."

"Just tell them."

Nessa stood taller in her boots. "My father's final appointment was at the University of Göttingen. He died of a stroke six months ago."

"Did you ever visit him in Germany?"

Her reply came through gritted teeth. "No."

"When was the last time you saw him?"

Nessa looked stung but resolved to defeat Oppenheimer, or at least, concede nothing. I learned something about her then as Oppenheimer gnawed at the obviously complex and difficult relationship she'd had with her father: Dr. Nessa Newmar was so much more than the towering wave of idealism I'd envisioned back at the ASA. That idealism had not been forged in the crucible of sunny California and what I'd assumed to be the kind of idyllic childhood necessary to produce a human so desperate to worship in the church of the future and ever-new. Just beneath that impulse bubbled legitimate human pain.

I couldn't bear to look at her face anymore and put my body between them. "Dr. Oppenheimer, that's enough."

Nessa pushed me aside, refusing to back down.

"I asked you a question," Oppenheimer said coldly. "When was the last time you saw your father?"

Nessa refused to break his gaze. "His will requested his body be donated to science without any kind of ceremony. Things were super busy at Google, and I didn't see any point in flying out to Germany if there wasn't even going to be a service. The last I saw him was two years ago before he went abroad."

And with that, Oppie's expression finally rescinded into the Cheshire cat smile I'd grown accustomed to. "That's all I wanted to know, Dr. Newmar. Now was that so hard? Really? Jeepers. Now follow me, children. Follow me. Let me show you what really happened to Dr. Elgin Newmar. I'll give you a hint: he never boarded that plane to Germany."

#

We rode the monorail in silence. The train was crowded at first, but with each new stop, more and more scientists and lay people disembarked until finally it was just the four of us. I assumed we were traveling to one of the furthest edges of Oppenheimer's Perro Caliente Research Lab, and every time I screwed up the courage to ask the doctor where we were headed, I was put in my place by the flat expression of Nessa's face. I considered wandering over and suggesting that maybe she should purchase an antacid from one of the many drugstores we'd zipped by during our trip, but before I could, Dr. Delbar Javari crossed the aisle and sat next to her. She straightened her skirt suit and spoke loudly enough for Oppenheimer and me to hear. "It's going to be ok," she said. "It's going to be ok." I was impressed by Dr. Javari's extroverted kindness and watched Nessa's expression go from grim surrender to something a little more confident, a little more steadfast. I was amazed that even here, miles beneath the fresh, tart surface of the Earth, friendship could bloom. I'd never really been good at making friends and couldn't recall the last person I'd shared a real human connection with post the departure of that ghost nymph Wren Wells. Perhaps this was my best opportunity to once again experience legitimate camaraderie, to prove to the world and myself that I was more than The Copeland Principle, that I was Teddy Copeland, a well-adjusted human being who might befriend the optimistically powerful duo of Drs. Newmar and Javari. I smiled and even thought about joining them on the other side of the train, but the moment I rose from my chair, the speakerbox above came to life and bellowed, "End of the line! End of the line!"

We exited onto a steel platform that overlooked a green meadow a tad larger than the University of Alaska's lacrosse field. It was so eerie to be confronted with this—the ludicrous neon green of the great outdoors—deep within Oppenheimer's techno-funhouse, and that sense of foreboding was amplified by the dome ceiling above and the unreality of its pristine SimuSky. Perhaps it was the surreal nature of the place that caused me to miss exactly why Oppenheimer had dragged us here in the first place. Dr. Delbar Javari pointed at the field, her face incredulous. "Is this a cemetery?" I had not entered a cemetery since high school and my grandmother's long expected death.

Oppenheimer climbed down the stairs, and the three of us hurried after him. It felt colder in the cemetery than it did elsewhere in Perro Caliente, and I found myself once again considering the fact that Dr. Oppenheimer was directly responsible for the atomic deaths of close to three hundred thousand people. Perhaps his stabs at becoming a self-sacrificing world savior were merely a front, and there was a more sinister side to the seemingly jovial physicist.

"Perro Caliente's been in operation for twenty-five years," Oppenheimer explained as we marched across the field, careful to avoid where people had been buried. "Some of our most devoted scientists have requested to be buried underground so that even in the afterlife they may remain close to our unique and special endeavors."

It was not long before we came upon a simple, marble headstone with the name Elgin Newmar etched atop the epigraph *He Devoted His Life to Science*. Just like Nessa claimed, his date-of-death revealed that Elgin Newmar had passed away six months earlier.

"How is this possible?" From the slight tremble in her voice, it was clear the sight of her father's tombstone had dislodged something hard beneath her skin. It was difficult not to pity her. How many first days at the new dream job began with a trip to Daddy's secret grave?

"Elgin joined the Manhattan Project as part of a US-Britain scientist exchange," Oppenheimer explained. "He was a real prodigy then, just a kid really, and I took him under my wing like you all. He was one of my first recruits when I began Perro Caliente."

"I would've been a child when you started this place. I don't remember anything about Perro Caliente or my father being involved with it. We lived in California."

"Remember the three conferences per year and entire summers he supposedly spent lecturing in Germany? He was here with me. Two years ago he moved down here permanently to devote himself fully to the cause. Göttingen was a front." Oppie placed a hand on the grave and turned his back to us. "So, Dr. Newmar, you wanted to know why you're here, and I'm happy to tell you. I tasked Dr. Copeland with choosing a partner from our pool of qualified chaos mathematicians, and when he chose you I wasn't surprised at all. Elgin spearheaded two massive projects for me over the last twenty-five years, one of them being The God Laser. Isn't it fitting that his daughter, a woman who by all accounts had no idea of her father's involvement with Perro Caliente, was chosen to continue his work? Our reality is a machine as precise and weighted as any clock."

I hid my hands in my pockets. This was all too convenient, and I wondered what other surprises Oppenheimer had in store. He'd arranged the twelve candidates, and just like Nessa guessed, all of them were twenty-somethings. Dr. Javari put an arm around Dr. Newmar's shoulders and encouraged her to speak, to release whatever it was she was holding back.

"You said he spearheaded two projects," Nessa said. "What's the other one?"

Oppie smiled like a grandfather with a Christmas morning secret and started back toward the platform. "Let's not blow all my revelations in the very first week. Come on, gang, we have worlds to save! Infinite worlds!"

A few hours after our graveyard excursion, our first true day of work drew to a close. The majority of the other physicists had already abandoned their computer terminals, but even as eight o'clock approached, Nessa and Delbar burned on my right and left, their fingers skating faster over their keyboards than I would have thought humanly possible. We hadn't spoken since returning from the cemetery—what did you say to a new colleague after a trip to her father's secret tomb?—and I busied myself by imagining a world where ethanol was the dominant form of fuel and the complex mathematics that would make such a deviation from our reality's equation possible. In many ways, I was not unlike a misguided Neanderthal attempting to carve a Picasso into a cave wall. But that truly was the beautiful part about believing in The Multiple Worlds Interpretation of Quantum Mechanics and the existence of a Multiverse. It accounted for all possible realities. A world that relied on ethanol was out there somewhere. We just had to sniff out the correct combination of numbers to find it.

It was Dr. Javari who finally snapped me from my trance, tapping me on the shoulder. She stood behind me cracking her knuckles. Dr. Newmar was oblivious on my right, a pair of expensive headphones suctioned over her ears blasting an upbeat techno thud I was proud not to recognize.

"She had a pretty rough day." Dr. Javari pointed at Nessa. "Let's take her out."

"To the surface?" I asked.

"No, dummy. The Nightlife District. You think Oppenheimer would move all these people underground without giving them a way to blow off steam? He's nuts, not stupid."

"The Nightlife District," I parroted. "Sure. Great. Why not?"

Dr. Javari pulled down Nessa's headphones. "Lady. It's been a long day. Like super long. Let's go kill some brain cells, k?"

Fifteen minutes later, we spilled onto the streets of Oppie's fabled Nightlife District. I was reminded of clips of Chicago I'd YouTubed after reading a thrilling paperback about sexed up scientists boozing their way through the Midwest mega city on sabbatical. Here was the same roar of trains overhead, the sidewalks packed with hurrying people of high intelligence, the buildings clawing their way ever upward. But, of course, there were a few significant divergences. The aforementioned buildings and sidewalks and even the train tracks themselves were tinted the light blue of Oppenheimer's hologram, and many of the denizens of Perro Caliente wore lab coats even after quitting time, as they entered a movie theatre or gym or sushi joint. In Perro Caliente, wearing a lab coat was the equivalent of showing up to a club in a limo or buying a diamond chain: it designated you as a rock star. Our trio passed the open windows of a restaurant called The Fish Dies at Midnight, and I peeked inside, stunned by the sight of a sushi chef sharpening his blades in front of scientists slamming down sake at the bar. How did Oppenheimer convince sushi chefs to relocate underground? How did he even advertise for such a position? I was about to ask Dr. Javari that very question when we came upon two bars directly across from each other. The first, Rum/p Shakers, vibrated with an electronic heartbeat that reminded me of the dumb churn of sweaty collegiate bodies fueled by Miller Lite specials that echoed all the way from downtown to my messy abode in Templewood Apartments. The second, The Trinity Tavern, was all brick, and through the front window I spied an old man with a creased forehead frowning into a glass of bourbon. I found it most charming and delightful.

Dr. Javari flashed us the kind of neutral smile I expected from a toothpaste commercial. "Your choice."

"Uh, Trinity," I said.

"Definitely Trinity," Dr. Newmar agreed.

Dr. Javari shook her head in relief. "Thank Christ. If you picked Rum/p Shakers, I'm not sure we could be friends."

The Trinity Tavern was dank and quiet, the kind of dive bar haunt I'd been drawn to from the moment I reached legal drinking age. The chatter of boozed up scientists pontificating in booths and on well-worn stools filled the humble bar, and I was moved by the wooden wall, that even here, miles underground, Oppenheimer cared about authenticity and providing his employees a suitable place to unwind with a bourbon or two after a long day's work. We selected a booth near the back, and I was delighted by the long list of specialty liquors sketched on a chalkboard above the bartender, a petite man in suspenders, his face all smiles and beard.

He bowed faux-regally at our booth. "Welcome! The name's Thomas Arm, and I'm your resident artisan mixologist. I studied under Leonard Babbage at Momofuku Toronto. My dual specialties are American prohibition and new wave Portuguese cocktails." He put his palms together in faux-prayer. "What will you embark on this evening?"

Dr. Javari ordered an aged whiskey neat, I stuck with my trusted Eagle Rare, and Dr. Newmar was the lone brown liquor holdout, opting for the same vodka Red Bull she'd selected days before in Indianapolis. To his credit, Thomas Arm's face betrayed only a millisecond of disappointment before he hurried off to fetch our drinks. After the day we'd endured—especially Nessa—we might have then descended into the murky despair of the post-work drink. But Dr. Javari recognized the potential for the evening to go south, for Dr. Newmar to tumble through the looking glass of parental memories and regret. Del asked Thomas Arm to fetch her the biggest Cuban they had, and when he returned, she lit up and blew a humongous puff in our faces.

"All right. Let's cut the bullshit. No more Dr. Javari, Newmar, Copeland. Afterhours it's Del, Nessa, Teddy. If we're going to survive down here cut off from the rest of the world for god knows how long, we're going to have to be friends I guess." She took a long pull from her whiskey. "No sob stories. Where are you from? What's your deal? Nessa, lady, let's start with you."

These underground women were full of surprises, of that I was sure. When I'd met Dr. Javari—I mean Del— only a few hours earlier, I'd expected the kind of business person portrayed in the media, the kind of singly-focused machine who existed only to reap and maim and expand their coffers. What I hadn't expected was the whiskey drinking, cigar chomping, ice breaker playing engineer before me. The vodka went straight to Nessa's cheeks, and it didn't take much prodding from Del to get her to begin.

"Like I said before, I'm from California. My dad taught at UC Berkeley. Didn't want me going into science, so what did I do? I got my PhD in Chaos Math from UC Berkeley. Finished and went straight to Google."

Del tipped her whiskey in Nessa's direction. "Why'd you leave?"

"I explained it to Teddy two days ago. Whose world are they improving exactly? They're not trying to stop famines, genocides. They're making things better for a very narrow set of middle-to-upper class first worlders."

The Trinity Tavern was filled to half-capacity, maybe two dozen people scattered across the booths and bar. Someone played an old funk song on the '50s style jukebox in the back, and I felt buzzed and hoped the Trinity had cheeseburgers. I figured if they had solid-to-good cheeseburgers, this could definitely become my go-to underground bar. Cheeseburgers are very important to me, I thought as I fiddled with my tie.

"So you think Oppenheimer wants to save the world for everyone?" Del repeated. "Ok, cool. Interesting point. Let's remember that and circle back to it later. How about you, Teddy? What's your deal?"

I was beyond impressed by how Del handed herself in social situations. She navigated the flow of our conversation, had initiated our going out in the first place, and subtly steered us toward her preferred Trinity over Rum/p Shakers across the way. It was easy to imagine her as a presidential candidate or maybe even a presidential assassin. If I hadn't seen those tablets she'd come up with earlier, I might have even doubted her abilities as an engineer. How could someone this at ease in the world find comfort in the isolated landscape of numbers and laboratories?

"Me?" I said. "I'm an open book."

The story I gave was the Cliff's Notes version I'd learned to deliver to fellow graduate students in Alaska. I covered my fairly predictable working class upbringing in Binghamton, my retroactively idyllic maturation in the incubating farmland of Susquehanna, and my triumphant move to Anchorage. Highlights included the publication of The Copeland Principle and completing my PhD the year prior. Lowlights included my floundering postdoc scanning quantum heterostructures for nanoscale electron self-organization, a task of dubious merit I considered below my abilities, a mere gateway year when I might recalibrate and decide whether I wanted to transition to academia or pure research. Removed completely were any references to my deceased secret bride. Removed completely was the long bout of depression I'd suffered in that lonely and overrun Alaskan apartment. I finished my tale with a gaudy thumbs up, a suitably awkward tell that hopefully signaled to my new colleagues that I was fine, a cutely awkward cosmologist on the make. I looked from Nessa to Del back to Nessa again and was surprised to discover the suspicion in their faces, the raised eyebrows that said without saying anything at all they knew I was withholding vital bits of my backstory, that I'd delivered an expository speech long practiced in front of my bathroom mirror. Before either of them could dig any deeper, I finished my bourbon and signaled Thomas Arm for another, prompting both Nessa and Del to the do the same. Before we could return to that dubious topic—the subject of the endlessly flawed Teddy

Copeland—I pointed my empty at Del and asked, "Now how about you? What's your deal?"

Del blew another cloud of smoke in our faces. She ran the cigar back and forth under her nose before asking, "Are you sure? Do you really want to know?"

We were buzzed. We were underground. The third funk song in a row blasted on the jukebox. Of course we wanted to know.

"All right." She leaned deep in the booth. "I grew up outside Tehran. My dad was a surgeon. He sacrificed quite a bit to get me a visa to Britain when I was eleven. I studied at Oxford, then I took a post as Lead Engineer at the Large Hadron Collider before Oppenheimer approached me a few weeks back."

Nessa and I exchanged glances. Del's life story—minus the chipper "All right"— amounted to a measly four sentences, even less than what Nessa and I divulged. I thought I was obvious, but Delbar Javari could teach a master class in withholding. It was Nessa who broke the silence, futurist Nessa who asked the question it was clear we were expected to avoid.

"Why'd you leave Iran?"

Del stubbed the Cuban in the ashtray and looked Nessa dead in the eyes. "My older sister was taken by militia for wearing a Weezer pin on her veil in the wrong part of the city. We never found out what happened to her. After that, my father made it his mission to get me out, then my mother, then him. Neither of them ever came. I stopped hearing from them two months after I moved to England. Probably the militia."

We stared at her and, for a time, said nothing. Nessa had withheld the particulars of her flawed relationship with

her father, and I had completely glossed over my dead wife. And here was powerful Delbar Javari revealing that not only had her sister been brutally slain by religious zealots in the country of her birth, but probably her mother and father as well. It immediately put both our tragedies into perspective, and for the very first time—and I'm more than humiliated to admit this—I considered the obvious likelihood that perhaps my pain and suffering did not tower over the rest of the world's like some grieving monolith.

"Come on, guys." It was Del who tried to buck up our spirits, not the other way around. "It was almost two decades ago. But it's kind of exactly what I wanted to talk to you about. Nessa, you said you left Google because it was only trying to make the world better for a small, select group of people. You think Oppenheimer's really that different?"

I turned the question over in my head. Oppenheimer claimed to want to use The God Laser to push back the apocalypse be it in the form of water shortages or global warming or nuclear winter or some other currently unforeseen catastrophe. That sounded pretty selfless to me. Nessa, on the other hand, didn't quite think so. "You're saying: why bother stopping the apocalypse if we can't also stop the kind of thing that happened to your family in Iran?"

"Bingo. I don't just want to save a select group of people, I want to save everyone, not just middle-to-upper class first worlders. But I'm not really getting that vibe from Oppenheimer. Our generation didn't cause any of these problems, but we have to be the ones to solve them. Oppeneheimer's been a hologram for twenty-five years. That had to warp him, right?" She wrinkled her nose and stood up from our table. "Christ, who keeps playing this lousy funk shit? I'm going to feed a dollar in the jukebox. Order me another Cuban from Suspenders, will you?"

We watched Del leave, and Nessa shook her head. "She would've made a great Googler." I agreed. We were silent then and shy. Del had been the driving force of the conversation, and suddenly we were on our own, rowers without paddles. Nessa pushed her glasses up over her forehead and finally spoke. "Hey, thanks for bringing me underground."

I nodded, unsure how to respond. I couldn't articulate why exactly, but Nessa made me feel awkward. "No problem. Your file was the best. And after our conversation at the ASA, I thought you'd be perfect."

"I'm excited. I really am. I think the three of us can accomplish something really special down here. It's just so thrilling." She paused. "Did you know about my father?"

I finished my second bourbon, unsure if I should order another, if I was ready to let my new colleagues experience Teddy Copeland drunk. "I read in your file that he was part of The Manhattan Project, but I didn't know he was buried here."

She nodded, satisfied. "I'm curious what he did down here. What that other project was."

We were quiet then and heard Del yelling at a German scientist for buying twenty dollars' worth of funk songs on the jukebox.

"By the way, I might have been a little harsh on you at the ASA," Nessa blurted. "The whole 'nostalgia is nihilism' thing. I still believe that, but I don't even know you, guy. I jump to conclusions. I hate waiting, patience. People say patience is a virtue, but it's not. Not really. It's just something people tell you so you'll happily wait for good things to happen.

It's the opposite of taking charge, being ambitious. If you're here, you must be a pretty future-oriented kind of person."

I wanted to tell her that it was ok. I wanted to tell her that she'd been right at the ASA, that I did consider myself a nostalgic, that I viewed the past as an overwhelmingly superior option to the present. What surprised me, however, was this: my desire to tell her that I wanted to change, that I desperately wanted to become the kind of person who looked forward not backward, that perhaps here, in Oppenheimer's great underground crucible of brazen, wacky hope I might at last touch the full sum of my potential. I looked into Nessa's face, Nessa's eyes, and wanted to reveal myself. But then, predictably, inevitably, that familiar gust of guilt. I felt it coursing through my body, the neurons firing in my brain like popcorn. Wren Wells. It was not an unfamiliar sensation. Whenever I found myself on the cusp of looking beyond the solipsistic scope of my personal tragedies and subsequent hangups, I immediately began dwelling on stupidly sepia-toned images of Wren forever frozen as an undergraduate, on the unfinished poems she wrote on her powder blue typewriter and taped to the walls of her dorm room, on the way her voice warbled during the most intense moments of Femme Furies songs. I felt guilty for even considering focusing on the future instead of the monument to Wren I'd constructed in my mind. I turned away from Nessa's confidently optimistic face toward the bartender and the shelves of whiskey behind him. They looked like harbingers of death, doom, decay, of everything that might potentially happen if our efforts at Perro Caliente failed: annihilation!

"Look," I said, "I've got to get going. Want to be at my best tomorrow. Tell Del I said goodbye."

She shrugged indifferently. "Suit yourself, Cope."

I practically jogged out of Trinity and returned to the monorail platform high above the raucous bars of Perro Caliente's Nightlife District. The train that would return me to Housing Unit Seven swooshed by, but I didn't board it. Instead, I waited, waited, waited for the train to The Control Center and the unquestioned gem of Oppenheimer's underground funhouse: The God Laser. I'd sketched a plan the very moment Del explained how we would interact with The Theory of Almost Everything, but I couldn't bring myself to follow through with it until I was melancholy, buzzed, and appropriately self-flagellating. Something about Nessa's face pushed me over the brink, and I was ready to repent at the heels of Wren's omnipresent ghost. A live testing of The God Laser was scheduled in a week's time. Soon we would enter parallel worlds!

The Control Center was almost spooky in the afterhours dark. The terminals were left on overnight to process the near infinite amounts of data collected by Oppie's physicists during the day, and collectively they warbled a mechanical song that left me unnerved in the darkness. I didn't bother with the lights, and instead, went directly to my workstation. Each terminal had a perfect vantage point of The God Laser behind that cylinder of glass, of the two electromagnets emerging from both ends of the particle accelerator and the stone walkway that rose in between. This was where we would birth wormholes in a mere seven days. This was where my journey into parallel realities would truly begin.

I logged onto the algorithm generator and began pecking at the keys, not the way the nuns taught us in typing class so long ago, but with just my index fingers, the flawed method I'd employed ever since I was the boy with the off-the-charts science scores. I opened a new file and named it "The Wren

Algorithm." It was the solution I'd glimpsed as a self-medicating grad student hidden beneath the snowy shroud of Alaska. A world without leukemia surely existed if all possible outcomes were accounted for across the grandiose Multiverse, but that would take too long to search for, too long to code the perfect sequence of math that might lead to such a beautiful reality. But a world with a slightly lower occurrence rate of leukemia in women was surely more feasible. All I had to do was code it.

This was how I might see my wife alive once again.

This was how I might finally make things right.

The Copeland Principle: An Examination of Parallel Worlds in Three Parts (Part Two of Three)

By Dr. Theodore Copeland

INDEPENDENT VARIABLES

After the Battle of the Bands, Wren and I transformed into something no doubt familiar to the throngs of people across the nation who attended small, liberal arts colleges, places where everyone knew not only each other's names, but their business too: we became one of the fabled campus couples. No longer were we individuals. "Teddy" and "Wren" were erased, replaced with "Cope and Wells," matching sparticles/superpartners, the type of golden puppy love many of our co-ed brethren aspired to. The prophecy I'd gleaned in Wren's old suite—that alongside her I might happily become a unique and memorable person, weird for lack of a better terminology—had turned out to be true. In her company, I felt more confident—able to start conversations with strangers, able to march into seedy concert venues all across Pennsylvania, able to acknowledge how much my life would differ from my parents' in working class Binghamton. I felt like the best possible version of myself, that fabled, elusive Teddy Copeland Prime.

But then, in the summer before our final year at Susquehanna, everything changed. I was reading an essay about the Friedmann universe of spherical space on my parents' porch—I'd taken 20 credits a semester plus six each summer and was on track to graduate a year early—when Wren texted that I should come to her parents' home in Wilkes-Barre immediately. This wasn't a completely out-of-the-ordinary request, as the WB was only an hour-long hop across the New York border. But I was unnerved and drove quickly. Wren had caught the flu that had been going around the dorms during finals week, but unlike our pals, she hadn't kicked the bug when the semester ended. It remained, festering, leaving Wren woozy in bed, unable to resume her summer job at Café Metro, the favored punk club of northeastern Pennsylvania.

I didn't understand how totally everything was about to change when I arrived and saw the rubbed raw faces of Wren's fitness crazed mother, the barely concealed fright in her father's eyes. I didn't get it when I saw her aunt and uncle—teachers from Pittston—in rocking chairs, their faces fat and flush with sympathy. Wren sat at the head of the table, her head dipped, beatific. She took my hand and led me into the backyard where only a year prior we'd sat on lawn chairs with her high school chums and argued about who was better, Kurt Cobain or Eddie Vedder—Saint Kurt obviously. He hadn't lived long enough to sully his legacy. We sat down, and Wren told me she'd been diagnosed with leukemia.

I did everything that was expected of me in a crisis and focused on the few tangible goals I could accomplish. When the semester began, I retrieved work from professors so that Wren could maintain the illusion that she was still working toward her degree. I drove friends to her hospital in Wilkes-Barre. I held her hand during chemo, and together, we watched daytime talk shows and made jokes about the sad lives of the people therein, how lucky we were to be on our side of the television screen. Whenever I had a feeling of any kind, I buried it deep down and refused to think about it. Whenever that didn't work, I walked the mile from my dorm room to the townie bar where I knew I wouldn't have to face our sympathetic classmates and could medicate my depression with one stiff drink after another until I could barely stagger home. To Wren's eternal credit, she was strong and upbeat. Even when she had to drop her classes. Even when she lost her hair, even when the medication caused painful acne flare ups across her back, even when she could no longer taste food, even when the first round of chemo was unsuccessful, even when the second round of chemo was unsuccessful, even when she could only go into public wearing a dust mask and paper boxes over her shoes like some type of lunatic fretting over the apocalypse. But this *was* the apocalypse. Our apocalypse. And I was totally powerless to prevent it.

As fall gave way to winter, I applied to a handful of physics PhD programs across the country, the closest NYU, the farthest Alaska, and entertained the same fear most undergraduate couples experience near the end of college: would we remain together, or would upheaval tear us apart? The only difference was it looked less and less likely that Wren would even make it to graduation. When the biopsy results in February revealed the third round of chemotherapy had failed, the doctors made the inevitable clear: Wren Wells, the great love of my young life, had weeks to live at best.

Marriage was an abstract concept we danced around occasionally, but it was always so far in the distance, a star studded coast of adulthood which we could scarcely peep through the fog of our post-adolescence. During our leukemia year, we rarely talked about that possibility, as if even mentioning such an outcome would jinx us and our chances forever. Two weeks before the end, I was walking around town—I'd begun taking long strolls to clear my mind when self-medicating with bourbon couldn't do the job—and came across the small vintage shop behind the Laundromat. I'd watched Wren purchase heaps of clothing and records over the years, and it wasn't an odd thing for me to step inside and look around. But that day, something else entirely caught my eye: two simple wedding bands glimmering beneath the glass counter. I didn't consider the ramifications of what I was doing and, in many ways, felt like an observer to my own life. There I was, using my credit card to purchase two wedding bands. What would happen next? I eagerly awaited the next thrilling turn like a slack-jawed yokel in the darkness of a movie theatre thriller.

What happened was I called Wren and asked if I could see her alone. Her parents, eternally understanding, agreed, and I arrived at her house in less than an hour. It wasn't even noon yet. She lay in her childhood bed, a television propped up on a nearby dresser, lit journals spread over the comforter, her laptop looping ska songs she'd recorded with the Femme Furies only a year earlier, when she'd been twenty-one and healthy, the rest of her life hazy in front of her but as real and thick as concrete. I'd almost grown used to this new Wren. She was bone thin, her skin yellow. Her hair had grown back, but it wasn't the same. It was more like auburn peach fuzz than human hair. I took her right hand into mine. We hadn't had sex in months. Before her first round of chemotherapy, the doctors extracted a batch of her eggs and froze them in case she wanted to have children via surrogate later in life. The chemo, they explained, would nuke her productive system barren. It was difficult to feel sexy after that.

"Hi, Wren," I whispered.

"Hi, Teddy." She forced a smile.

I stroked her hand and dropped to one knee. I reached in my pocket and produced the ring. I felt more like the protagonist of a romantic dramedy than Teddy Copeland, aspiring physics graduate student. "There's a place in Atlantic City where we can get married today. We can go there and come back later tonight."

"Ok?"

"'Ok' what?"

"Are you proposing?"

"Yes."

"Then give me a real proposal. Don't just focus on the practical stuff. Gosh, you can be a real idiot sometimes." She didn't look flattered or even excited. Her annoyance was as plain as the crease in her forehead.

I cleared my throat. "Wren Wells?"

"Uh-huh."

"Will you marry me?"

"Fine."

We ended up at a hokey church on the edge of the boardwalk. The owners tried to make it resemble the places of worship from our youth—wooden pews, an altar—but the stained glass windows betrayed exactly how far we'd fallen. There were no deities or apostles, no angels or martyrs other than the version of Wren I'd constructed in my mind. The Little Church of the East Wedding Chapel had instead elected to depict casinos and amusement park rides in its windows. We stood in front of the minister not really listening to his spiel. I couldn't focus. My whole body was sweaty, and looking over at Wren, I still thought she was the prettiest bride I'd ever seen in her worn jeans and black hoodie, red scarf atop her head. The minister pronounced us man and wife, and I kissed her deeply, sweetly, keenly aware that I had made her family, that we had done something that could never be undone. This was adulthood.

When the ceremony was over, I bought the most expensive bottle of champagne I could find—it was less than fifty dollars at a nearby liquor store—and the two of us snuck onto the beach, practically abandoned during the offseason. It was windy, and Wren had to walk very slowly and take frequent breaks, and I knew we had to be home soon, that it was growing late and we hadn't even told her parents we were leaving. I owed them so much more. But I felt a stronger duty to my new wife, and what Wren wanted more than anything was to sit on the sand for just a few minutes and watch the waves crash against the beach. We settled on the edge of a dune, and I felt foolish for not packing a blanket. Ever since Wren's diagnosis there had been this layer of wave decoherence between myself and the world. Surely the younger, more innocent Theodore Copeland would have remembered to pack, or at the very least purchase, such an essential item from a boardwalk vendor. No longer was that the case.

I tried to put my arm around Wren, but she huddled away from me. She drew her legs up close to her chest and set her chin between her knees. Unlike the blanket, I'd remembered my camera and retrieved it then, snapping a photo of Wren looking forlornly into the horizon. It was the same one I'd lock in my mini-safe along with my ring just two weeks later. Wren ran the ring back and forth across her knuckle—it was too loose, another practicality I hadn't taken into account—and said, "Let's not tell anyone, ok?"

I stared into the ocean. "What?"

"I don't want to tell anyone what we did here. Let's keep it a secret."

"There's legal documents." I almost took them out to show her.

"I want it kept a secret."

We didn't dare look at each other and, instead, watched the waves crash. Finally, Wren said, "This isn't what I imagined for my life."

I wanted to reply, "Obviously," but I knew that was uncouth and insensitive, and if there was one trait I had cultivated during Wren's cancer, it was repressing my emotions.

"I don't mean the cancer." Wren hugged her knees tighter. "I mean you. I mean us. I mean us getting married."

More than any other moment during her illness, this one took me by surprise, the revelation that she doubted me in even the slightest. "What's that supposed to mean? We talked about marriage even before."

Before was how we talked about that mythical period before the disease. It seemed as remote as our primordial ancestral past. We'd been Neanderthals hulking around Susquehanna not even sensing the Ice Age lurking for us in the not-too-distant future.

"I know that," she said. "But we're just kids. Do you realize how long the average life is? I might have lived till I was a hundred. You still might. I wasn't totally sure about us. I'm still not the person I might have grown into. Who knows if those people, our adult versions, would have been right together? I wanted so much more from my life than this. I had hopes and dreams totally independent from you."

The grief counselor told me Wren might lash out at me, that she might say things she didn't really mean. "Wren," I said. "I love you."

She thought about that for a long time. "I love you too, but we're not soul mates. I never really believed we'd get married. You should know that." She refused to take her eyes off the ocean. "I'm cold. Take me home."

We drove back to Wilkes-Barre in silence and never discussed our marriage again.

THE CONTROL

In my more rational moments, I understand I played no part in Wren's death, just like I understand that my inability to save her is inexorably linked to my interest in saving the world, a selfish-cum-altruistic savior complex. But so what? Is that really so terrible an affliction?

We were together for three years. I spent more time with her than any other person in my life with the exception of the parents who raised me. We shared so many conversations, so many memories, yet the one of us on the beach is the one I replay over and over again in my mind. In my more optimistic moments, I consider the possibility that maybe, just maybe, Wren was planting a seed of doubt in my mind so that I could move on after she died, meet another woman, fall in love, and start the type of life we'd talked about as freshmen and sophomores. But that hypothesis is dashed whenever I remember her eyes, the flat, little line of her mouth, the honest-to-goodness pain etched across her face. Wren Wells was many things, but an actress she was not. And it's in these more realistic moments when I have to acknowledge that we probably wouldn't have gotten married, that our affection for one another was simple puppy love brought on by our new environment and experiences. We'd conflated collegiate excitement with love.

And yet I still can't escape that unlived fantasy. Every time I meet someone new and interesting and challenging, I wonder what would have happened if Wren lived, if I met her again now, as an adult on the pernicious precipice of 30. Would we have wound up together? Could we have been happy? Was she really my soul mate? Or was I simply obsessed? Had I deluded myself into thinking my collegiate loss was somehow different from all the other losses accrued by mankind? Maybe I was a solipsistic goon forever unworthy of love and affection and humanity.

Regardless, I still remember the dissonance of ocean waves and Wren's voice.

I still can't escape the pitch of her voice.

PIZZA WORLD

On the eve of The God Laser live test, Drs. Newmar, Javari, and I found ourselves splayed out across the trio of couches in the fourth floor common room of Housing Unit Seven. After fourteen straight hours of coding, Oppenheimer exiled us from The Control Center—"Get some rest!" he shouted. "Tomorrow's a big day."—and we were so exhausted that we couldn't even rouse ourselves for a fortifying burger and beer from Thomas Arm at The Trinity Tavern.

"Ooooooh," I moaned, hand over eyes, toes quivering. "Ooooooh."

"Del," Nessa said weakly. "Del, will you bring us food? Del."

"No."

"Del."

And so, we arrived at an impasse. A week had passed since my arrival underground, and in the interim my life had fallen into a happy and predictable pattern. Each morning, I rode the monorail from my apartment to The Control Center where I spent the next ten hours—and often beyond—computing algorithms that might lead us into parallel worlds and subsequent salvation. In the evenings, Nessa, Delbar, and I went to Trinity, but the reassuring comfort of my newfound colleagues wasn't enough to curb my extracurricular activities at The God Laser. Each night when our tab was paid, I bade a fond farewell to Nessa and Delbar and rode the monorail to The Control Center and The Wren Algorithm. I saw little harm in the enterprise. If it didn't interfere with my work during the day, then what was the problem if I spent my evenings trying to claw my way into a world where Wren was still alive, where she was twenty-nine and not eternally frozen at sickly twenty-two? How was it any different from a Google executive who spent her evenings building miniature ships in bottles or marathoning B movies on demand? Before I fell asleep each night, I told myself that I was ok, that I was saving the world, that I really was the good person I desperately wanted to become.

Nessa rolled on her back and dug in her pockets for her phone. "Guys," she shouted. "I saw a pizza place near Trinity a few nights back. Salvatore's? Mario's? Rinaldi's? Do you think they deliver? Do you think they'll deliver us a pizza?"

Delbar limply waved. "Call it in. For the love of god, call it in."

We listened intently as Nessa ordered an extra-large half-pineapple, half-bacon pizza—how deeply this rankled my east coast sensibilities—as Delbar and I rubbed our palms and licked our lips like a pack of over-the-top cartoon wolves.

"This is so great. Pizza. I love pizza." Delbar pointed at the blank television. "Can you put something on for us, Nessa? Do you know any shows that pair well with pizza?"

Nessa thought about it for a second before her lips curled into a grin. "Do you guys ever watch K-dramas?"

"What's a K-drama?" I asked.

"Jesus Christ, Copeland." Delbar shielded her eyes so she wouldn't have to look at me.

"Oh, man." Nessa was up and pacing now. "They're awesome. They're sort of like telenovelas but better. I just started one before Oppenheimer brought me down. It's basically a combination of *Friends* and *Star Trek*. I have Season One on Blu-ray in my room."

"Get the Blu-ray," Del demanded. "Now."

Nessa hurried off to her apartment, and a few moments later, we assembled around the common room television to bear witness to the unfolding spectacle of *Your Romantic Star-Filled Journey*. Just as Nessa promised, her beloved K-drama focused on the intergalactic exploratory efforts of the good ship Mocha Mocha and its crew of flannel-sporting, grunge-inspired, '90s-bathed Koreans. Leader of this coffee shop-cum-spaceship was protagonist Kim, a beautiful commander still sporting The Rachel haircut made famous in the mid-'90s. Although the pilot episode occasionally made vague references to the Mocha Mocha's larger, peacekeeping mission, much of the runtime was spent establishing the love triangle between Kim, Park—a handsome but dumb warrior of the Captain Kirk variety—and Kwan—a sensitive alien civilizations sociologist with green skin. Our trio of ambitious prodigies hooted and hollered. We shouted at the screen. We toasted to the plight of Kim with pizza and tap water and quickly dissolved into two factions: Team

Park—Nessa and Delbar—and Team Kwan—lonely Teddy Copeland. And when a rando engineer from India walked by and asked what we were watching, we invited him to join and happily explained the plot. It wasn't until much later, just before I fell asleep in my narrow apartment bed, that I started to really wonder what exactly had happened. Was this the golden glow of friendship, the inverse of my Alaskan isolation?

#

The next morning, Nessa, Delbar, and I assembled in the bodega across from our apartment building en route to the live test. The corner store had quickly become one of my favorite underground haunts. I'd never had access to bodegas in my life aboveground and took a demented joy in the owner's surly attitude. A thick, middle-aged man in a threadbare cardigan, Old Man Reeves acted like he had no earthly idea he'd relocated underground. When asked if he preferred Perro Caliente to wherever it was he hailed from, or why exactly he'd moved beneath the surface in the first place, Old Man Reeves always responded in exactly the same way—"What's it matter?"—before reiterating that loitering wasn't allowed and we best be on our way. We never saw him anywhere other than the bodega, and the only activity he actually seemed to enjoy was sitting quietly behind the register while listening to an ancient radio warble out catastrophic Cubs games. I asked him how it got reception all the way underground once, but he only grunted and spat a litany of sunflower seeds onto the linoleum.

I set my extra-large mug of coffee on the counter and gave Old Man Reeves my most charming smile. "It's so wonderful to see you this morning, Mr. Reeves. Have you heard about the live test? It's today, you know? Big day, big day."

He nodded grimly. Nessa and Del had already paid for their coffee and bagels and loitered near the entrance casting stink eyes in my direction.

"Dollar fifty," Old Man Reeves grunted.

"Dynamite price for coffee. Just dynamite."

Old Man Reeves accepted my cash and flexed a newspaper open in front of his face, ending our conversation. Delbar grabbed me by the bony elbow and almost had to drag me away. Once we were outside and out-of-earshot, she loudly announced, "You're a rube, Copeland. A country-fried rube."

Coffees and bagels in hand, our trio ascended the monorail platform and boarded a train en route to The Control Center and live test. In less than twenty minutes, Nessa and I would sail through the first ever manmade wormhole, but we were at that moment content enough to eat bagels and avoid thinking about how dangerous our lives were soon to become. For Nessa, that meant spouting one practical application for chaos math after another.

"Algorithms," she continued, "could be used to track and predict when athletes will suffer injuries based on when older athletes of similar builds suffered injuries. We could use it to trace how and why a specific segment of the population developed an immunity to—let's say the flu—and then reverse engineer that into a vaccine. We could analyze the results of the financial crisis or the Great Depression and then institute a financial warning system for future generations. We could—"

Del grabbed Nessa's coffee. "Christ, woman. I get that you're nervous about the test, but seriously? Can you stop? Can you calm down and stop?"

Nessa looked down at her Forces.

"Oh, come on now." Del rolled her eyes and sighed, clearly annoyed she had to deal with actual human emotions. "I'm just kidding. Haha, right? Haha. The two of us are enjoying a good joke right now, huh? Jokes! But seriously, our goals for today are just making sure The God Laser's working properly and that you can comb another universe for data. That's it. Calm down. Think UC Berkeley. You'll be there so soon!"

Earlier that week, we'd decided to visit the UC Berkeley of this alternate universe. The idea was to go somewhere familiar and safe where we knew the terrain, and nothing was more familiar to Nessa than the sprawling campus where her father had taught for decades, where she earned her PhD. "UC Berkeley," Nessa told herself. "UC Berkeley." The monorail darted into the northern tunnel that led to The God Laser, and our faces were consumed by shadow. "I got this. No problem. I know that place like the back of my hand."

The particle accelerator flashed alongside our windows. "Your dad taught advanced particle physics, right?" I asked.

She nodded.

"You think that plays into his secret project?"

"Maybe, but I'm not sure. We didn't exactly have the best relationship, especially the last few years."

I wanted to say something comforting, something that signaled to Nessa that she was understood and among friends, but the best I could muster was a feeble, "Totally." Delbar again rolled her eyes, and we were silent then until the monorail mercifully deposited us at The Control Center.

A palpable electricity coursed through The Control Center. Physicists who were usually glued to their workstation terminals now stood at attention and awkwardly saluted, eager for their first glimpse of The God Laser in action. Delbar handed us our Calabi-Yau Computation Tablets, and before she slipped upstairs to stand alongside Oppenheimer, she left us with one final kernel of advice. "No pressure, bros." She winked, and Nessa and I at last entered the holy center of The God Laser: that seemingly-mythical stone walkway that reached up into the emptiness between the dual electromagnets of Oppie's collider. From the base of the walkway, we could see the many physicists, their faces pressed to the glass of the cylindrical Control Center. I could hardly reconcile the myriad ways in which my life was changing—Saving the world! Oppenheimer! Strong and confident friends! The Wren Algorithm!—with my humble origins, that innocent childhood in Binghamton that had first stoked the coals of scientific inquiry. I stood there oddly recalling the ISC Rising Stars science competition that rolled into Binghamton mere days after my twelfth birthday. Fifty local kids with the best standardized test scores were selected to participate, and I was one of them. How vividly I remembered the gaudy set erected in our downtown civic center, all faux-starship backgrounds and steaming prop-beakers. I remembered the host, a British scientist, round and saccharine, the way he fired off question after question from a stack of yellow index cards. I remembered the competitive experiments, how we raced to see who could build an electromagnet or potato battery the fastest, how I survived through the very last cutoff to face little Laura Leery in the final blitzkrieg of rapid fire questions, my parents sweating in the audience, cheering me on. I remembered winning, how the neon balloons rained from the upper echelons of the civic center, how the grandfatherly British scientist handed me an oversized check that signified a minor college scholarship. I remembered that early encouragement into the world of science and could not connect it to Oppeneheimer's God Laser. I was sweaty and nearing a panic attack. I reached for Nessa's hand, and she squeezed it as hard as she could.

"Dr. Newmar? Dr. Copeland?" Oppenheimer's voice boomed over the loudspeakers, and we saw him standing alongside Delbar on the top floor, his face pressed close to a microphone. "I'd like you to meet Dr. Percy Fenton here." A pudgy man with crumbs in his beard gave a flirty little wave. "He's the one who coded our experiment today. Tell them, Dr. Fenton, exactly what you changed within The Theory of Almost Everything."

Dr. Fenton cleared his throat, and a painful screech rang throughout The Control Center. "Oh, dear." He sniffed. "Ahem. Yes. For this first test, I knew we wanted to alter some event mostly irrelevant to history so we could send you into a world mostly like our own, so I went into the code and located this moment thirty years ago when I had pizza at Pequod's in Chicago. I remembered that I ordered a deluxe because this was my one and only time in Chicago. I was visiting my Aunt Virginia, and I really wanted this pizza to count. I'm from outside Philly originally and the pizza's flat there. If I was only going to visit Chicago once, I wanted the deluxe, but I did, however briefly, consider ordering the veggie instead on account of advice from my doctor. Acid reflux. Although really, I shouldn't have even been eating pizza at all. I never do now." Another clearing of the throat. "So that's what I changed. I went into the theory and coded a world where I ordered a vegetarian pizza thirty years ago instead of a deluxe."

Oppie snatched the mic away. "That's the world we're sending you to, and the idea is it should be pretty close to our own. We just want to make sure all our equipment works. All right, you two ready down there?"

We stood twenty yards back from where the wormhole would appear. I was totally and utterly unable to speak, but Nessa found my gaze and spoke for the both of us. "We're ready!"

"Bully!" Oppie called. "The entire planet is depending on you. Be brave, be intelligent, be daring!"

Dr. Oppenheimer threw a comically oversized lever, and suddenly the underground cavern filled with ear-shattering noise, the behemoth wails of a hundred mile collider churning to life. It felt like being in the heart of a tornado, and my teeth chattered like a terrified school boy as the dual quadrupole electromagnets spun slowly at first, then wildly, bits of white electricity crackling in the air between. Faster and faster they spun, the lightning blasts growing larger and larger until finally they struck in the middle with enough force to knock Nessa and I back on our rears. We sat there stunned as the laser grew into a black egg surrounded by a growing cloud of fizzing electricity. Nessa drew to her feet and held out a hand to pull me up, but for a moment I could do nothing but stare at the wormhole summoned before us, the terrifying Einstein-Rosen Bridge I had conjured from my grief. It was a truly religious experience, and I suddenly imagined my parents receiving the Eucharist in Binghamton. Had they ever experienced something like this, I wondered. Had anyone? A moment of pure religious ecstasy.

"Teddy, come on!"

Nessa pulled me up, and we ran straight at the center of the wormhole. In the split-second before we tumbled through the dead-eye portal, I considered the possibility that The Copeland Principle was wrong, that I hadn't figured out the lone perceptible difference between wormhole gateways and black hole dead ends, that in fact, we'd assembled a black hole underground that would now disintegrate our bodies before moving onto the planet and eventually the entire universe itself. But luckily for all our sakes, that absurdist fear was short-lived. We hurled ourselves into the black egg and appeared instantaneously atop a collegiate quad as lush and as green as a brochure. I touched my head, chest, genitals, yes, they were all there. No body parts had been vaporized during our cross-dimensional trip. I found Nessa on my right, the same look of happy stupefaction on her face. We had done it all right. We had definitively proved that not only were parallel worlds real, but you could enter them as well. Our reward was the sunshine warming our faces, a phenomenon neither Dr. Newmar nor I had experienced in days.

Nessa ran a hand through her hair. "Holy moly, we did it."

I slapped her on the back and assessed our surroundings. Unlike Nessa, I hadn't grown up in the nurturing incubator of Berkeley and had never been to California in my life. My first impression was the same one I had whenever I visited another college for an academic conference or student exchange. Be it the sprawling southern charm of the University of Alabama or the compact boxy-ness of SUNY Binghamton, all colleges possessed a certain sameness, sort of like wandering past fun house mirrors and seeing so many stretched out images of the same face. No college was complete without the brick academic buildings, grassy knolls swollen with sunning teens in springtime, the mighty sororities and fraternities, the sensation that this was a place to be serious, studious, a place where true knowledge might be at last unearthed. Berkeley was no different. A bell tower illuminated by the bright morning sun rang out, and we watched as students filed out of buildings, throngs upon throngs of them on their way to their next class.

"This is North Field," Nessa said excitedly. "Over there's Morrison, Barrows. That's the gym. It's so wild being here, Teddy. It's exactly how I remember it, but it's not my Berkeley. It's a totally different universe!"

"Not that different," I reminded her. "The only difference here is Dr. Fenton ordered a veggie pizza thirty years ago. How different could it be?"

A line of students cut through the field en route to the gym, and each one passed us with a shy, little smile. A young woman in sandals and a yellow sun dress bowed her head at Nessa and cheerily said, "你好!"

I blinked at her. She was Caucasian. Even though I'd never been to UC Berkeley before, I assumed blonde students didn't wander around greeting people in Chinese.

"你們兩個失去?" the student asked.

Nessa gawked at her, confirmation that this truly was out of the ordinary, that I wasn't just behind on my Berkeley societal norms. And then I noticed something even stranger. All of them were talking in Chinese. Nessa realized this too and poked the sandal sporting student in the shoulder to determine whether or not she was real. "What's going on?"

The student appeared scandalized, physically disgusted by the blunt phonetics of the English language. She leaned into Nessa and hissed, "What the hell's your problem? Stop speaking English. Are you a dumb Gamma Delta or something?"

The woman hurried off, and just as quickly as it had begun, the bell tower rang again, and one-by-one the vast sea of students disappeared into the many buildings flanking North Field or the few paths that extended into the broader world of UC Berkeley. We were alone.

"How'd a veggie pizza cause that?" I asked.

"Don't talk to me right now." Nessa was already furiously swiping the screen of her Calabi-Yau Computation Tablet, her brow furrowed, her cheeks illuminated by the artificial blue light of Delbar's machine. To passersby we would've looked like anyone else checking e-mail on the quad. But I knew what Nessa was up to and why Oppenheimer wanted a chaos mathematician in the first place. It was Nessa's job to calculate how exactly Dr. Fenton ordering a veggie pizza instead of a deluxe pizza in Chicago had led to throngs upon throngs of UC Berkeley students speaking Chinese. This went far beyond her work on Google Now, was so much bigger than predicting whether or not you wanted to see the Knicks score before you actually Googled "Knicks score," and the intellectual strain was obvious on Nessa's face.

"Wow," she whispered. "According to this, Dr. Fenton not eating that pizza thirty years ago caused an absurdly complex series of events that led to the collapse of the American economy and eventually China purchasing the western half of the United States." Her eyes flew across the screen. "There's too many variables. Way too many variables. I'm going to try and scan them, maybe collect them so we can examine them later at The Control Center, but this is crazy." A few more swipes and bang, a series of loud pops emitted from her tablet, then a tiny cloud of smoke, the miniature mushroom cloud of Hiroshima. She showed me the dead screen of her tablet, then reached for mine.

"Uh, are you sure?" I reluctantly handed it over. "If this one breaks, we're stuck here."

She shook her head. She was speaking so fast I could hardly keep up. "No variables this time, no variables. There's too many for the tablet to take in all at once. I'm just setting up an environmental scan. That way we can compare it to ours and see how it differs once we're home." A few more swipes. "It should take a half hour." Nessa grabbed me by the shoulders, her eyes wide and—forgive me—a tad crazy. "Do you understand what this means?"

I had an inkling, but chaos math wasn't my specialty.

"It means," she continued without waiting for a response, "that every single cosmic event—everything from ordering a pizza to the atomic bombings to the microscopic movements of space dust—leads to an extremely high number of variables. Way higher than we originally thought. Oppenheimer guessed that this world would be exactly like ours, that an event as 'historically unimportant' as ordering a pizza would barely alter the flow of time. But clearly that isn't the case at all. Every variable causes a massive chain reaction. Or at least, that's my theory." She palmed her forehead. "This means locating a world free from the threat of extinction is going to be way harder than we first thought. It could take decades. It could take forever."

Nessa sat on the grass, my tablet still clutched to her chest. I recognized the look on her face, the anxious, shallow breaths, a panic attack in purple bloom. I'd experienced so many in Alaska and could almost sense what Nessa was thinking. What if this was all too big? What if we'd strayed beyond the purview of man's scientific interests? What if we'd slipped into the muddy waters reserved only for gods and titans? What if everything was doomed?

I sat next to her and put my arm around Nessa's shoulder. "Hey," I said. "Hey. Look at me."

She looked me in the eyes. Her breathing was still shallow, and it was obvious from the pressed line of her mouth she didn't want me thinking her weak. Nothing could be further from the truth.

"Breathe," I said. "Breathe."

She took a deep breath. "This is crazy."

"I know."

"I didn't expect this."

"I know."

"What else do you think is different?" Nessa seemed a little calmer now, her voice signaling the return of her trademark curiosity.

I nodded at the tablet. "Check it out. What do you want to know?"

She brought up the web browser and navigated to Google. We started with the American government and were tickled to discover that in this world, a woman—unknown to both of us—had won the presidency not to mention re-election. We searched for bands and movies and restaurants and found no traces of them. On this earth, they'd been replaced with bizzaro alternatives. Everything before Dr. Fenton ordered that now infamous pizza thirty years ago was exactly the same as it had been in our world, but everything after was radically altered, almost unrecognizably so. I remembered that feeling outside the conference hotel at the ASA, the sensation that the world was divided into halves. We sat in the grass waiting for the scan to finish, and suddenly I remembered why Nessa had opted for UC Berkeley in the first place. She'd grown up here. She knew it intimately. Her father had taught here for years.

"Google your dad. See if he still taught here."

Nessa typed in her father's name, and a moment later we were reading his obituary. In the very first paragraph it mentioned his decades of service not to Berkeley, but Stanford.

"So weird," Nessa said. "I wonder what that means for my mom?"

She swiped in another name in the search bar, and I watched helplessly as her face dropped. One minute we'd been laughing about how in this reality people still used America Online, and the next, she was sprinting toward the nearest academic building, our lone functioning tablet in hand. I'd never been much of a runner. Even as a child, when it was acceptable or even fun to run around like barbarians in pursuit of a pal or a flag, I always declined. Let life come to me, I thought, even as a boy in ruddy Binghamton. But in that alternate universe where China owned half of America, I had a very different opinion indeed. Nessa possessed the only way to return to our world, and I didn't think myself up to the task of learning a new language so late in life. But by the time I stood up, my knees popping loudly as I did so, Nessa had already disappeared into the building across the quad. I thought about calling out to her more for the dramatic image—an intellectual dandy lost in a parallel world!—than any legitimate hope that said call might be answered, but my self-preservation instincts kicked in at last, and I realized I'd been left with no other alternative but to sprint after my partner.

I'd spent the last decade of my life in a collegiate setting, and I knew immediately where I was the moment I entered the building. Oddly thick doors with tiny glass peepholes. The dissonance of some unseen dweeb tuning his tuba. A quick-footed professor striding by with a scarf and megaton levels of flair. This was the music building, and I arrived just in time to see the squat outline of Dr. Newmar hurry up the stairs at the other end of the hallway. I darted after her—or at least, my slightly quicker-than-normal gait was my version of darting—and climbed the stairs. Perhaps Nessa harbored some deep seated anger toward music students and every event in her life—the PhD, working for Google, even her strained relationship with her father—had been part of an elaborate campaign to gain access to these defenseless musicians fiddling with cymbals in rehearsal spaces. There was no trace of her on the second floor, but I turned into one of the open doorways and found her paralyzed with fright in a waiting room. An administrative assistant—no doubt close to eighty-years-old, a Stephen King romance spread eagle atop her desk—called out to her in Chinese, then reluctantly in English. "Are you ok?" she asked.

Dr. Nessa Newmar turned from the row of offices beyond, no doubt the slim jail cells of an aging professoriate. Her face was shaken, and she looked about ready to throw up. I anxiously scanned the room for a trash can.

"Is Dr. Newmar in today?" Nessa asked.

The admin smiled like a mother welcoming home a prodigal son, and it was clear she didn't exactly relish having to speak Chinese every day of her life. She set a receipt in her book and pointed down the hall at an open doorway. "Right over there, hon."

Nessa nodded but didn't move. I didn't understand what was going on. We'd read her father's obituary. He'd taught at Stanford, not Berkeley. But maybe obituaries were different in this universe? I had no idea but understood Nessa's motivation completely. Who wouldn't want to see a dead loved one again, especially if the ending hadn't gone quite as you'd hoped?

Did it matter if said loved one was from an alternate universe and had never even met you before? Not to me it didn't. It was the most human desire in the world.

"I thought your father was dead here too?" I asked.

She didn't look at me. She just kept staring down the hallway at her father's office and the door left tantalizingly ajar. "It's not my father's office. It's my mother's."

#

I found a sherbet stand on the other side of North Field, and Nessa and I sat on a bench outside Morrison Hall—that fabled music building—eating politely in silence. Students streamed by chatting in Chinese. We had ten more minutes before the data scan was complete, and Nessa still had not explained what she'd said in the music department. I remembered the proclamation she'd made in the Indianapolis convention center: *Nostalgia is nihilism*. It felt like a prophecy of some kind, and I wanted to burn Nessa's message in the green of North Field for all those Chinese-speaking Berkeley students to see. *Nostalgia is nihilism*. Between spoonfuls of sherbet, Nessa retrieved a tiny piece of paper from her pocket and folded it in a series of complex machinations until it became an origami crane. Then she made another and another, setting them around her like a miniature bird army.

"You make cranes?" I asked.

"When I'm stressed. When I want to brighten my environment."

"Cool. That's really cool." I coughed into my fist. "Are you ok?"

She folded another paper bird. Then three more. "My mother's been dead seventeen years," she blurted. "My father met her in his late fifties. She was still so young. Just a grad student at Berkeley in music. I never got to see her perform live, but I've digitized a bunch of her recordings and uploaded them to YouTube, SoundCloud, the works. Kind of like a digital monument." She paused here. It was clear the phrase "digital monument" pleased her, and I wanted to tell her it was a nice expression. Instead, I scraped the bottom of my cup. "It was a six car pileup on the freeway," Nessa continued. "Three people died. Five in critical condition. It was started by—you guessed it—a drunk. Thad McClane, a librarian from Marina Bay. He survived the accident, got clean, sends everybody's family an apology each Christmas. Has a kid now. A girl. She's interested in science too. I chalked it up to randomness even back then. A tragedy, sure, but clearly random. But it broke my father. That's when he started burying himself in his basement lab even though the accommodations at the school were so much better. That's when he stopped teaching undergrad classes and applied for all this research time so he could sit twiddling his thumbs all day with the exception of the lone graduate course he taught on Wednesday nights. That's when our house turned into a mausoleum. He wouldn't even let me update any of the furniture. Nothing. He never even moved her clothes out of the closet. Christ, that house probably still looks exactly the same, and no one's even lived there for years. I told you he never wanted me to pursue science. He always pushed me toward the arts even though he knew I despised it. I can't carry a tune to save my life, Copeland."

It wasn't hard to trace the origins of Nessa's worldview via my own brand of chaos math. Nessa's life had been cracked down the middle by what she dubbed randomness. She was then presented with a choice. She could either wallow in the past like her devastated father, or she could stride bravely into the future, never looking back. Of course a woman like that would end up at Google. Of course a woman like that would put "Futurist" smack dab in the middle of her business card. In her view, the past was pain, and the only salvation lay in the future.

"In this world," she continued, "Dad died in the accident, and Mom became a professor just like she always wanted." She was speaking slower than I'd ever heard her, and I have to admit I was a tad disturbed. "I looked up what happened to me too. I still got my PhD in Chaos Math, only from Stanford this time. This world's me works for some shoddy sounding think tank in Austin. Can you imagine that, Teddy? There are other versions of us walking around this Earth. It's crazy."

I imagined how this scenario might play out if our roles were reversed. Let's say—for hypothetical sake—that it was Wren Wells no less than two floors away in an unlocked office. Would I demolish our last remaining Calabi-Yau Computation Tablet and profess my undying love to my resurrected bride? Would I somehow try and explain my sorry tale about how I'd traveled from another universe to find her? I couldn't say exactly, but I sure as hell wouldn't be finishing up sherbet with a co-worker I'd known for barely a week and a half.

"Go talk to her, Nessa."

Nessa's reaction was swift and unavoidable. She looked as disgusted as if I'd casually proposed we spend our remaining moments on this earth beating up orphans and terrorizing puppies. "Are you joking? That would be so out of bounds, Teddy. We're scientists, and Oppenheimer entrusted us to use The God Laser for the betterment of mankind. I'm not going to use this technology to pick at my own emotional scabs. What good would that do? Besides, it would be so utterly unfair to that woman in Morrison Hall. She didn't die. She already has a Nessa. What gives me the right to go interfere with her life? I'm not god."

I wanted to spar with her, to make her understand that what I was proposing wasn't diabolical but necessary and harmless. Oppenheimer expected us to enter parallel worlds, assess the situation, observe the data scan, then return. What did it matter if we engaged in some idle wish fulfilment in the process? And I wasn't exactly suggesting that Nessa march on up to her other mother's office and explain the entire story about The God Laser and parallel worlds and how in our reality she'd been the one who'd died instead of her husband. Nessa could simply go up and impersonate this world's Nessa. Then she'd get a couple of minutes to actually talk with her mother! Surely that wasn't a violation of scientific ethics, now was it? But luckily, I never had to engage in that particular conversation. Because less than a minute after Nessa explained exactly why everything I was planning to do with The Wren Algorithm was self-destructive at best and potentially world-dooming at worst, the alarm buzzed on our tablet. The scan was complete, and already the data had been transferred across those magical radio waves Oppenheimer had told me about on my first day underground. Our first jaunt into a parallel world—stressful and bizarre as it was—had drawn to a close.

Nessa didn't wait for me to respond to her accusations about the proper uses of The God Laser. Instead, she swiped in a command on the tablet, and I heard the same, dull churn from when Oppenheimer teleported away from my StayRomp hotel room. We dematerialized in a flash of pulsating light and appeared a moment later atop the stone walkway between the dual electromagnets of The God Laser. It felt like going down the first drop of a roller coaster, that initial moment when it feels like your stomach's been ziplined out of your body. But it was a swift recovery, and soon Nessa and I were gazing at the dozens of familiar physicists behind their terminals. One-by-one they rushed out of The Control Center and joined us. They clapped and cheered. They hooted and hollered. They happily stomped their feet, and I realized they weren't yet aware of how radically altered Dr. Fenton's pizza world truly was. They were still blissfully ignorant of the massive workload dumped before us.

"Teddy! Nessa!" Delbar Javari pushed through the crowd to embrace us. "You were great, just great. Parallel worlds are real, and we can actually enter them! We know a hundred, no, a thousand times more about the Multiverse than we did a few hours ago." She shook her head. "We keep applying this data to The Theory of Almost Everything, and we may actually build an algorithm for a world free from human extinction."

It sounded so nice, so sweet, and although Nessa and I understood we'd have to tell them about the students speaking Chinese and how so many lives and events had been altered by Fenton's veggie pizza, in that moment it was enough to let their collective hope wash over us like an artificial waterpark wave. I heard the pop of a champagne bottle, and before I knew it, the men and women of Perro Caliente lifted Nessa and me high above their heads, shouting, "Hip, hip, hurray!" We were on the hypothetical verge of saving the planet, and as I glanced conspiratorially at Nessa, I recognized this as the type of moment I'd fantasized about for years, maybe ever since building electromagnets in my childhood basement: a tingling sensation that everything might turn out ok after all, that through the manifest destiny of scientific inquiry we might reach out beyond the stars and shout, "No, we won't go quietly into the night," rebuking the skeletal caress of death itself. If I couldn't keep Wren's love, perhaps I could earn the love and admiration of the entire Multiverse.

Curiously, the Hologram of Robert Oppenheimer was nowhere to be found.

#

The champagne and camaraderie shifted from The God Laser to The Trinity Tavern, and soon, all of us were drunk, boasting, arm wrestling, toasting to Thomas Arm's artisan cocktails and the bright future and discoveries we were all soon to make. Nessa and I drunkenly explained to Delbar what we'd observed in the parallel world—excluding, of course, the visit to Morrison Hall—but she only nodded. "It's just the first one. Maybe Fenton's pizza is inextricably linked to Chinese-American relations. Let's see how it plays out." In the buzzed haze of the Trinity, that seemed like reassurance enough for me.

Our trio settled in at our familiar booth, and try as I might, I could not relax. Maybe it was all those students speaking Chinese. Maybe it was the disappearance of Oppenheimer. But something felt off, staged, simplistic. "Guys," I said, as we started our second round, "do you have the feeling that all of this has been a little too—easy?"

Nessa and Delbar stared at me expressionless. "All of what?"

"This." I gestured at our surroundings trying to imply the entirety of Oppenheimer's underground endeavor. "Our invitations to Perro Caliente. How quickly we entered parallel worlds. Our acceptance by Oppenheimer. I mean, honestly everything from grad school on has been shockingly simple."

Delbar scratched beneath her cleft. "Uh, maybe the whole entering-a-parallel-world thing has been a tad on the easy side, but that's about it for me, Copeland. A childhood of oppression in Iran. Growing up without my immediate family in a foreign country. Trying to climb the ranks of a field that's notoriously a boy's club. Overcoming a century's worth of institutionalized racism where brown means bad. Yeah, so easy!"

I looked to Nessa for support.

"Nope."

"But–"

"Nope. Nope. Nope. Teddy," she finally said, "if I had to choose a list of adjectives to describe my life, 'easy' wouldn't crack the top one million. Maybe that's true for you, but not for women in the sciences, especially women who look like us."

I conceded my admittedly privileged and naïve argument and surrendered to the fact that perhaps I was just being paranoid, that so many days cut off from the outside world had left me foolish and strange like Dr. Kwan from *Your Romantic Star-Filled Journey* after his imprisonment on Soda World 4. We hurried through our drinks, but before we could place an order for dinner, I received a peculiar text message from none other than the missing Dr. Oppenheimer. *Take the eastbound monorail to the end of the line. Bring Drs. Newmar and Javari. No one else. Secrecy is the spice of life, kiddies. But seriously, don't bring anyone else. For real.* I held up the screen for Nessa and Delbar to see.

"That sounds totally normal and not at all insane," Del said.

We did as instructed and caught the next eastbound train. It was almost empty at that time of night, just us and an

Argentinian scientist whose job was experimenting on hyper intelligent horses, and even he disembarked a few stops short of the eastern tunnel that led out of the Mezzanine. So we sat and waited, strips of yellow light racing across our faces, before the speaker box shouted, "End of the line!"

We disembarked onto a platform overlooking a surprisingly vast desert punctuated by an old log cabin. It was Delbar who figured it out as she led us down the stairs, removed her heels, and started across the sand.

"Doesn't that look oddly similar to Oppenheimer's aboveground cabin?"

I squinted. She was right. Here, miles beneath the Earth's surface, the Hologram of Dr. J. Robert Oppenheimer had erected a replica version of his tiny surface ranch, the underground yin to his aboveground yang. I was about to comment on how unusual this was, how peculiar our lives were becoming during that sweetly strange spring, when our old pal Oppie upped the ante. We heard music blasting from inside the cabin. Not just any music, but the high sopranos of a children's choir backed by an overwhelming orchestra. We trudged along, the cabin growing larger and larger against the horizon. There was something unfamiliar about the lyrics. Were they singing in Chinese? Japanese? Had Oppenheimer been infected by the chipper students of Dr. Fenton's pizza world as well?

We arrived on Oppenheimer's doorstep, and while I hesitated and wondered whether or not we should knock, Delbar turned the knob and went right on in. Nessa and I followed close behind, and the music was so loud that I almost reached for my ears, a weak-willed impulse Wren Wells had taught me to ignore during the many punk/ska shows we'd attended in State College and Harrisburg. The inside of the ranch looked exactly the same as its aboveground counterpart where Barb from HR first introduced me to the exciting world of Perro Caliente. The only difference was we found Oppenheimer sitting by a Victrola near the fireplace, his face as somber as I'd ever seen it.

"Ah, children. Welcome," he said, reaching for the needle.

"What was that?" Delbar asked.

"It's a record put out by the Children's Choir of Hiroshima in response to... our work in Los Alamos." He cleared his throat and closed his eyes, his chin tipped skyward. "'In a flash, we became fire. In a flash, we became ghosts.'" He gestured to the loveseat and drink cart. "Sit down, have a drink."

We were as obedient as the school children on Oppenheimer's record, only instead of belting out a song of national mourning, we filled our glasses with Oppie's liquor. Delbar and I immediately went for the browns, while Nessa frowned and scratched her neck. Apparently, Oppenheimer was no fan of Red Bull. She awkwardly poured herself a glass of sherry and sat next to me on the couch.

"So," Delbar said, "you built a replica of your cabin underground? That's cool and not crazy."

"I'm over a hundred years old. A man gets used to certain habits, and the best periods of my life were spent in that cabin. Don't judge me." He crossed his legs. In many ways, he was the living definition of the intellectual dandy I'd always dreamed of becoming, but also a stern reminder of how quickly that fantasy could decay into nightmare. The significant accomplishment of his scientific life was the eradication of hundreds of thousands of civilians. "A toast," he said, holding up his glass, "to you three. I'm tremendously impressed by the work you've done in such a short period. It's just been outrageous. To you and your continued accomplishments, my trio of ambitious prodigies."

Delbar, Nessa, and I each took a sip from our drinks, but Oppenheimer held his glass to his mouth, his Adam's apple bobbing up and down, until every last inch of rye was gone. He smacked his lips and looked at us aghast. "Ah, don't be modest, kids. Let's do this Manhattan Project style. Back in Los Alamos, whenever we toasted some scientific achievement, we always finished our drinks." He pointed a slightly trembling finger at Nessa. "If it was good enough for your father, it's good enough for you. Tut, tut, gang."

I shrugged before finishing my drink, and Delbar and Nessa did the same. I wasn't sure about them, but as I watched Oppenheimer collect and refill our glasses, I knew that the whiskey in combination with my earlier drinks from The Trinity Tavern had rendered me drunk. The room wasn't spinning, and I wasn't slurring my words, but I felt the familiar red-cheeked smile on my face, the weightlessness in my legs that signaled I had crossed an imperceptible but vital threshold.

Nessa accepted her refill and frowned. "We shouldn't be toasting. Everybody in the world we visited was speaking Chinese. Fenton's veggie pizza caused millions, maybe trillions of little changes to our Theory of Almost Everything. You know how hard that's going to make it to accurately predict what any other changes will cause?"

Oppenheimer waved her off. "It was the first test. Calm down. The first time we tested the atom bomb, I almost blew up half of Nevada." Oppenheimer sank back into the armchair and let loose a contented sigh. "No more about work this evening. Let's just sit back, relax, and get to know each other."

And that's exactly what we did. One-by-one we recapped our life stories, a drunken reboot of the conversation our trio had shared in The Trinity Tavern a week prior, only this time Oppenheimer interjected, commenting about faculty he knew at Delbar's Oxford or on something Nessa said that reminded him of her father. He even relayed much of his own experience, and even though I had an intimate understanding of the narrative of his life from his bio, it was oddly pleasurable to hear those same stories remixed by the man himself. Wild tales about uranium and fission experiments conducted in the shrouded mystery of Los Alamos. Staffing gambits that had shaken the military head of Los Alamos to his core. And one after another the drinks kept coming, and it was all so weirdly pleasurable, weirdly carefree. Or at least, it felt that way until the clock struck midnight, when a laughing Oppenheimer stood from his chair, his face newly rigid and strangely sober. We were much too drunk to pick up on any nefarious scheme, but the way he so suddenly shot to his feet took me by surprise. I felt rooted to my chair and couldn't even imagine making the brief trek across the desert to the final monorail station on the eastern line.

Oppenheimer checked his pocket watch. "It's almost time to call this evening to a close, but before I do so, I'd like to play a game I introduce to all my most promising new hires. Is my assessment correct that you're all impressed by the scientific resources I've gathered underground, kids?"

It was Nessa who spoke first, Nessa who excitedly jiggled her foot, Nessa who had seen the inner sanctum of Google's futuristic sunshine lair. "Absolutely."

"Bully. Then let's engage in a little thought experiment. I want you to each tell me what you'd do with Perro Caliente—everything from The God Laser to the workers to the money—if you were in charge." He waggled his hologram eyebrows. "No need to rush. Take your time, children."

The moment Oppenheimer finished, Delbar spoke. "First thing I'd do is reprioritize The God Laser. Right now, it's focused solely on solving global extermination threats like nuclear fallout, global warming. What about searching for a world without poverty, a world without hunger, a world without racism?"

Nessa nodded and clapped. "Yeah, yeah, definitely. Me too. But I'd make The God Laser tech available to the public at large. Let's give access to every scientist and government in the world. Right now we have the processing power of a few thousand scientists. But what if we had the processing might of every scientist, not to mention computer, in the world?"

"Oh, perfect idea, girl. Perfect. Instead of using The God Laser merely to save the world we have, we can use it to imagine a utopia, a place totally devoid of problems. We can use it to save everyone, not just a chosen few."

Dr. Oppenheimer's expression revealed nothing, but I didn't think he was too moved by Delbar's desire to save everyone. I remembered Hiroshima and Nagasaki. I remembered what Del had suggested during our first evening at the Trinity. *Oppenheimer's been a hologram for twenty-five years. That had to warp him, right?* He took another sip of rye before turning to me. "And you, Copeland? What would you do?"

I didn't immediately respond. The future was something I rarely considered and actively avoided. But now that I was drunk, I allowed myself to wonder where I belonged. Did I belong anywhere? I finished my drink and tried not to dwell on these admittedly sophomoric—yet impossibly vital!—concerns and instead focused on Oppenheimer's hypothetical. What would I do if I was in charge of Perro

Caliente? First, I considered what I'd done so far with my limited access to Oppie's vast resources. Outside of following every order he gave us, I'd used my free time to compose The Wren Algorithm, a fantasy in which I might see my wife alive once again, a delicate equation I was getting closer to solving with each and every day. While Delbar and Nessa suggested disseminating God Laser tech and using Oppie's resources to save everyone, I fantasized about seeing my long dead wife.

"The truth is I probably wouldn't change much. I'm not sure revealing The God Laser, or even the existence of this place for that matter, is a good idea. Wouldn't some people use it for evil, destruction? And I'm not sure how practical it is to save everyone. It's noble. It sounds nice. But isn't stopping the apocalypse good enough for now? I want to believe in everything you're saying. I really do. But it's hard for me to imagine it."

Again, Oppenheimer gave no indication if I'd passed his exam, or if this "thought experiment" was important to him in even the slightest. But one look at Nessa or Delbar made it clear I'd failed a very important test in their minds. Our roles were cast then as solid and permanent as steel. Nessa was the futurist, Delbar the tough-as-nails savior, and I was the cynical nostalgic. It was a strange triumvirate to be sure, and I wondered if we could really do it, if we could reach out beyond the stars and actually solve the problem of the end of everything.

Oppenheimer retrieved a clove cigarette from his breast pocket and lit up. "Intriguing answers, children, but we best say goodnight. The last train leaves the station in fifteen minutes. Get a good night's sleep. We have important work in the morning. We always have such important work."

The Copeland Principle: An Examination of Parallel Worlds in Three Parts (Part Three of Three)

By Dr. Theodore Copeland

PROCEDURE FOR THE EXPERIMENT

Two weeks after our Atlantic City wedding, Wren Wells died. Let me tell you where I was: at the movies with my old roommate The Bull. Wren had fallen into a coma and this period of knowing-but-not-knowing dragged on for six days. I camped out with the hospice nurses in the Wells' living room, and on the final day her family told me to take a break, to go see a movie. The consensus was she still had another week. So I called The Bull and we met at a movie theatre to see a comedy about a school security guard with a raging flatulence problem. My co-ed brethren had been raving about it for months, christening it as that term's cinematic gem. I laughed. I forgot my cell phone in my car. Her parents tried to call, tried to retrieve me, but as my secret wife Wren Wells died, I sat amid darkness laughing at a farting comedian.

By the time the film was over, night had fallen across Selinsgrove. I returned to my car and listened to three missed voice mails, each from Wren's father, the first imploring me to return as quickly as possible, the second telling me that her suffering was over, the third thanking me for being such a large part of Wren's life and that he'd get back to me with details for the viewing and funeral. I sat with the windows open. It was only March, but the weather had warmed considerably since our chilly beach excursion. What was I supposed to do now? There was no reason to return to her parents' house. I wasn't truly part of their family, and I had no intention of breaking Wren's request and telling them we had married. I hadn't even worn my ring since leaving Atlantic City. Already, I had purchased that accursed mini-safe.

After Wren's death, my life returned to the suddenly false normalcy of undergraduate life. Like the coward I was and possibly still am, I bailed on Wren's funeral and never even came within fifty miles of her grave. It all felt too final, too sci-fi unbelievable, and instead, I showed up to classes periodically or drank myself stupid in townie bars. Professors showed me too much sympathy, and I was allowed to turn in projects late or not at all without much penalty. Weeks before my collegiate career drew to a depressing close, I swung by my mailbox near the cafeteria—the first time I'd done so in months—and discovered the future in fat, thick letters from the nation's top graduate schools. I hadn't fared as well as I'd hoped. Portsmouth and UT-Austin replied with a summary no. But I'd done better than many of my friends who were about to trade the comforts of academia for an America tipped toward economic breakdown. I returned to my dorm and opened up two acceptance letters from NYU and the University of Alaska. I could either return to my home state and become a true Manhattanite or venture into the deep north, a self-imposed exile from the continental United States where I might spend the next section of my life in scholarly isolation studying the very nature of the universe itself. It wasn't much of a choice, and I booked my flight to Alaska that afternoon.

EXPERIMENTAL DATA

I flew to Anchorage in a plane so small we had to climb down a flight of stairs onto the tarmac before scurrying toward the warmth of the airport. I disembarked and stopped dead in my tracks on the runway, my effeminate crimson scarf—a near replica of the one Wren had worn on the beaches of Atlantic City—flapping wildly in the wind. A heavy snow was falling across Anchorage, a solid four inches already accumulated at my feet, the sky dotted with the bright yellow lights of the international airport. I had been reassured by future professors and fellow grad students alike that Alaska, especially Anchorage, was not exactly how the media portrayed it. It wasn't all snow and cold and darkness, they told me. Sometimes you even forgot you'd elected to spend years of your life severed from the rest of America. Snow whipped through the air and stung my eyes, and I recognized their collective lie and grinned. This was the perfect place to stage my self-imposed exile, a period when I might use science to make up for my inability to save Wren, a wife who hadn't even wanted to marry me.

I attended classes with blunt titles like "The Wave Functions of Virtual Particles" and "Equilibrium Statistical Physics" and afterwards holed myself up in my dorm room to listen to Femme Furies CDs and drink myself into something resembling a functioning human being. What I discovered was that if Wren Wells spurred me to become the best possible version of myself, her permanent absence transformed me into a husk, a ghost, a simpering malcontent. Life with her at Susquehanna had been Technicolor, and now I trudged through the black and white isolation of Alaska alone, Dorothy forever seeking Oz after her return to prosaic Kansas. I drank most days until my head felt aglow with neon cotton candy, and it was in this period of eternal half-stupor when I was seduced to the dark side of physics, to cosmology and the tutelage of Dr. Ernest Rodriguez, a hippie-cum-cosmologist who'd become famous for sussing out the consequences of the various string dualities in M-Theory. I discovered I liked being considered an outsider, a rebel, the scientific equivalent of what Wren had tried to sculpt herself into amidst the farmlands of Susquehanna. And it was under Rodriguez's guidance when I first began toying with what would soon become The Copeland Principle.

It started near the end of my second semester, a period when Anchorage only received a few hours of light each day. We were spared the perennial darkness of those unlucky souls toiling away north of the Arctic Circle, but it was still terribly depressing to only experience sunlight for less than the length of a Hollywood blockbuster. Professor Rodriguez was explaining a theory to our "Cosmic Horizons" class about the origin of the universe that I'd no doubt heard before without fully extrapolating the consequences. He stood at the board, his hands caked in chalk, and told us that one cosmological theory hypothesized that our universe was like a bubble in a vat of oil breaking off from another bubble breaking off from another bubble breaking off from another bubble. "Boiled down, The Many Worlds Interpretation of Quantum Mechanics posits that every event causes a branch point to a new parallel universe." Rodriguez reached inside his coat and produced a single red die. He rolled it on his desk and held it up for us to see. "Six," he announced. "That means according to The Many Worlds Interpretation of Quantum Mechanics, there's another universe where I rolled a five, and another where I rolled a four, and another where I rolled a three, and each of these unique universes is vibrating one on top of another." He made sure to stress that this was a theory that couldn't yet be tested, and although class continued for two more hours, I don't know if I heard another word he said. You can probably already imagine what I was envisioning huddled beneath my parka in the vast lecture hall Professor Rodriguez ruled like a titan. I imagined a universe parallel to our own where Wren Wells never contracted leukemia, where she was still alive, where we might at last uncover whether or not we were truly soul mates.

I became obsessed with the idea of infinite Wrens, healthy Wrens, Wrens living out their lives unencumbered by leukemia throughout the vibrating eternity of Rodriguez's Multiverse. But what good were any of them to me if I could never venture inside any of these universes and hold Wren again myself? I allowed myself to wallow in self-pity and spent so many sleepless nights staring at my ceiling asking, "What would you do to see her again?" How desperately I wanted to return to my best possible self, to trade this black-and-white world for the land of color.

In a haze of drunken mourning, I linked The Many Worlds Interpretation of Quantum Mechanics to The Black Hole Information Paradox. If there existed an infinite amount of universes vibrating against one another and wormholes could conceivably take us to said universes, all we needed was a method to separate wormholes—the gateways—from black holes—dead ends. I applied for internal grants, lab space, research assistants, and was just barely funded. Years later, I stumbled upon the truth: black holes emit barely perceptible bits of Hawking Radiation. Wormholes do not. The Copeland Principle was published, and even though I assumed the technology required to actually test my principle and sail off into other universes was a century away at best, I was sated by the fact that I had accomplished something honest. I had at last honored Wren's memory. I hadn't been able to visit her grave, but I had managed to imagine other universes where she might still be alive.

RESULTS AND CONCLUSION: THE COPELAND PARADOX

After graduation, I applied for and received a postdoc with one of Rodriguez's ancient colleagues scanning quantum heterostructures for colossal magnetoresistance and nanoscale electron self-organization. It had little to do with my research, but I foresaw no way to apply The Copeland Principle to the tangible world. The postdoc was merely a stall tactic, a last gasp effort to try and decide what path my life might take post-Alaska, a road that led me to the ASA and eventually Oppenheimer and Perro Caliente. What I did not realize as I fiddled with Alaskan undulator beams was that Harvard researchers on the other edge of the continent had taken on the Herculean task of predicting the likelihood of any one person finding their soul mate, the calculus of love and affection. Their formula borrows heavily from The Drake Equation—$N = R_* \times f_p \times n_e \times f_l \times f_i \times f_c \times L$—a mathematical litany astronomer Frank Drake developed for Project Ozma and their search for extraterrestrial life. The final number is different depending on where you live—the so-called Soul Mate Formula takes into account how many single people in your age bracket live close by—but the median says most Americans have a 1 in 285,000 chance of finding their ideal mate. That means you have a 0.0000034% likelihood of meeting your soul mate on any given day. If we assume that I already met my soul mate once during that now sacred Battle of the Bands, logic dictates that at 28—18 months away from 30!—I will not be lucky enough to find a second ideal mate with whatever time remains to me upon this dying earth. The results are in. Wren Wells was my only chance at happiness, my only chance at becoming my best possible self.

I dwell on that percentage—the dreaded 0.0000034%!—when I can't fall asleep no matter how much I drink, no matter how many cosmic strings I count. I find myself confronted with that old riddle that haunted me in my messy Alaskan apartment: *What would you do to see her again*? I see The God Laser illuminated by a chorus of glowing angels. I see it birthing not a wormhole, but an actual doorway cracked ajar, the tender face of an adult Wren Wells waiting for me beyond, beckoning to me, asking me to discover once and for all if we might truly be soul mates.

Her voice is still exactly the same.

THE STEADY STATE ECSTASY OF SIR FRED HOYLE

We ran. We ran down the brick alleyways of New Berlin City, Nessa clutching the Calabi-Yau to her chest as a flurry of shocktroopers shouting in German chased after us. The moon washed the alley in its familiar pale light, but it wasn't our moon, not exactly. Someone—I'm assuming Mecha-Hitler and his Panzer Science Force—had carved a swastika onto the craggy surface of this unfamiliar moon. We had arrived in a parallel world where Hitler had won World War II, a parallel world where the decaying corpses of FDR and

Churchill had been strung up outside the Führerbunker for over six decades.

We darted down a corner, and I pointed at a nearby dumpster. It was a self-aware gesture, and for a moment, I felt as though I had tumbled into the world of big budget popcorn spectacle. I fought every impulse to shout, "Come with me if you want to live," as I grabbed Nessa's hand and climbed into the dumpster. Surely, Saints Arnold and Sylvester never had to suffer the indignities of ducking amidst soggy garbage water as 21st century Nazis ran by, shouting feral cries of purification and woe.

"How much time before the scan's done?" I asked once we couldn't hear their footsteps, my breaths shallow and sharp.

"Ten minutes." She held her nose. "Hiding from super Nazis in a dumpster wasn't exactly part of my job description. We had free massages at Google, you know. Amazing sushi. Free access to Segways. It was pretty good is what I'm saying. It wasn't hiding in garbage water, but it was neat."

I shifted my legs and stepped into wetness that came up to my knees. I understood why someone would use humor to mask that they were terrified. Our voices were drowned out by the chop-chop-chop of helicopter blades overhead, and when it was gone, I asked, "All this happened because we changed something about Henry Ford?"

Nessa swiped at the tablet, her face newly aglow with its faint blue light. "They thought maybe if we changed reality so that Henry Ford had gone into energy instead of cars that might somehow positively affect CO_2 emissions or even global warming. All it did was cause the Nazis to win World War II and sink the planet into a so-called Thousand Year Reich."

She dimmed the tablet, and I was glad Nessa couldn't see the grim expression on my face. Two weeks had passed since our first foray into parallel worlds, and things weren't looking so hot. It didn't matter if we altered some seemingly insignificant detail like Dr. Fenton's veggie pizza or if we adjusted something of more historical significance like Henry Ford's career. Either way, the changes we made resulted in parallel worlds with massive, near infinite changes that barely resembled the present we were familiar with. The true problem lurked just beneath the surface. If every change we made to The Theory of Almost Everything led to some totally unpredictable world, how could we ever figure out what changes were necessary to generate a portal to a world free from human extinction? And even if we did, how could we determine exactly how to reverse engineer said solution for our own world? So far, none of these questions had been articulated, not by our weird little trio, and especially not by Dr. Oppenheimer. But there was an underlying depression beneath the banter and camaraderie of the thousands of scientists who toiled away within Perro Caliente, and I feared what might happen if that negativity pierced its way to the surface.

Another platoon of shocktroopers jogged by, their boots heavy on the pavement. When they were gone, Nessa leaned toward me and whispered, "Cope. I buy into the general spirit of Perro Caliente, a gathering of the world's greatest minds to tackle its biggest problems. But I'm not sure this is going to work. What are we supposed to learn about extinction from a world overrun with Nazis?"

"It's only been two weeks," I said weakly.

"Sure, but the scope and power behind The God Laser—it's limitless. We could do so much more with it. Imagine if we opened it up to all the scientists across the world. Then we'd really have something." She tapped her tablet again, so I could see the sincerity on her face. It was a quality I admired, a quality I strived for in myself. "I keep thinking about alternate uses for The God Laser. Alternate uses for Perro Caliente. Oppenheimer's biggest flaw is his stubbornness."

I searched her eyes. Her voice was steady and knowing, and I sensed she was withholding some vital piece of the jigsaw. "What do you have in mind exactly?"

She dimmed the screen so I couldn't see her. "Nothing specific just yet," she said. "Just ideas. Inklings of ideas really."

I wanted her to let me in. I desperately wanted to see what harebrained, world-saving scheme a self-proclaimed futurist would come up with if given the limitless resources of Perro Caliente. "What are you doing tonight? After we get home, I mean? You want to grab a beer at the Trinity?" I asked. "Maybe we can hash everything out."

"Can't. I have rehearsal."

"For what?"

"A play with the Perro Caliente Community Players. It debuts next week. I was a huge theatre nerd in high school, and I told Barb from HR when she brought me down from the surface. She made me audition."

An underground theatre. I shook my head. Nessa had a way of constantly surprising me. "Can I see a performance?"

"Sure," she said breezily. "That would be nice. Thank you."

I squeezed her shoulder. It was a sweet little moment of friendly affection even as futuristic Neo-Nazis ran past our secret dumpster, a sweet little moment even as the fate of everyone everywhere hung in the balance.

I made a hasty retreat to Old Man Reeves' bodega after our return from the Nazi world and returned to my apartment with a microwaved burrito. Something felt off about the entire day, as if the ground beneath our feet had tilted a degree in either direction. I knew I couldn't count on Nessa that evening—the aforementioned rehearsal—but hoped I might instead grab a burger and drinks with Delbar. I'd invited her after our return home, and she politely turned me down, said she was dead tired and wanted to get an early start tomorrow. But tomorrow was no different than today: another journey into a parallel world. This or something like it had been happening more and more frequently since our initial trip to that alternate UC Berkeley. Usually Nessa or Delbar would blow me off while the other accompanied me—perhaps in order to distract me—to The Trinity Tavern and Thomas Arm's Momofuku-inspired beverages. We still gathered, however, to watch *Your Romantic Star-Filled Journey*, an event that had now ballooned to include most of our neighbors—young-to-middle-aged scientists happily bemused by how quickly the love triangle shenanigans of the good ship Mocha Mocha devolved into raiding lizard cat planets for fuel cells—some of whom even made "Team Park" and "Team Kwan" signs in between episodes. Perhaps I was just being paranoid.

I finished the burrito and actually threw the wrapper into the trashcan, something I probably wouldn't have done in my astoundingly gross Alaskan apartment. I looked around my studio in Housing Unit Seven and was almost surprised to realize it was clean, almost impeccably so. My mourning squalor had not followed me underground, and although I was unable to fully articulate why, I realized that part of the reason hinged on how much time I was spending away from my apartment, usually with Nessa or Delbar. In my old life, I spent nearly every waking minute outside of work at home, leaving one beer bottle after another in random locations on the floor. But in Perro Caliente, I spent my time with people.

I remembered what Nessa whispered to me in the Nazi dumpster, her suggestion that perhaps there were alternative ways to utilize The God Laser. Was it possible they were working on some secret project without me? Or was I just being unreasonable, a response from my guilty subconscious over The Wren Algorithm, my own secret project that had no world-saving ramifications? It was simple wish fulfillment, nothing more, and thanks to late night coding sessions fueled by equal parts coffee and bourbon, The Wren Algorithm would soon be ready. By my estimation, I'd have access to a world with a reduced leukemia rate for women in around a week's time, and since I had nothing better to do that evening, I left Housing Unit Seven and returned to the monorail that would shuttle me to The Control Center and my secret vanity project.

My train arrived, and I heard a peculiar noise as I climbed to the top floor of The Control Center. I heard the familiar click-click-clack of fingers against keyboard, the symphony of the machine. I flattened myself against the stairwell and inched ever upward, careful to be as quiet as possible. I didn't want anyone to see me and ask why I was hanging around afterhours, but I was very much interested in who else had returned to The Control Center and for what exact purpose. I craned my neck and recognized the sculpted hair of one Delbar Javari.

"Del?"

She minimized her screen and spun around in her chair, an awkward smile across her lips. A notebook covered in scribbles lay open on her desk, and Dr. Javari closed it as fast as a teenager caught reading porno by their grandmother.

“Oh, hey, Teddy. Hey.” She opened her desk drawer. “Want a Cuban?”

“No.”

“Mind if I light up?”

“No, but—”

“Great.” She chomped the end off the cigar and sparked it. “Nothing like a Cuban after a long day’s work. Feels better than unhooking your bra, you know?” A hurried, little puff. “I was just working on a little task Oppenheimer put me on. No biggie.”

I didn’t believe for a second that whatever “little task” Oppenheimer had given Delbar had anything to do with the minimized screen and closed notebook. This was sleight of hand distraction, a tactic I knew all too well from the one lousy summer I’d tried my hand at becoming a magician as a twelve-year-old dorkboy. Delbar wasn’t any better at lying than I was, but I understood the need to keep secrets. All she had to do was ask why I’d returned to The Control Center, and I’d be toast.

“Let me show you what he’s put me on,” Delbar said before taking me by the elbow, another attempt at steering me away from her computer and notebook. “Have you ever seen The Control Center servers?”

I followed Delbar into the downstairs lobby, a room so sterile it could have doubled as a doctor’s waiting room. Some dour soul must have tried to liven up the atmosphere by adding a drooping peace lily, but Delbar pushed it aside, revealing a basement door not unlike the one from my childhood home in Binghamton. That particular door had been used for coal storage at the turn of the century, but I assumed Oppenheimer’s basement had a slightly more modern use. Del produced a key from her lab coat and fit it into the lock.

"Life's so dope here, isn't it?" she asked. "So many cool secrets."

The staircase was pitch black, but Delbar led the way, illuminating the darkness with her phone. Down and down we climbed, until at last Oppenheimer's basement came into view. The stairs fed into the top of an antechamber that stretched out in all directions, far larger than any structure I'd ever seen, even bigger than the basketball court at the University of Alaska, a sweaty building I only entered once for a speech about Kerr black holes. Oppie's basement was packed to overflowing with computer servers, tall machines stacked in neat rows that reached all the way up to the ceiling. There were millions of them beneath the floor of The Control Center. And as Delbar and I descended toward the epicenter, I spotted beaucoup cooling towers puffing friendly clouds of mist every few seconds. I'd read about the massive server hubs erected in dingy towns by Microsoft, Apple, even Nessa's beloved Google. But none of them were this big. It was difficult even for me—a cosmologist who thrived in the arena of the hypothetical—to wrap my mind around how much processing power Oppenheimer had amassed underground.

"What is all this?" I asked.

Delbar's heels clicked against the floor and reverberated throughout the cavern. "It's beautiful is what it is. These are 79,000,000 servers, the biggest processing marvel in the entire world. I don't like to think of it as millions of separate computers though, it's really one large machine daisy-chained together." Del lovingly ran a hand across one of the servers, and I was again reminded of how strange the world of engineers was even compared to the life of the cosmologist. "The problem is it's so powerful, so vast that Oppenheimer sees no need to open his tech up to the public. At Microsoft or

Google, they use the cloud for really intense processing jobs. They farm out queries and problems to the combined might of the connected corporate computers from all across the globe. Oppenheimer doesn't do that. He has a stockpile right here, but if he put them online and connected them to the cloud? He'd triple his processing power easy. Think of what the world could accomplish if they had access to the world's fastest machine. It could change everything."

I was moved by Delbar's sense of pragmatic justice. Oppenheimer was only using one third of the resources available to him. Why not max out especially when we were struggling to prevent the apocalypse? "What's he use them for?"

"That's what I was doing upstairs. Oppenheimer tasked me with overseeing data analysis for every parallel world you and Nessa enter. It'd take humans too long, and all our scientists are busy working on algorithms to open up more parallel worlds. We can use these computers to analyze the data in a fraction of the time."

It was all very plausible, and I didn't doubt that Oppenheimer entrusted her with this important task and the key to his underground compu-lair. But I didn't buy that this project was what she minimized on her desktop, that this was the staggering culmination of that notebook. It felt like a front, but I didn't press her in the hopes she wouldn't grill me about The Wren Algorithm or my own suspect motivations. "How's the analysis coming?" I asked instead.

She shrugged. "I should have an early estimate of how long it will take us to find a world free from extinction in two weeks. Oppenheimer's Apocalypse Hypothesis says we only have sixty-to-seventy years before the human race is snuffed out by global warming or water shortages or nuclear fallout, right? So, if the early estimated range edges past sixty years—Kaboom." She shook her head. "But it'll just be an early estimate. It'll take another three days or so after that before we know exactly how long it'll take to find a world free from extinction in the Multiverse."

So there it was: a ticking clock. If Delbar Javari's report came back negative at the end of just seventeen days, our entire endeavor was worthless. I chewed at the skin around my fingernails, a childhood habit reactivated in times of stress. When Wren was first diagnosed with leukemia, I bit my fingers to bones. "A month ago I was a postdoc," I said.

"Life is change, Copeland. That's the definition. It's not something to be afraid of. That's why we got into science in the first place," she said with a quick, little wave of her cigar.

I didn't look up from the husk of my thumb. I had the feeling that Del and I became interested in the sciences for very different reasons indeed. I feared change. Science allowed me refuge from the boys on the playground, the fast-paced antics that even as a child scared me to pieces. "How did you get interested in all this in the first place?" I asked, gesturing at the humming servers.

"I lived with my great aunt in Britain after fleeing Iran. I was always a really smart kid. You know the drill. Aced every test, top of my class. But I don't remember liking science more than art or English until I was twelve. Leeds was chosen to host this traveling science competition run by some scientist. It was kind of lame in retrospect. The ISC Rising Stars Challenge?"

I stared at Delbar and her deadpan expression. I remembered the Rising Stars Challenge well, had even nervously recalled it before entering Dr. Fenton's pizza world. But I'd never met someone who'd actually heard of the competition, let alone someone who participated.

"I won Rising Stars back in Binghamton."

Delbar bugged her eyes. "Wow. Really? No one ever even knows what I'm talking about when I bring it up. I won it too. It gave me this huge boost of confidence. Not too many people were encouraging brown girls to go into the sciences."

"This is a pretty big coincidence, don't you think?"

"I guess." But she didn't sound convinced. "A lot of people who make it this far in the sciences have similar backgrounds, similar achievements. It's not weirder than any of this." She nodded toward the servers. "Life's been pretty consistently strange for me." She checked her watch. "Well, it's getting late. I better get going and leave you to your—what are you doing here so late again?"

I bit at my nails. "Just a little afterhours coding."

"Oh, right. Sure."

Del led me back to the lobby, and I walked her out. I brewed a pot of sludge in the break room and poured in three fingers' worth of bourbon from the bottle Oppenheimer hid between the Hi-Ho cookies and Spam. I returned to my computer for a bout with The Wren Algorithm and discovered a curious little trinket atop my monitor. It was one of Nessa's purple origami cranes. That chaos mathematician-cum-amateur actress had left one behind not just for me, but Delbar too. Something about that crane sent me into a tailspin, and I set my head on the keyboard and was endlessly grateful that the long ago boy who'd won the ISC couldn't see me now.

Something even stranger than exploring Delbar's server dungeon occurred the next afternoon at work. The translucent figure of Dr. Oppenheimer snuck up behind me at my workstation terminal and gripped my shoulder so hard

I thought my skin might bleed. “Dr. Theodore Copeland,” he whispered ominously, “do you want to go on a horseback ride through the digital mountainside?”

What choice did I have? We rode the monorail to his desert estate, but unlike my previous foray to Oppenheimer’s living quarters, this time he did not take me inside. We curled around the back of his wooden cabin, and Oppenheimer produced a tiny remote as analog and retro as my grandfather’s television clicker. I slid my hands in my pockets and tried to determine exactly why the father of the atomic bomb had dragged me here. There were no mountains behind the cabin, just the vast, flat SimuDesert and a trio of docile horses tied to a wooden pole.

“Nice horses,” I managed.

“The Argentinians are running genetic experiments on them, but I have them drop a few off for me every Wednesday. You know how to ride, son?”

“Me? No. I’m from Binghamton.” As if that explained anything.

“I go on rides once a week. It calms me. You can walk for today.” Oppie pressed a red button on his remote, and the SimuDesert quickly transformed. Jagged red mountains rose from the earth, no different from those I had seen on my ride through the Pecos Valley with Jin. They rose and rose and rose, and a flat path cut between them, a mind-cleansing gateway not unlike the one I’d attempted before returning to the StayRomp back in Indianapolis. Oppenheimer climbed his steed, and together we moseyed into the sweeping vista of simulated wilderness. “Now, Copeland,” Oppie began, “I know I can be somewhat of a trickster, a goof, a madcap wild card, but I want you to remember something: I’m a man, well, a hologram if we’re getting technical, who accomplished quite a bit in my day. We're both physicists, and I've always felt a duty to mentor my younger colleagues, and if you don't mind, I'd like to share with you some of my personal philosophies. What do you say about that, Copeland?"

I was taken aback by this new side of Dr. Oppenheimer. When I first agreed to relocate to New Mexico, I imagined myself enjoying the tutelage of one of the greatest physicists history had ever known. But for the most part, Oppie threw his trio of ambitious prodigies in headfirst. We learned by doing, and this kind of direct mentorship took me by pleasant surprise. How nice it'd be to return to the familiar role of the dutiful student. "That would be great," I said.

"Bully." We wandered between two dusty mountains, and Oppenheimer happily bounced up and down on his horse. "I'd like to let you in on one of the most crucial elements of being a successful man of science. Isolation. Not just physically like we are here underground. But from other people in general. We need to be able to examine situations objectively, from a higher viewpoint than your average joe at the sawmill. That requires keeping yourself mentally and emotionally apart from other people. Separate. Do you think we could have engineered an atomic bomb if we imagined the faces of the people of Hiroshima and Nagasaki? Absolutely not. We're not monsters. We're human beings of a higher calling, and because of that, we must remain above the emotions that cloud most people's lives. We must look upon them from above. Does that make sense to you, Copeland?"

It did, but I wished it didn't. Oppenheimer's call for isolation was a notion I understood far too well. Wasn't that what I'd attempted during my Alaskan exile: a self-imposed removal from the trials and tribulations of everyday people? But, on the other hand, wasn't my work underground in direct contrast to Oppie's suggestion? Wasn't I trying even in my own flawed and confused way to claw myself back to the known world? We ventured deeper into the mountains, and Oppenheimer told stories from the old days, about his work at Los Alamos and Princeton, about what it was like partnering with Einstein and Bohr and Nessa's father. But he was also curious and asked about my own experiences, about my tutelage at Susquehanna and Alaska, about the precise motivations that had led me to cosmology in the first place. I avoided all mentions of Wren Wells, but Oppenheimer didn't seem to notice. He was mining for something deeper, something truer. What he seemed to want to know was what I envisioned for myself beyond The God Laser, maybe even beyond Perro Caliente. The conversation was pleasant, but there was a gnawing in the back of my mind, a splinter I couldn't dislodge. Why had Oppenheimer chosen me? I imagined Delbar monitoring the near infinite servers beneath The Control Center. I pictured Nessa rehearsing her play which was set to debut in just a few days' time. Why did Oppenheimer think I'd be so receptive to his call for isolation, and if he was as flawed as I thought he might be, what did it mean if he viewed me instead of them as his protégé? I remembered Hiroshima and Nagasaki, the thousands dead.

When our trip around the mountains drew to a close, Oppenheimer reached for my shoulder, and I had to fight the impulse to recoil. There was something about his touch, something strange and otherworldly like the grasping tentacle of a ghost. I stared at him beneath the peak of a simulated mountain and told myself this was what I wanted, this was exactly what I'd yearned for wandering the streets of Indianapolis at the conclusion of the ASA.

"I ride once a week. I can teach you if you let me. What do you say?" he asked.

"Yeah. Sure. That'd be nice."

He nodded. "I'm glad you're here with me."

"Me too."

#

I found it odd that Oppenheimer had constructed a theatre space in the scientific wonderland of Perro Caliente, but in retrospect, I guess it was consistent with his manic flair. The Bergsonian Theatre was a towering three-story on the western side of the Mezzanine, four stops away from Housing Unit Seven. Unlike the other neon blue buildings of Perro Caliente, the Bergsonian had been built to resemble a movie theatre from the 1950s, complete with a glowing marquee that announced the many show times for *The Steady State Ecstasy of Sir Fred Hoyle* over the upcoming weekend. Truly, it was a spectacle to behold, and it wasn't difficult to imagine the Hologram of Robert Oppenheimer pointing at this empty spot 25 years earlier and instructing his initial crews to build the type of theatre he remembered from when he'd been on top of the known world.

Four days had passed since my horse ride with Oppie, and I was beyond excited to see Nessa's play. Even as a postdoc, I'd been too busy to go to the movies or the theatre, and I couldn't remember the last time I'd given myself up to the titillating drama of actors and narrative. Each morning for the last week, the friendly voices of The Communications Center pointed out the many show times and whipped we eager scientists into a frenzy. After purchasing an enormous tub of popcorn with two gregarious pulls of melted butter, I followed the Hologram of J. Robert Oppenheimer, Delbar

Javari, and the throngs of energized scientists inside the darkened theatre. I fidgeted in my chair and remembered something I'd read in Oppenheimer's biography. If he hadn't been a theoretical physicist, he would have become a poet. Perhaps all scientists secretly longed to be artists. Perhaps that's all anyone really wanted: to express their inner beings to the world. I chomped my popcorn loudly, as the lights dimmed and the show began.

The Steady State Ecstasy of Sir Fred Hoyle was a strangely invigorating performance. I'd done very little research about the show before arriving—with most movies or dramas or books, I preferred to go in blind and couldn't relate to my Alaskan colleagues who obsessed over upcoming movies, reading script excerpts and plot summaries a year, or sometimes even two, in advance—and was surprised to discover that the actors had swapped gender roles. The show began when Nessa rushed the bare stage, bursting to tell us about the steady state theory of the universe. She was dressed in tan slacks, a dress shirt, and lab coat, her already small breasts tamped down even further. She played Sir Fred Hoyle with the enthusiasm of a child who had just learned a fabulous secret they had to share with the world, and I must admit I was more than charmed by her frenetic energy. I sat munching my popcorn and came upon a strange thought: Nessa Newmar is objectively beautiful. For normal people, that wouldn't have been a peculiar notion at all. Surely my contemporaries ranked and re-ranked the young bodies they came into contact with all the time. But for me, still in the weeds of my seemingly eternal mourning process, finding another flesh and blood human attractive was truly a cause for anxiety. I'd admitted that various movie stars or pop singers were gorgeous when pushed by my former classmates, but

I couldn't remember thinking that someone I knew in real life was empirically beautiful. At least not since Wren Wells, and I knew exactly how that story ended.

"The big bang!" Nessa Newmar/Sir Fred Hoyle shouted. "The big bang! It doesn't make sense, right? Think about it. Something can't come from nothing. We know that. So who started this vulgar big bang theory? I'll tell you who. Georges Lemaître in his quest to prove the existence of a higher power. Hooey! Hornswoggle! The big bang is just an excuse to say our universe was created by some god, and I just don't believe that. No, sir. Let me throw something out there, all right?" Nessa was talking at a fantastic clip even for her, and it was nearly impossible for we scientists of the Perro Caliente Research Laboratory—myself included—not to enjoy this cross-dressing chaos mathematician-cum-actress's passionate performance. "We have always existed. This has always existed. The universe. It's bigger than our ideas about religion, about afterlife. It's all too big! It's always existed. This, my friends, is the steady state theory of the universe. This, my friends, will be my great contribution to the world." She winked at us. "I'm going to live forever!"

As the play continued, more and more gender-swapped characters were introduced. I was surprised that no one touched upon the fact that Sir Fred Hoyle, a crotchety Brit famous for his rudeness and penchant for sci-fi, was being played by an African American woman, but no one ever did. Hoyle's wife was portrayed by The Trinity Tavern's Thomas Arm, and Nessa/Hoyle dealt with him/her in a most tender way, stroking his/her cheek and explaining how much she/he loved him/her even though she/he was spending so much time in her/his lab working out the math with her/his PhD students that might prove the steady state theory victorious over the big bang. The quickness with which Nessa/Hoyle spoke reminded me of all the fast talking dames I'd fallen in love with during my screwball comedy kick shortly after arriving in Alaska. Their black and white wisecracks eased my loneliness upon my arrival to a strange, new land, and oh how I longed to crawl in through my television set and enter their back lot-rich world.

"It's going to be all right," Nessa/Hoyle explained to Thomas Arm. "I love you. I always will. But this theory is so much bigger than me, than us, than our love. I might be able to prove that the universe will go on forever. Do you know what that means? I can rebuke Darwin and finally make it clear that humans will live forever! I can disprove the existence of god and in the process become one myself."

Oh, the hubris of scientists! Nessa/Hoyle's antagonist, The Big Bang Theory originator Georges Lemaître, was portrayed by none other than Barb from HR, the woman who had first led me from Oppenheimer's ranch into this underground wonderland. The two squared off in a round of intense BBC debates where Nessa/Hoyle accidentally coined the phrase "big bang," which is what she/he would eventually be remembered for. We scientists of Perro Caliente were particularly moved by this segment. How easy it would be to go down in history for something you didn't view as your most altruistic work. Just imagine Oppenheimer. Say his name to any non-scientist, and they don't remember the decades and decades of service rendered to the physics community, they picture the dual mushroom clouds over Hiroshima and Nagasaki and the legion of corpses and cancer-ridden beneath.

As the play tipped into its second, inevitably tragic act, I trembled with narrative excitement. More and more results came back reaffirming Barb/Georges Lemaître's big bang theory. More and more results came back poking holes in Nessa Newmar/Sir Fred Hoyle's steady state theory. Nessa/Hoyle clung to her/his ideals long after the scientific community abandoned her/him, long after the media abandoned her/him, long after the PhD students abandoned her/him. Even in the futuristic nineties, Nessa/Hoyle would not give up the ghost of defeating god. The final scene was a monologue. Nessa/Hoyle had been given a long white beard meant to signify old age. Her/his wife had left her/him—a fictional deviation from reality I got a giddy kick out of—and now Nessa/Hoyle was alone, in the last laboratory in Britain that would give her/him refuge. Truly, it was a tragedy we scientists could relate to. We only wanted to help better the world, and what was our reward? Loneliness. Pain. Regret.

Nessa/Hoyle sat in the center of the small, wooden stage looking exhausted. She/he spoke slower now. "All right. I can admit that minute parts of the theory were wrong, but the overall impulse of the thing, its spirit, was correct. I refuse to believe we appeared out of nothing. I refuse to believe in chaos, in giving up human order for belief in some higher power. I refuse! I will concede where I have to. I'm working on the quasi-steady state theory of the universe. It will fix the holes in my original theory and blow Georges Lemaître and big bang and all those religious zealots who nihilistically mistrust humans out of the water." She/he looked up at the crowd, tears rimming her/his big, brown eyes. "I have to keep trying, right? That's all any of us can do, right? Am I right? Please tell me I'm right. Please tell me this hasn't all been in vain."

The curtains swept across the stage. The darkness lifted. And we scientists of Perro Caliente rose to our feet and clapped with wanton abandon. I glanced across the theatre and saw men and women who had lived underground for god only knew how long with tears streaming down their cheeks, and it was only then when I realized I too had been deeply affected, that the artistry of Nessa Newmar had moved me to genuine emotion. While the other scientists filed out of the theatre one-by-one, I remained rooted to the gummy carpet, paralyzed by what I had seen and experienced. Nessa had unearthed something hard within me, and I desperately wanted to believe that somehow I had been changed. Nessa Newmar, the genius idealist who might save us all. Nessa Newmar, the sweet, smart whiz kid who left origami cranes on my workstation keyboard. Nessa Newmar.

"Great performance," Delbar said, her eyes the driest in the house. "Dazzling."

"'Twas, 'twas. A glorious reminder that even our brightest and most daring scientific minds might be wrongheaded if well-intentioned." Oppie wiped a hologram tear from his hologram cheek. "Say, I feel like a game of billiards. What say you, children? Want to strike the old cue ball with old Oppie?"

Del agreed, but I declined. "I want to see about Nessa," I said. "You know," I backpedaled, "to congratulate her."

They left, and I walked through the door that led into the mysterious world of the theatre backstage. Men and women hurried in mid-undress changing out of their scientist costumes and into their scientist uniforms. I stumbled upon a row of dressing rooms far back from the curtained stage and saw Nessa's name Sharpied big and green upon a Post-It note cut into the shape of a star. I knocked, and Nessa called to come in. There she was still wearing her shocked white Fred Hoyle wig and lab coat, her skin radiant under the soft mirror lighting.

"Hey," I barely managed. "Hey."

She showed her teeth and laughed. "Hey to you too." There was a new and uncharacteristic shyness to her voice. "How'd I do?"

I wanted to say something clever. I figured that after watching someone bare themselves onstage that I should say something complex and witty, something that undeniably proved that I'd absorbed the artistic kernel radiating out from the core of her performance.

"You were great."

"Yeah?"

"Yeah."

Nessa removed her wig. She was so pretty to me then, and I felt so idiotic for not recognizing it earlier. A peculiar notion occurred to me. How simple it would be to walk across the room—the mere six feet that separated our breathing bodies—and take Nessa Newmar into my arms. The air in the dressing room was charged, and it felt like she wanted me to or, at the very least, was receptive to kissing me. How unbelievable it was that this lovely futurist delivered to us from the sunny shores of Google might be interested in me, a wormhole enthusiast wreck. Was it possible that Ness Newmar like Wren Walls might unlock the best possible version of myself? Wren Wells. Her shadow overcame me then, and I wanted to melt on the floor. Wren Wells. There was still so much guilt. How could I even think about another woman when The Wren Algorithm was so close to completion, when I was mere hours from potentially seeing my bride once again? Wren Wells. Wren Wells. Wren Wells.

"I'm a widower," I blurted. I'd never before uttered that word, and it sounded strange on my tongue, the way I'd felt as a boy when I put on my father's adult clothes when no one else was home. *Widower.*

Nessa looked taken aback at first, and I finally recognized how strange the scene was. There we were in an underground research lab containing the world's most powerful particle accelerator, my fingers and lips still greasy from popcorn, Nessa in her Hoyle drag, as I explained that I was a twenty-eight-year-old widower. But she quickly collected herself and gave me her most reassuring smile. It was Nessa who crossed the space between us, Nessa who did not kiss me but wrapped me in a hug.

"I'm sorry," she whispered.

"It's ok."

"It's not."

"No. I guess not."

She held me like that for a long time, and I was surprised by how perfectly her head fit against the top of my chest. It had been so long since a woman had held me. I'd forgotten the sweet machinery of it.

"The other actors are all going to Rum/p Shakers," she said. "You want to come with?"

"No. You go ahead." I snaked free from her grip and ran my hand through my hair. "Thanks. And you really were great up there."

She smiled. "Thanks, Teddy."

I left her dressing room and immediately felt equal parts wretched and foolish. How could you betray a ghost? Especially one who hadn't even wanted to marry you in the first place? I knew it was illogical and desperate, but it was the way I felt, and no amount of mathematics could change that. I hurried out of the Bergsonian and boarded the first available monorail with little to no idea of where I might go. I was too jazzed to sleep and too unnerved by my encounter with Nessa to immediately resume coding The Wren Algorithm. But then, the light from Rum/p Shakers appeared in my monorail windows and the promise of an old fashioned nightcap—or even just an Old Fashioned—at the Trinity Tavern below. Perhaps what I needed at that moment was the sensible ear of a friendly bartender. Perhaps what I needed was the vim and charm of one Thomas Arm.

#

Two Eagle Rares later, I sat at the empty bar across from Thomas Arm flipping through ancient sitcoms on the flatscreen overhead. The picture fuzzed, and Thomas whacked it with his palm twice to no avail.

"The reception down here's terrible, huh?"

"I haven't really noticed," I said.

We'd barely spoken since I'd entered the bar, but while considering Thomas' complaint about the overall Perro Caliente picture quality, I began to really wonder about the state of his life. How had this man from Momofuku Toronto—whatever that meant—in his neon New Balances ended up underground of all places? I wanted narrative, hyperbole, anything to make me forget my failure in Nessa's dressing room.

"So, Thomas," I tried, "how long have you lived down here?"

He leaned his elbows against the bar and squinted into the distance at some invisible calendar. "Jeez, almost two years now?"

"You like it?"

"Like I said, the TV quality's garbage and sometimes there's this weird burning smell around Housing Unit Four where I live, but other than that, yeah. I really do. I see my family in New Jersey a few times a year. They still think I'm living in Toronto. There's a lot of people here my age. The bike trails are rad. Good improv scene. It's pretty cool."

"But how'd you get here?"

"The same way most laypeople do." He grinned. "Probably the same reason you're here. I was living a mildly successful life. I was bartending at Momofuku, and I was really proud of the work we were doing there, but I also felt kind of empty. Like I wasn't adding anything especially positive to the world. We all know about climate change, water shortages, but what was I doing about it? Going out with friends and serving whiskey slushies to food bloggers. I got depressed, and one day I came across this flyer in Little Portugal that basically asked straight up if I wanted to make a difference, if I was ready to commit myself to the cause of saving the world. I thought it was a joke, maybe a publicity stunt for a superhero movie or something, but I called the number and went through all of these psychological tests. After I signed a nondisclosure agreement, I met Barb from HR and she invited me to work at the Trinity. I know I'm not directly contributing to The God Laser project, but hey, I'm keeping you guys relaxed, right? I'm doing my part."

I stared into my drink. Like Nessa and Delbar, Thomas Arm's intentions were altruistic and pure. Surely there were no wifely skeletons in his closet prodding him into unknown worlds.

"The God Laser," I said, slightly buzzed now. "Let me ask you a question. We all know it has the potential to save the world, right, the entire Multiverse even. But what if you could also use it to see dead loved ones again? Would you? Would you use it for that too?" I searched Thomas Arm's eyes. I never would have been able to express this desire to Nessa or Delbar or Oppenheimer, but something about the combination of alcohol and the well-established cultural institution of bartender-as-armchair-psychologist put me at a sudden and surprising ease with Thomas Arm. I wanted so very badly for someone to give me permission. It didn't matter who.

He thought it over a long time before finally saying, "Cope, I think I would. I know it's selfish and kind of lame, but I'd love to see my uncle one last time. He used to take me fishing on Lake Pearl. Massive Red Sox fan. It'd be awesome to tell him they finally won the World Series."

I resisted the urge to hug him. "Thank you, Thomas. Thank you."

I settled up and traded Trinity for the monorail stop overhead, passing Rum/p Shakers as I did so where surely Nessa was celebrating with her amateur underground thespians. I boarded the train en route to The Control Center and turned over that familiar question: What would it be like to see Wren again, not as the twenty-two-year-old college student I remembered, but as an adult woman with experience and regret? If I tumbled into a parallel world where we'd never met, would she still fall in love with me? Could I somehow disprove the notion she'd whispered in front of the Atlantic Ocean—*I love you too, but we're not soul mates?*

What if she was wrong?

I settled in at my workstation and furiously coded through the night fueled by a mix of coffee and Oppenheimer's break room bourbon. I coded and coded and coded, pleasantly stupefied by the waves of green numbers, the slow churn of mathematics that would alter The Theory of Almost Everything so that the leukemia rate among women would be reduced by a single percentage point. As the SimuSun appeared above the Control Center, I released a small yelp of joy. Finally, I'd done it. I'd come to the end of my equation. All those years of longing and loneliness, of unlocking my safe and returning my wedding band to my finger like a delusional malcontent, all those sleepless nights staring at my ceiling while wondering if we'd still be together had she lived. That compulsion, that obsession, had led me here, underground, twisting reality to satisfy my darkest curiosities, the most shadowy crevices of my mind and soul. The only thing left to do was power on The God Laser, leap into the new world I'd summoned, and scan the environment for the existence of one Wren Wells. I oscillated between vomiting and crying. It had been over six years since Wren had died. Six years, and I might finally see her again.

Before I could change my mind, I charged The God Laser—had long ago faux-innocently asked Oppie to demonstrate how —and watched from the lobby as the black egg of infinity revved to life between the quadrupole lasers. There was no turning back now. I had an hour max before my fellow scientists would appear for work. I took a deep breath and sprinted into the portal. A moment later, I appeared on an American main street so average, so positively mundane with its glowing rah-rah patriotism that it might as well have been a Technicolor Hollywood backlot. Tiny shops lined the canyon of three-story buildings, and in the distance I could make out the sun rising above a cluster of small mountains. A young mother and her toddler son wandered out of a drug store and waved as they passed. The boy clung to a smiley face balloon, and I saw that trinket as a fortunate omen of all the goodness yet to come.

I ran a quick, cautionary scan on my tablet to determine if Wren Wells existed in this world, if she had avoided leukemia, if she still lived. Sweat gathered on the back of my neck, and I understood that this was the culmination of all those once-impotent fantasies in my cluttered Alaskan apartment: the chance to see Wren Wells alive once again. The Calabi-Yau beeped, and I tapped the results. Wren Wells was alive. In this reality, she'd never even attended Susquehanna and had moved to DC after graduating from a small school in Maryland. She'd never even met this world's version of Teddy Copeland. The tablet tracked her to a coffee shop in Eastern Market. All I had to do was punch a button, and I'd teleport in front of the bistro. I tried not to focus on the significance of the situation. I rubbed my thighs, closed my eyes, and tried to free my mind from anxiety, a tactic I'd relied upon in the wake of Wren's death. Focus on your breathing. Focus on your breathing. I inhaled and pressed the virtual button.

I'd never been to DC before, not in this world or my own, and when I imagined our nation's capital as a Binghamtonian lad—which was surely a rare occurrence indeed—I pictured the White House and men in suits squawking at each other like the cardinals in the oak tree across from my grade school. I didn't expect cobblestone streets and fruit stands, a row of brick, artisanal shops that would make the few hipster PhDs I knew swoon with delight. The coffee shop was located on a corner. A small crowd had gathered outside the windows, and I couldn't see inside to the customers. I took another series of deep breaths before approaching the coffee shop, and that's when I finally noticed something off about the tangle of young men arguing and gesticulating wildly outside the entrance.

There was something strangely familiar about each of their faces, something wrong and impossible, vaguely immoral. I reached the outer edge of their ranks and realized they were all versions of me, a half-dozen Teddy Copelands clutching Calabi-Yau tablets and screaming at each other.

"What the hell is going on here?"

They turned to face me, identical looks of exasperation on their faces. The one nearest to the coffee shop door waved his hands and snapped his fingers. "Guys? Fellow Teddy Copelands? Can we all calm down a second? Things are getting out of control."

Behind me, I heard the steady gurgle of a Calabi-Yau Teleportation, and sure enough, another Teddy Copeland appeared looking just as indignant and confused as the rest of us. Then another. Then another. Then another. Until the tiny street swelled with Teddy Copelands—fat Teddys, skinny Teddys, Teddys in pea coats, and Teddys in Hawaiian shirts, a snaking, expanding mass of dubious Teddy Copelands replicating like leukemia cells, the whole of DC a facsimile of Wren's delicate body.

"Guys!" the Teddy Copeland nearest to the door shouted again. "Guys. Can you please calm down?" He climbed the stoop of the coffee shop and raised his hands.

Immediately, I sensed that this Teddy Copeland was constructed of sterner stuff than I. He was more muscular, his voice lower, his hair a tad more faux-bedheady. I imagined he was smarter than me, more caring than me, produced harder erections than me. I can't explain why, but I was overcome with the sensation that this was the Teddy Copeland I had always dreamed of becoming—powerful, confident, a true man!—that here, in front of a coffee shop window filled with panicking customers, I had come face to face with Teddy

Copeland Prime, the best of us. Unattainable. Wizard. Demon. Teddy Copeland Prime!

A Teddy Copeland with an English accent yelled from the back of the now hundred-plus crowd, a mass that was still growing at an exponential rate with each new teleportation. "What the hell is going on here?"

"Guys. I've been here the longest," Teddy Copeland Prime explained even as more Teddy Copelands teleported into the area, even as innocent bystanders stopped and screamed and dropped to their knees in prayer. "You're all here to see Wren Wells, right?"

"Yes," we shouted in unison, and then some of us pushed closer to the coffee shop window, so eager for a chance to see Wren Wells once more. The customers inside pressed their faces to the glass, but none of them were Wren. She remained hidden from us, as always.

"Look. As we all know," Teddy Copeland Prime screamed over the steady churn of the crowd, "The Many Worlds Interpretation of Quantum Mechanics accounts for all possibilities within the infinity of the Multiverse. That means there's an infinite number of universes where we all had to go through Wren Wells' death. That's why you're all here, right? To see her again?"

"Yes!" we shouted again.

"That means there's an infinite number of universes where we experienced Wren's death *and then* were summoned to Perro Caliente to solve extinction using The God Laser *and then* used that power to track down a world with a smaller leukemia occurrence rate, and that brought us all to this place."

More Calabi-Yau Teleportations and more and more and more. The street was now filled to overflowing with Teddy Copelands, and all I could see in any direction were other versions of myself, solipsistic creatures hellbent on proving to a collegiate flame that she truly did love us. I felt disgusted, the way I had in college after gorging myself at the Chinese buffet, that over-full feeling when you knew you had no one to blame but yourself. What had I done? What had we done? Why couldn't we just cast off toward the ruddy coastline of adulthood?

The British Teddy Copeland again raised his hand. "That can't be right. I grew up in Britain, but you have an American accent. We can't have led the same lives."

"You're right. We might have all led different lives, but the one thing that connects us, just a small fraction of the infinite Teddy Copelands spread out across the Multiverse, is that those of us here today all lost Wren Wells and parlayed that into a position at Perro Caliente. That's what we share in common. That's what brought us here." Teddy Copeland Prime ran his hand through his hair, a duplicate of my go-to gesture when nervous. "Look. There's too many of us. We have to all agree to leave, to never come back. We all think exactly the same way. If any of us decide to return, so will the rest and this'll just keep happening. We have to go. We have to leave. We can't overwhelm this Wren who never even met a Teddy Copeland with an army full of them. It's the only decent thing to do!"

"Just let me talk to her one more time!" a random Teddy Copeland yelled over the crowd. "I just need to hear her voice one more time!"

"Just let me talk to her one more time!" another cried. "I just need to hear her voice one more time!"

"Just let me talk to her one more time!" another cried. "I just need to hear her voice one more time!"

"Just let me talk to her one more time!" another cried. "I just need to hear her voice one more time!"

"Just let me talk to her one more time!" another cried. "I just need to hear her voice one more time!"

"Just let me talk to her one more time!" another cried. "I just need to hear her voice one more time!"

I wondered how many of us there were. I remembered the time Wren and I had jetted off to Warped Tour between freshman and sophomore years and how intimidated I was by the undulating wave of humanity assembled in the Pennsylvania fairgrounds. I took a deep breath. How many other Teddy Copelands were recalling that exact same memory, or at the very least a facsimile, the concert changed, the venue changed, the season changed? I was but a physicist hailing from Binghamton, New York. I was not prepared for such ghastly visions, for my deepest, most selfish yearnings unleashed bare and monstrous.

"We all have to go," Teddy Copeland Prime shouted. "We have to promise never to return."

The Teddy Copeland in front of me—how I envied his fancy scarf—disappeared, returned presumably to the Perro Caliente of his native universe. Then the Teddy Copeland on my right. Then the Teddy Copeland on my left. Then the Teddy Copeland behind me. One after another, until a few minutes later, we were back to our original numbers, a half-dozen sad sacks clustered in front of the coffee shop, Teddy Copeland Prime still guarding the door, refusing entry to that sacred space still occupied by our collective ex-wife.

"Just let me talk to her one more time!" I begged. "I just need to hear her voice one more time!"

Teddy Copeland Prime's face finally softened. I knew he recognized my despair, the years of heartache that had driven the six of us Teddy Copelands remaining and the thousands of us already disappeared to this specific location in the infinite Multiverse. At last, he relented. "We all get one look, then we leave this place forever."

We six Teddy Copelands huddled together in front of the window, and there, looking absolutely terrified, was a living Wren Wells crouched beneath a table with another scared customer. She was shaking, but that didn't stop us from imprinting that image onto our memories forever. Her hair was shorter, spikier, her left ear filled with studs, her glasses thick and bulky, a simple brown cardigan over a green dress shirt, tight jeans, a pair of worn Adidas. This was the adult version of the love we had lost, and we had driven her to fear, to clutching a stranger beneath a coffee shop table, horrified at the mass of identical human beings appearing outside her window like a league of unhinged magicians. We Teddy Copelands said nothing. We drew back from the window and teleported back to our Perro Calientes in silence. I can't be sure, but I can guess what we all were thinking as we shut down our workspace terminals and washed our faces in our respective rest rooms. We remembered Oppenheimer's premonition when we first ventured underground. We remembered the father of the atomic bomb telling us that he'd kept Perro Caliente hidden from the various governments of the world out of the fear that technology like The God Laser might fall into the wrong hands. What if those wrong hands were ours? What if we weren't world saviors? What if we were the villains, an infinite mass of delusional maniacs ready to justify any act of evil if it meant a balm for our collective grief?

THE APOCALYPSE POCKET WATCH

The 14th Annual Michael Faraday Festival was held in a serene park west of the Mezzanine, and how reaffirming it was to stroll with Nessa and Del amid a surging crowd of Perro Caliente loyalists. Rows of food vendors—helmed by the head chefs of such underground staples as The Trinity Tavern and The Fish Dies at Midnight—and painfully earnest arts and craft stalls rimmed a small, manmade lake where scientists and lay people alike removed their dust-spotted spectacles and steered pedal boats beneath the black SimuSky overhead. Everything smelled of sweat and batter, and after momentarily excusing herself from our trio, Delbar returned holding a box of deep fried butter bacon ice cream balls high overhead, the greasy bounty of the atomic age.

"Guys!" she shouted. "Guys! This is the fucking greatest of all time!"

A week had passed since my dubious journey to Washington, and although I tried to accept that the world of The Wren Algorithm was forever closed off to me, I couldn't stop thinking about The Soul Mate Formula and my infinitesimal odds of meeting a second ideal mate as I approached 30 and my inevitable adulthood, a period that would culminate with my death. Surely, there had to be some way to see Wren minus the appearance of infinite Teddys, but so far I'd come up with nothing. I tried not to be consumed, to dwell on what I might become alongside Wren, and had instead doubled down on my work and unexpectedly active underground social life. I was chatty at the Trinity and cheered on my beloved Dr. Kwan during *Your Romantic Star-Filled Journey* common room marathons. Most of the enthralled scientists of Housing Unit Seven yearned to be strong if dopey Parks but reluctantly admitted we were curious Kwans or headstrong Kims. It was a strange and fantastic time.

"So, what do you guys want to do next?" Nessa asked. "See the Michael Faraday balloon statue? Check out the beer tent with Thomas Arm? Peep the diamagnetism exhibit?"

"I'm actually really into these pedal boats right now." Del nodded toward the lake, her cheeks full of butter ice cream. "You guys down?"

Down we were, and how genuinely sweet it was to part the crowd with Nessa and Del, to wave at Barb hocking homemade necklaces, Old Man Reeves trading baseball cards with a Cuban mathematician, even at the ever-silent Jin passing out life preservers near a row of neon boats. I was reminded of the many church festivals I'd attended with my parents in Binghamton, how those achingly tiny and intimate affairs would reel in the entire town, everyone who had outlasted IBM's exodus to Armonk and the collapse of the shoe and cigar industries. Our trio boarded a four-person pedal boat—there were no three-seaters—and ventured out to the middle of the lake, and there I realized exactly what we'd achieved in Perro Caliente beyond The God Laser and wormholes and our flawed if earnest stabs at galactic salvation. We had established a community, the kind of place with dopey festivals, neighborhood bars, community theatre, even the curling club Barb told me about on the very first day. We were all in this together, and I tried to take comfort in that as old Oppie himself blasted fireworks that popped and fizzed over the mirror of the lake, as Nessa leaned toward Del and loudly declared she loved it here and that Perro Caliente had become home. I remembered my life in Anchorage—my whittled down routine of lab work followed by isolation in my cluttered catastrophe of an apartment. In Perro Caliente, I was occupied not just with work, but with friends, living human beings, and I found myself regretting my behavior in Alaska, how I'd burned my twenties in Wren's eternal funeral pyre.

A trio of fireworks burst overhead, and I smiled toward the empty seat on my left, the void that might have been filled by Wren's body, not her twenty-two-year-old self, not the horrified creature in Washington, but another Wren, a different Wren, infinite Wrens. Still her ghost lingered, refusing to sail off into the great beyond.

The Googleplex wasn't exactly what I pictured. I can't say how often in my ordinary life I actually sat back and imagined the fabled Google HQ brought to life by those notorious boy wizards from the Human Computer Interaction program at Stanford, but I certainly never realized the incredible scope of their Mountain View campus. The Googleplex was no mere skyscraper reaching up into the cloudless heavens from the sun kissed valley of California. It was a sprawling university-style campus with the same kind of rolling greens and t-shirt sporting smiley faces kicking hacky sacks on the quad. Only here there was more everything. More greens, more fresh-faced twenty-somethings ready to tackle the world's problems and especially more buildings. Buildings for as far as the eye could see. Buildings not like the academic brick of Susquehanna or the functional concrete of Alaska, but buildings that rolled and curved, culminating in great, big waves of architectural whimsy, like something out of a cutting-edge video game. Like something that would naturally stem from the minds of two Stanford shut-ins who had smoked dope and played Nintendo in unlit dorm rooms on Saturday nights.

Nessa inhaled that familiar Google aroma. "It's good to be back."

This was a universe drawn from an algorithm of Nessa's design. She'd gone into The Theory of Almost Everything and upped John Atanasoff's 1939 grant from $650 to $65,000 dollars. Atanasoff had used this money to build one of the earliest computers at Iowa State, the egotistically named Atanasoff-Berry Computer. Thanks to Moore's Law, the scientific principle positing that processing muscle doubles every two years, Nessa assumed that technology in this new world where Atanasoff began with so much more funding would be 16 to 128 times more powerful than the computers of our own. She believed that armed with these super computers, the golden citizenry of this world—especially the mages of

Google—would surely have cracked the puzzle of impending apocalypse. She was to her core the "Chaos Mathematician/Googler/Futurist" who had introduced herself in the Indianapolis convention center.

Nessa swiped at the Calabi-Yau. She didn't speak, but the way her eyebrows scrunched said it all. Clearly, her hypothesis was wrong.

"What happened?" I asked.

"The computers here are 32 times more advanced than the ones back home, but so's the military. Drone soldiers. Drone missiles. North Korea's engaged in a struggle with South Korea, and everybody's picking sides. A world war's looming. Things don't look too hot."

"What about Google?"

"Handicapped by an isolationist government." She swiped in another command. "Environmental scan's started. Come on. You want a tour? I'm starving. Apparently I'm a Googler in this universe too. My fingerprint access should be the same here if anybody asks."

Nessa didn't wait for my response and set off toward destinations unknown. All I could do—if I wanted lunch that is—was follow. She pointed out the various buildings as we passed. "That's the Gmail team. And over there's Android. That's Product Management, where the founders' offices are, and that little shack is Marketing. No one gives a flying crap about Marketing." She didn't pause—in gait or speech—until we came upon a small pond encircled by picnic tables populated by happy young invincibles sampling charcuterie and bubble tea. Behind them rose a building comprised solely of glass, and inside I could see great big lines of people waiting for cafeteria food.

"The bubble tea is to die for. They load it with vitamins and artificial brain stimulants. So cool. So forward thinking."

Inside, we joined the snaking line of Googlers waiting for sushi, and I eavesdropped as Nessa struck up a conversation with a baby-faced engineer about Google Energy. Truly, Dr. Nessa Newmar was the high priestess of chaos math, a prodigy derived from the legacy of Los Alamos. She pushed her glasses up over her forehead, and it was becoming harder and harder to deny how pretty she was.

We ordered nigiri and were soon happily eating at a table near the back. Nessa snapped up a piece of octopus with her chopsticks and dunked it twice in a tiny bath of soy sauce. "Copeland, can you keep a secret?"

I furrowed my brow. Delbar's early results on The God Laser project were due any day now, and I was momentarily terrified that Nessa knew the fallout, the possibility that we were already doomed.

"I've been really curious about my dad," Nessa said instead. "Ever since Oppenheimer told me he'd periodically visited Perro Caliente the past twenty-five years. That's almost my whole life. What else don't I know about him? I thought he was an open book that started with The Manhattan Project and ended with the death of my mother." She popped a piece of salmon and chewed very thoughtfully, very slowly. "I've been doing some research in the library. Did you know Perro Caliente has a library? It's down in the Library District. I found out that my dad used to have a lab along the southeast edge of Perro Caliente that's been unoccupied since his death." She pointed her empty chopsticks at my face. "What if his old equipment's still there?"

My first impulse was to say "So what?" but then I remembered my own barely concealed desires to learn more about those who were beloved to me who no longer walked the earth. It was only natural that Nessa would want to seek out the space where her father had worked for 25 years. "Do you want me to go with you to his lab?"

"Do you think I should go to his lab?"

"I think you should go to his lab if you want to go to his lab."

She considered this a moment. "I think I want to go. You'll come with?"

I took Nessa's hands into my own. I liked the kind of person I was around her. "Yeah."

We ate nigiri until the scan was complete, and when it was, we returned to our world full and happy, ready to explore Dr. Elgin Newmar's laboratory—if any of it was even left—together.

#

At last we came to the end. At least we reached the season finale of *Your Romantic Star-Filled Journey*, Nessa's thumb paused precariously atop the Blu-ray remote. The fourth floor common room of Housing Unit Seven had filled to capacity with curious scientists from the entire building who had begun, one-by-one, to join our madcap dash through the twenty-two episodes of *Your Romantic Star-Filled Journey*. They arrived with six-packs, great, big bowls of popcorn, some even sporting t-shirts imprinted with the faces of Dr. Kwan, Captain Park, or even the coffee enthusiast Commander Kim. "I'll ship Kim and Park until the day I fucking die," a third floor physicist solemnly swore. We gathered around the television and sat on the floor like the children we must have once been, sublime and oblivious to the impending dangers of Oppenheimer's doomsday. I smiled at Nessa from across the room. We planned to find her father's lab immediately after the episode, but we refused to let our new friends down, to miss this, the appointed hour of the finale. Just forty-four minutes, I thought. Just forty-four minutes away from the apocalypse and our many underground burdens.

Nessa pressed play, and a thunderous clap—spurred on by none other than Dr. Delbar Javari—boomed across the common room, but that gleeful enthusiasm would be short-lived. After responding to a distress signal from a damaged fast food cruiser on the edge of Aquarius Nebulon 65, the Mocha Mocha starship was sucked into the slow gravitational spin of a wormhole, leaving Commander Kim a mere hour to plot her escape. The CGI effects were lackluster at best—like something from a summer popcorn muncher from the end of the previous century—but the creators of *Your Romantic Star-Filled Journey* were surely at a disadvantage in this particular screening as we had all seen legitimate wormholes born from the code on our computer screens. As the Mocha Mocha swirled the drain of infinity, Captain Park and Dr. Kwan finally confronted Commander Kim, explaining they were in love with her and she had to make a choice. Kim looked back and forth between them before staring straight into the camera, her subtitled dialogue proclaiming, "Very well. Then I choose..." Nessa clutched her knees so tightly her knuckles went white, but before Kim could finally make the decision we'd been waiting twenty-two episodes for, the camera smash cut to the Mocha Mocha zooming through the center of the wormhole. Unlike Nessa and I, the Mocha Mocha did not reappear in some other, better universe. It simply blipped out of existence, and the credits scrolled to a chorus of haunting screams.

Nessa stood, her mouth agape. "No."

A Finnish Mathematician hurled a handful of popcorn at the screen. An Aussie engineer cupped her hands to her mouth and booed. A biologist from Texas ripped his Team Park shirt in two.

"Is there a second season?" Del shouted from the back.

Nessa scanned her phone as quickly as she scrolled through the results of the Calabi-Yau, but this time there was no news of alternate presidents or toppled regimes. This time the story was written on her face. She held the screen up as if we could actually read it before announcing, "*Your Romantic Star-Filled Journey* was canceled after one season. The creators say the ending is supposed to imply that everyone died. It's over."

For a few minutes, no one left, no one spoke, no one moved. We just sat there, moved to reflection by what had once appeared to be mere escapist absurdity, a little afterhours pick-me-up when not even the comforting banter of Thomas Arm and his Toronto cocktails could do the trick. Commander Kim, Captain Park, and Dr. Kwan were dead, even though we all understood they'd never existed in the first place, that they were second-rate actors, that *Your Romantic Star-Filled Journey* was little more than puffed up fluff. But its downbeat ending felt like an omen, a warning from across the globe in Korea, a reminder of the end times we were collectively flirting with, the future ghosts we all soon would become.

One of the things I most loved about Perro Caliente was the efficiency of its monorail system. You could get almost wherever you wanted in under twenty minutes, and every destination was at maximum six monorail stops away. If, for some reason, you found yourself in the cemetery on the northern edge of the research laboratory and wanted to hit up Oppenheimer's replica ranch on the eastern side of Perro Caliente for some wacky-cum-salient advice, all you had to do was wait six stops, a far cry from the subway system in Manhattan, an unknowable gridlock I was bested by on a trip with Wren to see some punk band who only sang about ADHD-riddled werewolves. I still remembered standing beneath Canal Street with my wife-to-be blinking at the subway map like it had been written in an ancient and foreign tongue as removed from my life as the language of Atlantis. And that's why our ride to Dr. Elgin Newmar's long shuttered laboratory was so unnerving. At the fifth stop of our journey, everyone else—mostly the Argentinians who conducted horse experiments—disembarked. Twenty-five minutes passed, and still we had not reached the end of the line. Nessa stared at her reflection in the window, and for the first time since I'd met her, she didn't annihilate her anxiety with chatter. She was stoic, her chin tipped bravely skyward.

"Everything's going to be ok." I gave a limp thumbs up.

Nessa didn't look away from her reflection. "I know that. You don't have to reassure me. I'm fine." She no doubt recognized the hangdog look on my face and patted my knee. "I know you're trying to help, but I've come to terms with my relationship with my father and my mom's death. It's behind me. I'm not doing this for closure or anything like that. I'm doing this because I'm sincerely curious to see what my father worked on while he was underground. We are—we *were*—such different people, but we both ended up here." She shook her head. "I'm not depressed, just curious."

Dr. Nessa Newmar was one of the most well-adjusted people I'd ever met, and it was this very quality that drew me to her. She more than most understood and recognized the unordered chaos of the universe, yet she did not retreat into darkness or alcohol or some primordial cave, she marched bravely forward and cast the light of understanding wherever she went. I wanted to tell her this somehow, to articulate my emotions, but before I could, the monorail ground to a halt and the loudspeaker above announced that we'd reached the end of the line.

We disembarked, and unlike the myriad of other monorail platforms across Perro Caliente, this one did not lead to a wide open desert and replica cabin, the rolling greens of the cemetery, or even the noisy city streets of the Mezzanine. We exited the monorail and came face to face with a large metal door and a wall of earth, craggy and dotted with rocks. The platform was barely big enough for two people to stand, and the moment we stepped off the monorail, its sliding doors slammed shut and the train zoomed off in the opposite direction. We were stranded for at least another twenty-five minutes.

"That's encouraging," Nessa said.

I inspected the metal door. Where the handle should've been was a small QWERTY keypad and enter key. I typed a few letters at random, hit enter, and a tiny red LED light flashed above the buttons.

"It's password protected," I said. "You think Oppenheimer set this up or your father?"

Nessa pushed past me and pressed four letters. The LED went green and the door swung inward. "Guess it was my father. He always used the same password for everything."

"What was it?"

"Elsa. My mother's name."

I followed Nessa inside. "Elsa? Jeez. That's only four letters. Bet old Dr. Newmar had his e-mail hacked all the time."

She rolled her eyes. A thick canvas of darkness awaited beyond the password-protected door. It was sweltering in Dr. Newmar's secret laboratory, far warmer than anywhere else in Perro Caliente, and I wondered if Oppenheimer had turned off the temperature controls here and why exactly he would do so. We blindly stumbled along the walls until Nessa's hand brushed against a light switch. She flipped it, and the entire laboratory came into startling view.

The reveal was anticlimactic. There wasn't much left of Dr. Elgin's laboratory, and it was barely bigger than the common room of Housing Unit Seven where physicists gathered to watch television or sip coffee. The floor was bare save for a long U-shaped table that hugged the walls of the room, and everything was covered in a thick layer of dust. Nessa walked into the open center of the lab and slid her hands into her jean pockets. It was a heartbreaking sight. She wasn't me, gallivanting around the cosmos in the hopes of cauterizing an open emotional wound. She just wanted to learn more about her estranged father's work. Seeing her in the center of that empty lab that obviously hadn't been used for years short circuited something in my emotions. Nessa Newmar didn't deserve this, and the world didn't deserve Nessa Newmar.

"Hmmm," she said.

Clearly, Nessa wasn't having the same emotional reaction I was. Her face was the definition of steady calm as she crossed the room toward a small object I'd missed at first glance. A hollowed ring, slightly larger than a bathmat, sat dormant on the aforementioned table. I hurried over, and it instantly became clear that this object held at least a tiny bit of intrigue. The ring was outfitted with exposed microchips and diodes, and tiny projectors jutted out every few inches, all pointing up and inward. It was Nessa who spotted the small red button,

Nessa who grinned like a master scientist on the verge of a great discovery when she leaned over and pressed it.

The machine hummed to life and projected the light blue image of a black elderly scientist. He seemed to be constructed of the same Physicality Algorithm used by Dr. Oppenheimer, but I didn't immediately understand what was happening. Nessa's face gave it away. The way she reached for her mouth, tears rimming her eyes. It was her father. Just like Oppenheimer, he too had discovered a way to cheat the reaper.

He smiled benevolently but didn't look either of us in the eye. "I know what you're thinking, Nessa, and no, I'm not still alive. This is just a recording. I don't know whether that's a blow or a relief, but I hope it's a disappointment of some kind."

She smiled and shook her head, and it wasn't difficult to imagine the kind of father Dr. Elgin Newmar had been—a lovable trickster before the untimely death of his wife sent him forevermore into the sterile comforts of his laboratory. Nessa rocked back and forth on her Forces and whispered, "Dad." So significant, so simple. Nessa. I put my arm around her and drew her head close to my shoulder. Was this that fabled empathy?

"If you're here," the recorded hologram of Dr. Elgin Newmar went on, "that means one of my biggest fears has come true. That old bastard Oppie convinced you to come underground." He scratched at the wisps of hair above his plastic frames. "I always knew he wanted to recruit you. Always. And if you don't know why yet, you will soon. It's not my place to explain it, and you're a smart enough woman to figure it out on your own. You don't need Dad explaining every last mystery. You never did. Look, Nessa. Let me tell you the reason I've recorded this message. I know I'm not long for this world. I've smoked all my life and these bad boys—" he paused here to thwap his chest— "are stage three. I know you know this because I just called and told you. There were so many things I wanted to tell you on the phone, but I just couldn't bring myself to do so. I'm rambling, aren't I?" Dr. Elgin Newmar stood straighter on his heels and took a deep breath. "I want to apologize. What happened to your mother wounded me. I still see it as the event that single-handedly destroyed my life. But I realize now in my twilight that it didn't have to be that way. I still had you. I pushed you into voice lessons and tap not only because I wanted to keep your mother's presence alive in some small way, but because I didn't want you to turn out like me. I love the sciences, Nessa, but my life was exceedingly difficult. I faced a lot of prejudice in my day. I had to work five times harder than my colleagues. I didn't want that for you. I wanted your life to go smoother." Dr. Newmar shook his shoulders.

"I should have known better. Even as a child, you were more like me than your mother. I'm anxiety-prone, obsessive compulsive. When there's a problem I can't solve, I'm totally consumed by it. Your mother, on the other hand, was carefree, lovely, and curious. She could separate her pursuits from her family. I never could. I didn't want you to waste your life away in the darkness of a lab. I didn't realize that's all you ever wanted."

He removed his glasses and wiped the lenses with the bottom of his lab coat. It was a gesture I'd seen Nessa perform a thousand times and observing her father engage the same tick felt terrifyingly intimate, like walking in on Elgin and Nessa on Christmas morning. I held her closer. She just looked so happy, so moved, and I was thrilled for her, squeezing her fingers, an SOS made of flesh that told her I was there for her in any capacity she needed. How strange it was to feel connected to a human being who was still alive, someone who didn't have to hide beneath a coffee table at the sight of infinite Teddy Copelands multiplying across Washington like oversexed rabbits.

"I need to tell you about the obsession that has occupied my life these last twenty years," Dr. Elgin Newmar said. "Ever since your mother died, I've been working on The God Laser. I'm not sure how long you've been underground, but surely Oppie explained to you that I've been with him from the very beginning, ever since the original members, myself included, built this place twenty-five years ago and brought back his mechanically stored consciousness via hologram. Every summer I come here. Every holiday. And after your mother's—" Again he paused, and it was obvious he still had difficulty directly referencing her death all these years later. "—accident, I began work on The God Laser. It wasn't called that then. I wasn't even sure what it would do. At first I naively thought we could crack The Theory of Everything—we didn't know then it'd be an Almost Everything—and use it for time travel. Then I could go back and prevent your mother from driving on that fateful day. But we quickly realized The Theory of Almost Everything wouldn't help us with time travel. We settled on the idea that maybe we could use it to enter parallel worlds and dig out a solution to Oppenheimer's Apocalypse Hypothesis." He coughed into his handkerchief and continued.

"Nessa, look at this lab. Unless Oppie's moved somebody else in, it should be empty. That's not because I'm dying. Tomorrow, I'm asking Oppie to move all of my work to The Control Center to be handed over to the physicists there.

I'm going to ask to be reassigned to the farm lab. You know why? It's taken me almost 20 years, but I've come to realize what a selfish and arrogant person I've been. When I thought we might build a time machine, did I consider stopping the Holocaust or preventing any number of global catastrophes? No. I only thought about saving your mother. When I realized we might use The God Laser to enter parallel worlds, did I see what Oppenheimer saw, that we might find a world free from extinction and use their solutions here in our own? No. I only thought about finding a parallel world where your mother never got on that damn highway two decades ago. I shouldn't be allowed anywhere near The God Laser. I'm like an alcoholic. You don't let him in the bar."

I felt mildly sick to my stomach. There was no avoiding the parallel. Just like me, Dr. Newmar had planned to use the greatest technological spectacle the world had ever known not to save everyone like Delbar suggested, but to fix what had gone wrong in his own tiny, little life. I leaned forward, eager to hear what he'd say next.

"Nessa. I squandered the last twenty years of my life. Your mother is dead. There's nothing I or science can do to change that. If only I realized that earlier, I might have spared our relationship. I know I ruined things between us, and I know you're just a phone call away, but I don't know how to fix it. I helped figure out how to smash atoms, but I can't fix my relationship with my daughter. I'm a weak, feeble, old man. All I have for you is this: don't become me. Don't become so obsessed with your own personal tragedies that you waste your life. If your mother could see what I've done to us, she'd be ashamed. Please don't become me. Please."

The hologram blipped out of existence. The message was over, and Dr. Elgin Newmar was truly gone. I knew how I'd react if I discovered a posthumous hologram message from my beloved father, that Binghamton mechanic/aspirational scientist who encouraged my interest in physics and later cosmology, or even worse, if I stumbled across some letter from the beyond left behind by Wren Wells, that punk princess ghost struck down in her prime. I would have devolved into a sloppy mess of blithering emotions. But Nessa Newmar was not Teddy Copeland. She was a futurist, not a cynical nostalgic like me. All her worldviews were reaffirmed by her father's final plea, and she had long ago transformed herself into a walking pillar for good. It was clear from her tear-stained cheeks that she'd been moved by her father's message and, perhaps, had attained some unexpected closure after a particularly rocky relationship. But she didn't need her father's warning—*Please don't become me. Please.* The person who needed that message was me. Dr. Elgin Newmar was my ghost of Christmas future, a dire warning of the skeletal wreck that if not exceptionally careful I soon would become. I was sobered by his words and resolved myself to be good, more hopeful, a better, more evolved Teddy Copeland who could grow beyond the tragedy of my collegiate years. I turned to Nessa and again squeezed her fingers already arthritic from years spent hovering above keyboards.

"What he said was beautiful," I told her.

"Yeah. It was." She wiped the tears away. "It really was."

"What do you want to do now?"

"Let's go home, Teddy. Let's go home."

We returned to Housing Unit Seven a smidge after midnight. The common room on the fourth floor which was usually so full of activity—Icelandic scientists playing obscure card games, Brits screaming over televised soccer matches—was empty, and the only noise came from the humming vending machine, a song I'd never been quiet enough to hear before. It was oddly comforting, like coming home amid a symphony of crickets.

Nessa and I awkwardly paused between our respective hallways. It was time for sleep and separation, and there was something sour about that. I didn't want the night to end and couldn't remember the last time I yearned for company past the midnight hour. Nessa lingered too, and from the way she shyly met my eyes, it was clear she was considering the same quandary: she wanted to spend more time with me.

Nessa kicked at some invisible interloper on the floor with her sneaker. She removed her glasses and slid them into the front pocket of her lab coat. She radiated confidence, and it was all rather infectious. "Do you want to come to my room?"

I looked past Nessa into the hallway that led to her apartment. We were two adults in our late-twenties who shared many similar interests and common experiences. Our conversations were charged in a way I hadn't experienced since I'd been a co-ed trudging across the farmlands of Susquehanna. I had just witnessed something very personal about her, and she knew about my own hang-ups—*nostalgia is nihilism*—and past as a youthful widower. My contemporaries engaged in activities like this all the time. They met someone they were attracted to. They went to their apartments and kissed, groped, maybe even slept together. Television programs and the boasts of my Alaskan grad pals confirmed this reality and made it all seem so simple. All I had to do was say yes—so easy!—and follow Nessa into a more well-adjusted and happier life. It was right there for the taking if only I was good and brave enough.

And yet...

And yet I couldn't envision myself alone with Nessa in her apartment. It was like an invisible barrier separated me from her hallway, an unholy wall guarded by who else but the floating ghost of Wren Wells decked out in Femme Furies gear warbling her siren song of disaffected annoyance. A woman who hadn't even wanted to marry me! I felt like there was something cracked in the very core of my personality, a virus downloaded from one too many nights navel gazing my needy obsession that could not, would not be purged from the hard drive. I was a flawed and doomed wreck!

There was no doubt that Nessa recognized the hesitation and pain etched across my face as I thought and thought and thought before finally managing to say, "Um, not tonight I don't think." She nodded grimly, and from the way her shoulders slumped, I assumed her pride had been hurt. But then her eyebrows narrowed and a little snort came bellowing down her nose. Her confidence did not stem from me or anyone else. It sloshed in a great reservoir derived from years of scientific accolades and well-groomed self-esteem. Nessa Newmar was not hurt, she was annoyed.

"No worries, bro," she said as nonchalantly as if I'd turned down an offer of a post-work beer at the Trinity. "Teddy, I think you're interesting. But there's one thing I will absolutely never do." She paused here for emphasis. "I will not compete with a ghost."

She turned on her heels and left, and I watched her march down the hallway and disappear. I was once again left with nothing but memories of Wren, my wedding ring, and our nuptial Polaroid to keep me warm at night. I returned to my apartment—how badly I wanted a drink, how badly I wanted to ride the train straight over to the Trinity and drink until every last impotent feeling of mine was drowned in a thick, crashing sea of bourbon—and was shocked to discover the Hologram of Oppenheimer waiting beside my bed, a déjà vu nightmare of his sudden appearance in the Indianapolis StayRomp.

"Where the hell have you been, beef-head?" the hologram barked. "I've been trying to get a hold of you and Newmar all night."

I pulled out my phone. Seven missed calls from Oppenheimer and seven missed texts. I'd put it on silent the moment Nessa and I headed off in search of her father's secret laboratory. No need to have her moment of familial discovery tarnished by the beep-beep-bloop of my ringtone. "What's the matter?"

"Get Newmar. Then meet me and Javari at the replica ranch." Oppenheimer puffed a big cloud of smoke in my face. "The early results of The God Laser project are in, and kid, they look bleak as hell."

#

After Oppenheimer teleported back to his cabin, I slinked my way across the invisible barrier that separated our apartments and knocked on Nessa's door like a repentant buffoon. At first, she wouldn't answer. Another series of knocks, and I heard her yell from inside.

"Go home, Teddy. I'm already asleep."

"No, Nessa. It's not—that. Oppenheimer was waiting in my room. The early results are in. He wants us to come to the replica cabin now."

A beat passed before the door flung open, and Nessa appeared in her pajamas, a beyond wrinkled t-shirt that simply read "Gmail" and a pair of oversized soccer shorts that looked a decade old at least. She looked my face up and down to make sure I wasn't making the whole thing up, then nodded and said, "Let me get my glasses."

Our train ride to the replica ranch was awkward at best and soul crushingly silent at worst. There were no other passengers after midnight, and we didn't speak a word the entire way. We sat on the six person bench that faced the sliding exits, me on one edge, Nessa on the other. Occasionally I glanced over as the tunnel lights swept over her tense face, and at first, I assumed she was replaying the anticlimax of our evening over and over again in her mind like I was. Then I realized just how stupid I was being, how unbelievably arrogant. Nessa had just witnessed a posthumous message from her father. Then we learned that perhaps our project meant to save the entire known world might not actually work. Our sandwiched-in-between moment of human disconnection had surely been obliterated by those two other obviously more consequential events. Maybe she hadn't even wanted to bring me into the darkness of her apartment for a moment of shared physical intimacy. Maybe she just wanted to drink coffee and talk about the exciting developments in the field of gravity wave detectors. What did I know about women not named Wren Wells? For that matter, what did I even know about Wren Wells?

We arrived at Oppenheimer's replica ranch and found the door unlocked. Inside, Oppie and Delbar were arranged around the fireplace just like they'd been when the father of the atomic bomb engaged us in his Perro Caliente thought experiment weeks earlier. Two stubbed out Cubans peeked out from the ashtray at Delbar's side, and it was obvious from the tall glass of bourbon she gripped like a blade and the sweaty grin on her face that she'd been drinking a long time. She eyed Nessa and me up and down and waggled her eyebrows suggestively, no doubt assuming she knew exactly why we'd been irretrievable until almost one in the morning. Her mouth flexed open, but before she could get a barb in Nessa flared her eyes so that even Delbar Javari, fearsome Iranian power goddess though she was, knew enough to refrain.

Oppie cleared his throat, the junior high vice principal's tactic to bring the class to attention. "Children. Early results are in from your parallel world excursions, and they're not very good." He handed Nessa and me a printout flush with numbers. "We've combed the data of every universe you've entered so far, and every single one is doomed to annihilation via global warming or water shortages or some other unforeseen consequence within the next few decades." He removed his straw hat and poured us both drinks. "Using Advanced Probability Mathematics, we can conclude that at our current rate of exploration, not to mention how radically each change to The Theory of Almost Everything alters the earth in question, that there's an extremely high chance it will take us more than sixty years to locate a universe with a workable solution toward combatting human extinction. And as you all know, that's a tad beyond our window."

I stared at him. "'Extremely high chance?' What does that mean exactly?"

Delbar sipped her bourbon. "It's unclear. We'll have a more precise estimate on how long this project will take within the next three days, but obviously, things look really grim right now."

I waited for Oppie to reassure me, to remind me that there was still a chance the results might come back positive.

"If things don't improve," he said, "we're going to shut down The God Laser."

"Who else knows about this?" Nessa asked.

Oppie reset his straw hat. "Only the four of us right now, but tomorrow morning the rest of the scientists are going to come into The Control Center and see the early results. And we still need them working at full capacity." He paused. "My guess is the entire population of Perro Caliente will know about this within hours."

I couldn't imagine how that would affect the morale of the other scientists and lay people. Why even bother striving for a solution if we knew our attempts were doomed? Would they double down on their efforts or defect for the surface and the comfort of their loved ones en masse? No one had any answers, and for a while we just sat there sipping our drinks and listening to the flames of the fireplace lick the logs into ashes. A long time passed before Oppenheimer rose and put his back to us. "I'm tired, children. If you don't mind leaving, that would be wonderful."

We stood, but before we could even pile our glasses in the sink, Oppenheimer's voice boomed again. "Except you, Copeland. I want to talk to you alone."

#

Dr. Oppenheimer ushered Nessa and Del outside, leaving me to linger in the den. I wandered over to the mantle above the fireplace. I'd never had an opportunity to walk around and inspect anything before, and I picked up a lone black and white photograph in a dusty gold frame. I blew off the layer of dust and studied the four glowing faces of the nuclear family contained within. I recognized the younger Robert Oppenheimer—in his forties—from the many pictures in his biography. But alongside him were his wife and daughter and son, their handsome foursome posing in front of the Advanced Institute in Princeton, the early blueprint for Oppie's underground utopia.

"Is this your family?" I asked dumbly when he returned.

"Yes," he said slowly.

"Where are they now?" I regretted it the moment I said it. Simple mathematics told me where they were. Oppenheimer was more than a hundred years old.

"They're all dead, Copeland. Everyone I cared about when I was a flesh and blood human is dead. Now come on. Sit down. I want to tell you a little story, and there's no time for sentimentality."

I did as I was told. I'd spent a great deal of time with Dr. Oppenheimer over the past month and that continued proximity had not diminished my view of him as a scientific titan. I was still as awed by him as the moment I found him in the StayRomp. This really is the father of the atomic bomb, I told myself. This is the man who can help mentor you beyond the rigidly narrow career blueprint of the ASA. This is the genius who's taken a special interest in you, who's teaching you how to ride a horse! I smiled at him and wondered if he'd ever done this with his son. If he ever chased everyone away after an evening of drinking to share a man-to-man alongside a roaring fire. I was so anxious for him to tell me something comforting and inspiring and good.

"Most people don't know this," Oppenheimer began, "but in 1960, the Japanese Committee for Intellectual Exchange asked me to visit their country, specifically Hiroshima and Nagasaki." He refilled our glasses and smiled. "At first, I was hesitant. Why would they want to see me? Why would I want to see them? I'd gotten more than my share of up close and personal looks at my atomic handiwork through the films and photographs the military accrued during the occupation. My wife Kitty was the one who convinced me. 'Go over there,' she said. 'You'll be a god to them after what you've done.' I wasn't sure if that was true, but I liked the sound of it, Copeland. I liked it a lot.

"So I go over there and all these polite dignitaries show me around the country. I couldn't believe how friendly they all were, how they kept stressing they didn't blame me or my scientists or even my country. They blamed themselves, Copeland! Can you believe that? They blamed themselves for starting the war, not the US for wanting to show off their latest weapon to Russia. At Los Alamos, Elgin and I predicted Hiroshima and Nagasaki wouldn't be inhabitable for another sixty years, but in the fifteen-year interim, they'd already rebuilt schools and hospitals and parks. You have to hand it to them." He took a long pull from his bourbon. "But what I really enjoyed, what I truly loved, were the archives. Some ambitious Japanese had realized the opportunity in those razed cities for an oral history on destruction the likes of which had never been seen before by man. They rounded up everybody they could who was present for either of the attacks and had them record it all down for safekeeping in the atomic museums." Another pull. "I read each and every report. People back home thought I was taking a sightseeing tour, but I spent almost the entire time in the stacks like a graduate student. Let me tell you about one if you have a minute. It was written by a woman who was a teenager at the time. She went to school thirteen miles out from the hypocenter, but her family lived right in downtown Hiroshima not far from the initial blast radius. So the bomb goes off and this woman, this Katasumi, decides she has to go see about her family.

But she doesn't go home first—that's probably what saved her from getting cancer in the first five years after the blast, but surely she developed it later in life if she lived much past 1960. So she goes to the bank where her father works. Now this is only five miles out from the hypocenter, and by the time she arrives, her dad looks ok, but he's already done for. Internal radiation sickness. He's only got thirty-five hours to live, Copeland, but they won't realize how sick he is until the next morning.

"So Katasumi reunites with her father, and they make the bright decision not to leave the bank until the black rain stops. Another good choice. If they'd left for home in the black rain, Katasumi would've ended up with cancer in the next five-to-ten for sure. Plus she would have been ostracized by polite Japanese society and called a war bride. Instead, they sit in the bank and watch the red river overflowing with bodies, and then, the next morning, with the sky as clear and sunny as a picturesque New Jersey spring, Katasumi and her father—he's coughing now, hasn't showed her the rash on his belly and back yet, but you can bet he's seen it and is terrified and has an idea of what's to come—they march into the wasteland of downtown Hiroshima." Oppie sniffed and gazed at me hard over his glass. "Now here comes the sad part, Copeland, so bottom's up."

If the next section was the sad part, what did that make the opening exactly? It was now past two in the morning, and more than anything I longed for the simple comforts of my bed. I had to be up in four hours and had no earthly idea why Oppenheimer had chosen this precise moment in time to tell me one of the most horrifyingly unimaginable stories I'd ever heard in my life. Couldn't he have saved this for one of our weekly trips around the digital mountains? All

I wanted from him in that moment was comfort, and instead he delivered annihilation. I again remembered Delbar's warning: *Oppenheimer's been a hologram for twenty-five years. That had to warp him, right?*

"It takes Katasumi and her father all day tramping along the remains of annihilated houses and skeletons, but finally they find their flattened roof and where their house should be. Now by this point, the father is coughing up blood, and it's clear he's not going to make it. Everything's flat and bombed out, so they know they aren't going to find mama and little brother alive either. Katasumi's being exposed to radiation, and really they should've hightailed it away for the hospital on the other side of the mountain. Although, one man tried that and he went to Nagasaki and ended up getting atom bombed twice. So who can really say?" He shook his head. "So Katasumi and her father dig and dig and dig, and eventually she unearths the remains of her mother. Her torso and face, they're unrecognizable, but Katasumi is positive it's her from her dress and necklace. Her legs? They're pulverized. Her bones are dust. Now here's the sad part I alluded to earlier. Katasumi's crying, and her father's vomiting blood and picking at his radiation rash, and little teenage Katasumi decides she wants a memento. What do you think she takes, Copeland?"

I glared at him, still surprised by the occasional streaks of Oppenheimer's cruelty, similar to how he'd treated Nessa before bringing us to her father's grave. Was this the cost of mentorship? "The necklace," I guessed.

"Obvious choice, but wrong. Katasumi bends down and scoops up a handful of chalky, soft bone. Then she puts it in her mouth and swallows. She wrote in her account that it was the only way to keep her mother a part of her."

He let that image settle a bit before continuing. It was a difficult moment to explain. The depth of the story's sadness was almost too vast, too opaque to even grapple with. It was like trying to reason with the sun. You couldn't out logic it. The sun simply existed as plain and true as the earth itself, and you could measure it and hypothesize, but your interactions with it were inherently limited. It was a profoundly sad story that depressed me, and I resented Oppenheimer for choosing this time and place to tell it. I didn't need any assistance feeling low.

"Right before I left Japan, an NHK reporter stuck a microphone in my face. He asked me if after visiting I regretted The Manhattan Project or if I felt worse about my involvement. I thought of Katasumi swallowing her mother's bones as her father died of radiation poisoning. I told him that although I deeply regretted the suffering of the Japanese people and that the Atom Bomb had been used there, I didn't regret my choice to help with The Manhattan Project. We knew Hitler was working on something similar. Copeland, we had to beat Hitler. What happened with the bomb after that was a travesty, but we still had to build one to stop Hitler, an apocalypse made flesh." Oppenheimer stood and put his hand on the fireplace choker. It felt like a lifetime had passed since Barb pulled the aboveground cabin's choker and revealed the elevator that granted us entry into Perro Caliente proper. "The point of this story is that the luminaries of our field have to make extremely difficult decisions. You can't save everyone, like Dr. Javari thinks. And you can't share the top tech in the world with everyone like Dr. Newmar thinks. Maybe that works with Google when you're talking about e-mail or search engines or whatever hornswoggle they're peddling on the surface, but The God Laser is a different matter entirely. If we hand over the world's most powerful particle accelerator to everyone now, who knows what the terrorists will do, what the Russians will do, what the serial killers will do? Copeland, the world is full of terrible individuals, and as the world's top scientists, it's our job to keep this mangy mutt known as society in line."

Despite his brutish tactics, Oppenheimer was persuasive. I admired how optimistic both Nessa and Delbar were, but there were times when I found them a tad overly trusting. They believed in the power of the human being, the idea that when push comes to shove, most people will choose to do the right thing. I desperately wanted to agree, but it was difficult to see the proof even in myself. I'd been given the opportunity to toy with a machine that might radically reshape the entire world, and for the most part, I'd used it to inch closer to my deceased wife. What if people with even more selfish desires were given access to our gadget? What if they were even worse than me?

"It's time to get real." Oppenheimer pulled the choker, and just like aboveground, the bookshelf parted, and another secret elevator appeared. I put my drink down. Was it even possible to go deeper into the earth? "Follow me, Copeland. Tut, tut now."

I followed Oppenheimer into the glass elevator. The excitement of a new mystery stirred me awake, and I could feel the goose bumps on my skin as the elevator plunged even deeper into our planet. We appeared at the top of yet another dome—so much smaller than the Mezzanine, not even a tenth as large as Oppenheimer's server dungeon—at the center of which stood a towering super computer that looked at least thirty years old. There were levers and black-green screens all along its circular terminal, not to mention a thick layer of dust that made it clear Oppenheimer didn't go down there very often. A ten foot vat of neon blue liquid rose from the middle of the machine, and something shuddered behind the bubbles. It took me a moment to recognize it: a human brain. It hung suspended in the tube connected to the super computer via a series of wires cackling with energy and flirty bubbles. The elevator doors slid open, and Oppenheimer regally bowed. "Dr. Copeland, here lies the brain of Dr. J. Robert Oppenheimer."

Eternal life is something humans have dreamt about since the beginning of time. It's something I longed for during Wren's leukemia year and my Alaskan exile. But far beneath the New Mexico desert, under a ranch that was a replica of another ranch, I realized just how quickly that dream could evaporate into nightmare. Oppie's brain bobbed in the pulsating blue waters, and it reminded me of a chained puppy struggling to get free and explore the bright green yard of infinity.

"After my body died, I had my brain sealed in this machine until the original Perro Caliente scientists, Elgin Newmar included, cooked up a way for my consciousness to be projected into the hologram you see before you. It's brilliant really. When I take a drink, this little doodad dulls my nervous system. When I smoke, the machine floods it with stimulants." Oppie paused. "Don't try to hide that the look on your face. I know it's an abomination. But you have to admit, it's pretty wacky, huh?"

I turned away from the hologram and stared into the vat, the very center of Oppenheimer's century-old brain. Oppie bent low and opened a tiny door beneath the control panel, retrieving an elegant golden pocket watch. He turned it over in his palm to show me. The face didn't have the normal one-through-twelve layout. Instead, where midnight should have been was a small cursive *Apocalypse* and then two hands counting down from five and ten years. "Everyone honestly believes that beating back the apocalypse should be so simple. I understand why, Dr. Copeland. People can't wrap their minds around the end of everything, the expiration of civilization, of everything we've accumulated since our drunken stumble out of the primordial goo!"

I was still surprised by how diminutive he was. His reputation had grown exponentially over the years, but physically he was slight, even somewhat pitiful. It was not difficult to imagine larger boys stealing lunch money from the boyhood Robert Oppenheimer, terrorizing him with their working-class fists. "What are you saying, Doctor?"

"You're the only other person who knows. I'm trusting you, Copeland. Don't make me regret that trust. You wouldn't enjoy a vengeful Oppenheimer. Ask Katasumi about that one!" He slapped me on the shoulder. "I've told everyone that my Apocalypse Hypothesis shows we have sixty-to-seventy years before global warming or water shortages or nuclear bombs end the human race. That's not exactly the whole truth and nothing but the truth." He dangled the pocket watch. "I call this my Apocalypse Pocket Watch. It shows approximately how long we have left, and we don't actually have sixty-to-seventy years before we tip into irreversible global catastrophe, we've got five-to-ten. If my hypothesis if off, we may have even less than that. So, to sum up, shit's even worse than I said."

"You've been lying to us?

He bared his hologram teeth. "Look, if I'm going to get the best work out of my people, they need hope. If they think they're toiling away spending their final years underground, too many would opt for their families and poppycock distractions."

Delbar's early results said it would probably take over sixty years to solve extinction through The God Laser. My face must have sunk, because Oppenheimer immediately guessed what I was thinking.

"Maybe her calculations are off. Maybe mine are." He pressed the Apocalypse Pocket Watch into my hands. "Copeland. I'm tired. I thought I wanted eternal life. I built this place to protect humanity. I thought it was my penance for building a bomb that could eradicate everything. I thought it was up to me to protect the earth from that fate no matter what form it took. But I've seen too much. My family is dead. I want denouement."

"Can you die?"

He pointed to a flashing red button on the control panel. "All you have to do is push it."

I glanced from the button to the Apocalypse Pocket Watch back to the button again.

"All hope isn't lost. We have the best scientific minds in the world down here, and I've got them working at max potential because they still have hope. That's the key, Copeland. Well-intentioned deception." He put his back to me. "I need to ask you something now, and I don't want you to say anything just yet, kiddo. I don't even want to see your reaction. I'm going to tell you my plan, then you think about it and get back to me. Take your time."

I took a deep breath. I could scarcely believe this was my life. Maybe I should have listened to the many panelists at the ASA urging me toward the tenure track.

"I'd like you," Oppenheimer continued, "to take over Perro Caliente. Someone needs to shepherd this place after

I'm gone, and I think you're the man for the job. That's why I brought you and Drs. Javari and Newmar down here. I need a successor. They're too impractical. You're the one I want, Copeland. Think it over."

Oppenheimer left me then with nothing but my cluttered thoughts, the Apocalypse Pocket Watch, and the gross gurgles of his gray brain. I sat on the ground and remained very still. Once, at Wren's insistence, I'd accompanied her to a meditation class after she was diagnosed. Try as I might, I could not empty my brain of my many neuroses, all those thousands of neurons telling me to imagine burgers or Wren or SETI. My mind was a pinball machine bumping from one disconnected thought to the next. But sitting there next to Oppenheimer's abominable brain, I achieved the clarity that Wren had so often strived for. My mind was laser focused on one thought, just one nugget from the avalanche of revelations Oppenheimer had just unleashed: we had five-to-ten years before all of human life would end.

I was going to die.

I should have gone straight to bed. It had been an absurdly long day filled with one development after another, but as I sat on the shuddering train that would return me to Housing Unit Seven, I discovered that I could not stop fidgeting. I kept rubbing my knuckles, tapping my foot against the floor. It was nearly three in the morning, and I was totally alone. I sailed right on past the apartment buildings without even realizing what I was doing. The train was heading northwest, and I scratched and trembled all the way to the final stop of the line, the underground cemetery Oppenheimer dragged us to on Nessa's very first day.

I removed my Italian loafers at the edge of the cemetery and waded into the grass with my bare feet. I'd craved the familiar sensation of skin against plant and dirt all evening long the way some pregnant women craved pickles and ice cream as their due dates approached. What malignant form bloomed inside my body just waiting to earn access to the outside world and its treasures and indignities? I zigzagged through the cemetery careful to avoid walking across where anyone was buried. I told myself that I would put everything that had happened that evening out of my mind—Elgin's warning, the lingering moment outside Nessa's apartment, Oppenheimer's revelations and request for me to become the new director—and deal with it tomorrow. For now, it was simply enough to stroll through the grass, to remind myself that I was a flesh-and-blood human with choices and free will who wouldn't let the narrative of his life be overridden by apocalyptic catastrophe. I touched a stone marker and remembered how long it'd been since I'd set foot inside an aboveground cemetery. I'd never actually gone to Wren's grave. Her parents asked me to serve as pallbearer, but I just couldn't bring myself to do it—a failure I still deeply regretted. I often imagined what Wren's graveyard looked like and in my mind pictured something out of Oppenheimer's cemetery—green and flat and serene. The only difference was the scattering of dead pixels in the upper-left corner of the SimuSky, technology's acknowledgment that all rules and promises could be broken, that nothing lasted forever, not even holy silicon. Wren. I remembered the intellectual gauntlet thrown down by Teddy Copeland Prime, that other, better me. He told us, all of us, the ever-expanding snake of Teddy Copelands looking to right what once went wrong, that we could never return to that particular universe because we were all so alike that if one of us decided to do so, the rest of us would decide to the same.

But what if Teddy Copeland Prime's hypothesis was flawed? Or more importantly, what if Teddy Copeland Prime purposely obscured some truth so that he and he alone might enjoy the sweet comfort of seeing Wren Wells alive once again?

The solution came to me quite suddenly, and I can't say it was wholly unexpected. One of the final lingering problems of The Copeland Principle was solved in similar fashion. It was the end of my second year of graduate school, and Dr. Rodriguez had just broken the news that I hadn't been selected for an international fellowship to work at the Cavendish Laboratory and wasn't even one of the finalists. It was a huge blow to my ego, and I remembered walking out of his office and pacing the commons back and forth like a lunatic. I should have been figuring out alternative summer plans, but instead, I set my mind to work on that final mathematical stumbling block within The Copeland Principle. It came to me within the hour. Figuring out the inherent problem with how I'd approached The Wren Algorithm occurred to me in similar fashion. I recalled something peculiar from that wretched encounter in Eastern Market that had stuck out to me even then. I'd heard a Teddy Copeland with a British accent. I could assume that in his universe, my parents or their parents' parents, had immigrated to England instead of America. Even if that Teddy Copeland moved to the US as a boy, he couldn't have possibly led the exact same life I had. Maybe what we Teddy Copelands united in Eastern Market shared in common were not identical lives, but two important variables in many lives full of them: we had all met and fallen in love with Wren Wells who subsequently died of leukemia, and we had all studied cosmology and been invited by Dr. Oppenheimer to partake in The God Laser project. Everything else could have been totally different. And if that hypothesis held water, that meant I could pull up The Wren Algorithm on my workstation computer and alter it further. We Teddy Copelands had changed only one element of The Theory of Almost Everything: we reduced the leukemia occurrence rate in women by a single percentage point. What if I took that algorithm and applied another modification to my own life as obscure as Dr. Fenton who'd transformed a deluxe pizza in Chicago to a veggie? Presumably, if I chose something so small and insignificant in the grand daisy chain of events that constituted my life, it would be unique to me and me alone. I might then be able to enter a world with a living Wren Wells and not have it overrun with a sea of infinite Teddy Copelands!

I dashed back to my loafers and hopped a train en route to The Control Center. I tried imagining some mundane moment, anything, that I might flip to test my new and improved theory, the one that might defeat Teddy Copeland Prime, and therefore, myself. Should I pull a Dr. Fenton and alter a pizza? Maybe a missed foul shot in gym class basketball? Perhaps a brown pair of sneakers instead of blue? I recalled a board game I played only once with my father. It was shoddy, purchased from a drug store, a poorly-illustrated rendering gracing the box of two Indiana Jones-knock offs running down the side of a volcano with bundles of treasure in their arms. *Explorers of Verenzetti Island!* The game was ok at best, already outmoded by the primitive video games I then worshipped on my dinky television screen. In *Explorers of Verenzetti Island!*, you took turns navigating a cardboard marker representing one of four explorers around the aforementioned Verenzetti Island on the lookout for relics and hostile natives. Once every few turns the volcano in the center of the board would erupt, and little plastic fireballs randomly juked around the playfield. If your cardboard marker was knocked over, you had to go back to the very first tile. It was a mostly unremarkable game, but what I remembered most about that first play through was the penultimate turn. My father was one space away from a boat that signaled he would escape Verenzetti Island and win the game. I was seven away, and it was my turn. The maximum number of tiles you could move per turn was seven, so if I just spun the play wheel and hit that number exactly, I could still win. But I didn't spin a seven, I spun a one. My father won and promptly retired from all future games of *Explorers of Verenzetti Island!* so as to preserve his perfect record but also to avoid ever having to play the relatively dull game again.

And that might have been the end of the story—a predictable father/son board game romp I might recall fondly from time to time—had I not trudged up the stairs of The Control Center and fired up The Wren Algorithm. What if I took that universe where Wren never contracted leukemia and then made an additional change? What if I went into the calculus of the gods and changed that game spin from nearly two decades earlier from a one into a two? If no other Teddy Copeland experienced that particular game of *Explorers of Verenzetti Island!* or, at the very least, remembered it, then I could enter a world with a living Wren Wells devoid of an ever-expanding mass of grieving Teddy Copelands.

I coded until the yolk of the SimuSun appeared on the eastern horizon of the domed SimuSky. Control Center scientists—Nessa and Delbar and Oppie included—would begin filtering in a little after eight. That gave me barely over an hour to enter this new universe and return before being found out by my colleagues. I powered up The God Laser and watched from my computer as its dual quadrupoles birthed yet another miniature wormhole, the open gateway to a world with a living Wren, a beautiful Wren-world. I pressed my hand to the glass of The Control Center's walls. What if I found her? What if I saw her? What if I heard her voice one last time?

What if?

It turned out that in a universe with a reduced leukemia rate for women and one in which I spun a two instead of a one against my father, Wren Wells survived and ended up in Baltimore, land of harbors and titillating, award-winning crime show dramas. Or at least, that's what the Calabi-Yau informed me when I entered that strange, new Wren-full world. I waited at a bus stop on the fringes of downtown Baltimore. It was a crisp late spring morning, and the stop was oddly empty, just me and a college-aged boy entranced by the light of his phone.

The reason I had teleported to this particular bus stop was simple: the Calabi-Yau told me Wren was at that very moment riding the 61C. This was the next stop on the line, and Wren's bus—such a delicate, lovely phrase—was scheduled to arrive within the next three minutes. All I had to do was screw up my courage and step aboard. Then I could at last be reunited with my wife. Sure, in this reality she had never even met me, but I naïvely told myself that sitting near her would be enough. I didn't even have to talk to her. I could just soak in her presence and return to my world—to Nessa, Oppenheimer, and my impending candidacy for director. I could return home and continue my path toward perpetual improvement.

I checked my wristwatch for the fiftieth time that morning. So far, no sea of Teddy Copelands had appeared with the same sad longing to see Wren again, proving my hypothesis that although we Teddys all shared certain similarities, we hadn't experienced exactly the same lives, and thus, they wouldn't even know about the relatively unimportant game of *Explorers of Verenzetti Island!* I had altered. But I couldn't shake the feeling I was being watched, and every time I turned toward the row of buildings behind me, I imagined I spotted a shadowy figure ducking behind a corner. Who in a world where I knew no one would spy on me? It's true that I could have used the Calabi-Yau to scan the environment to find out what other changes my altered board game spin had caused—differences surely comparable to the ones we discovered in Berkeley and Mountain View—but I was too focused on Wren, Wren, only Wren.

I felt my stomach drop when the 61C at last rounded the corner, splashing up grimy water in the process. My hands were trembling, but I was slightly less nervous than when I'd tracked down Wren in Eastern Market. This was my sophomore effort, and the Infinite Teddy Copelands had prepared me for almost anything. I reassured myself that the worst case scenario was that I simply retrieved my tablet and teleported home. I handed the bus driver two crisp bills, and there, sitting by her lonesome in a row near the back, was lovely Wren Wells alive and healthy once again. I dared not move any closer and held fast to an overhead railing trying not to stare. Here was the lead singer of the Femme Furies resurrected from the dead and transformed into a real, living adult. She wore a faded leather jacket and her hair was done in a crew cut that magnified the beauty of her face, that sharp nose and raised cheekbones. When more riders boarded at the next stop, I had no choice but to move toward her, to abandon my station near the driver and slowly make that holy march to the end of the bus where an unwitting Wren Wells sat bopping her head to some unheard melody. If only she knew. If only she knew everything I'd endured to get here. How desperately I wanted to stroke her cheek.

But Wren didn't even look my way when I walked by or even when I sat directly behind her. I thought it might be enough just to be near her, to sniff that once-familiar Wren-aroma—even in this world she smelled vaguely of soap and whiskey—and then I would be ready to face my forever Wren-less existence. But in the actual moment of the event, I longed for her to turn to me, to somehow understand the significance of this moment and our relationship. I longed for her to ask me out for a cup of coffee, tangible proof that our love was destined and legendary, as star-crossed as Romeo and Juliet or Einstein and the atom. But Wren did nothing. And when seven stops later this other Wren reached up and pulled the stop rope, I felt my legs stand as if possessed by some phantom power. She walked up the aisle and off the bus, and my body carried me behind her, a mere six feet away. I couldn't believe how short she was. Had she always been this short? In the years after her death, she had grown so large in my mind that I wouldn't have been surprised if she was actually the size of skyscrapers, lumbering through Baltimore like an angelic Godzilla happily pulverizing we mere mortals into dust.

We stepped off the bus into a residential area comprised of cobblestone streets and old company duplexes. I followed Wren up a hill—it was just the two of us now—and had no plans, no grand delusions that I might call out to her and explain my strange story of cosmology and cancer. I just wanted to be around her a few minutes more, just a few seconds more, just a few anything. Wren. Wren. My Wren.

She turned down a side street, so I turned down a side street. And that was when she finally spun around and faced me, a can of mace brandished like a gun. "What the fuck, creep?"

"What?"

"I saw you gawking at me on the bus. I know my neighbors. I've never seen you before in my life."

"I'm... I'm... I don't mean any harm. I'm nothing. I'm nothing."

"Just get the fuck away from me. I've taken defense lessons, all right, prick? Turn around and get the hell out of here."

She stormed off, and I was left with no other alternative but to stand there and feel terrible about myself and all I had done. All my life I'd despised men who leered at women in public or jeered at them from cars, and now I had become much worse, tracking this stranger like some kind of deranged serial killer. Wren disappeared down a corner, and I already knew it didn't necessarily have to end this way. I'd glimpsed the possibilities the moment I formulated my *Explorers of Verenzetti Island!* hypothesis. If I wanted a do-over reunion with Wren, all I had to do was go back into the algorithm and change the game spin from a two to a three. If that encounter went as terribly as this one, I could again alter it from three to four and then four to five and so on and so forth until I changed the spin to the seven that would've caused my cardboard marker to land on the escape boat and win the game against my father. That meant I had five more opportunities to see Wren Wells again, and each Wren would have no memory of the previous encounter.

Before I could tease out the ramifications of my hypothesis, I again saw the shadowy figure gawking at me from behind a bush in some random Baltimorian's yard. This time there was no chalking the vision up to nerves or paranoia. He or she ducked when I spotted them, but there was nowhere to escape this time.

"Who are you?" I shouted.

They didn't answer, and before I could start toward them, I heard the familiar churn of a Calabi-Yau teleportation. The intruder was gone, either returned to my own native universe or some other land of God Lasers and Perro Calientes. I checked my watch. Oppenheimer and the others would be arriving within minutes for a full day of work, and I had to get home. I swiped in the teleportation command, all the while wondering if I continued down this road of exploring the five remaining Wren-worlds as I knew I would, did that mean I would encounter this mysterious observer again?

I materialized beneath the quadrupole lasers of The God Laser and hurried up The Control Center stairs to my workstation on the top floor. The building was empty, but not for long. I heard the smack of footsteps and spun in my chair to see Nessa, the first arrival of the morning. We hadn't seen each other since Oppenheimer revealed the early results of The God Laser the night before. She looked embarrassed and angry when she saw me, and I knew she was also thinking about the moment in Housing Unit Seven, when we both wanted to go back to her bedroom and guilt reeled me away.

"Morning, Nessa," I said, trying my best to sound chipper despite the steady ticking of the Apocalypse Pocket Watch in my lab coat.

"Hello, Dr. Copeland." Her voice was as cold as steel.

THE GENBAKU DOME

Old Man Reeves' bodega was abandoned, the front door locked with a hastily scribbled closed sign taped on the inside. You have to understand how truly ominous a development this was. During our tenure underground, I counted on two bedrock principles when the going got tough: the cavalier friendship of Nessa Newmar and Delbar Javari and the convenience food and coffee served to us by surly Old Man Reeves. After I declined Nessa's invitation into her apartment two nights earlier, I wasn't sure where I stood with Nessa, and now the bodega was closed to me too. I loosened my knit tie even though it wasn't yet eight in the morning. What unimaginable catastrophe would unfurl next?

I had ten minutes to kill before the train for The God Laser arrived, so I awkwardly sat on Old Man Reeves' stoop. A full twenty-four hours had passed since I'd returned from Baltimore to find Nessa and my fellow scientists arriving at The

Control Center for work. I'd sheepishly told Oppenheimer I was sick, that I needed a day off, and slept for the next sixteen hours straight. I'd missed the news of the results sweep through The Control Center and potentially all of Perro Caliente, and perhaps this was the genesis behind Old Man Reeves' absence. Maybe given the increased likelihood of our destruction, he'd opted for the surface. I fingered the Apocalypse Pocket Watch tucked safely in my lab coat. It was a burden I was not quite ready to bear. I'd been flattered when Oppenheimer asked me to become the next Director of Perro Caliente, but I didn't subscribe to his notion that Nessa and Delbar would necessarily make subpar directors on account of their omnipresent optimism. On the contrary, I had misgivings about my own candidacy precisely because of my lack of said optimism. How could I push back against an apocalypse lurking only ten years away when I had spent so much of my time underground secretly coding a route back to my dead wife? Oppie too was a man of secrets. His continued existence had been kept secret from the surface, and, when you got right down to it, that's all Perro Caliente was: the biggest secret never told. And where had that gotten him? Twenty-five years underground and sure, he'd cracked the unsolvable Theory of Almost Everything, but had that brought him any closer to beating back the skeletal embrace of an inevitable doomsday? No one could be sure. Perhaps it was time to reset Oppenheimer's paradigm. Perhaps it was time for Nessa and Delbar's Google-esque brand of disruptive thinking.

Nessa and Delbar emerged from Housing Unit Seven precisely on cue, their usually hopeful faces as grim as I'd ever seen them. They made an amusing pair, Delbar in her heels and perfectly applied makeup, that movie star cleft, and Nessa the queen of au natural with messy hair and her Forces and superhero t-shirt. They saw me sitting sadly beneath the neon bodega sign, and I was so relieved when they started in my direction. I wasn't sure how I'd survive without them and was startled to discover how much I relied upon my new companions. I was beginning to truly regret my behavior in Alaska, the seven years I'd spent avoiding other people, opting for the safety of the lab, the reassurance of the clutter in my apartment growing alongside my grief. Other people could potentially provide comfort, I thought. It was an intriguing hypothesis.

"He's not here?" Delbar pointed at the bodega sign.

"Gone."

Nessa said nothing. She shielded her eyes from the SimuSun and avoided looking in my direction. It was clear from Delbar's neutral expression that Nessa hadn't explained the awkward details of our apartment encounter, and for that, I was immensely grateful. I studied her face and again turned the Apocalypse Pocket Watch over in my lab coat. It occurred to me that I had to reveal what Oppenheimer had told me in front of his decaying brain. We didn't have sixty-to-seventy years left, we had five-to-ten. It wasn't my intention to betray Oppenheimer's trust, but I couldn't bear the thought of withholding such vital information from my two colleagues, my two friends. Didn't they have a right to know how much time we collectively had left? Didn't they deserve the option to return aboveground if that's how they wanted to spend their final years on earth? I was about to break down and tell them when finally Nessa spoke.

"He probably joined the protesters."

"Protesters?" I asked.

Delbar reached for my hand and pulled me up, and together we began towards the monorail platform. "You missed quite a show yesterday. Oppenheimer announced the early results to the scientists, and by lunchtime, everyone in Perro Caliente knew. People are totally shitting the bed. They don't want to waste their lives underground if the project's doomed anyway. A lot of them are even questioning whether or not Oppenheimer's Apocalypse Hypothesis is even accurate. They think he might be lying."

Nessa sighed. "They'd handle it better if he hadn't dismantled the elevator cars."

"What?" I asked. "He dismantled the main elevator and the service elevator? The cars are just gone?"

"The man built an atom bomb in the '40s. You think he can't dismantle elevators? He's claiming it's part of routine maintenance, but it's obvious it's to stop people from leaving. Teddy, those are the only ways out of here. Things are getting tense."

"What if they escape and spill the beans?" I asked.

Delbar shrugged. "There's the non-disclosure agreement we all signed. Plus, somebody tried that a few years ago and Oppenheimer had them totally smeared. The only outlet that even covered the story was *Weird World News* or something. Barb told me the snitch is flipping burgers in Antarctica now."

This new development changed things considerably. If I told Nessa and Delbar the truth now, it was clear to me they would reveal that information to the rest of Perro Caliente. What would happen if people like Old Man Reeves and the thousands of other underground employees realized that not only was the world ending in five-to-ten years, but they were also being kept against their will by Dr. Oppenheimer? I desperately wanted to explain everything, but I couldn't afford the risk to everyone's safety. We heard the familiar voices of The Communications Center and turned north to that powder blue tower. The lead officer's voice rang out steady and true for all of Perro Caliente to hear. "Good morning, everyone," he said uneasily. "This is just a friendly reminder from all of us at The Communications Center and dear old Oppie himself to remain calm. Please remain calm."

Our monorail arrived, and at last, I was given a front row seat to how drastically things had changed since my inter-dimensional trip to Baltimore. During most morning commutes, the monorail was filled to overflowing with scientists and lay people of all shapes and backgrounds chatting over coffee or one of the many newspapers Oppenheimer imported from all around the globe. That morning, however, the train was half full, the formerly buzzing scientists now quiet and reserved. One mathematician—a quiet Icelander named Stefansson or Sigurdsson—sat on the floor gripping a knife with what appeared to be a line of cocaine spread across the blade. Whenever someone approached him, he yelled, "Ég vil ekki að deyja! Ég vil ekki að deyja!" and I assumed it was best to leave him alone.

The monorail swept through the Mezzanine, and my bird's eye view of our underground utopia was barely more reassuring than Stefansson/Sigurdsson snorting coke off the blade of his knife. The jovial scientists I had come to know filled the Nightlife District well beyond capacity even though it wasn't yet eight in the morning. Some stood huddled outside, gesturing wildly and shouting about Oppenheimer, while the lunch ladies from the cafeteria had abandoned their posts to sit on stoops and spit and gossip. The most troubling scene occurred right before our train left the Mezzanine for the tunnel that led to The Control Center. We zoomed past the elevator shaft, the same one all of us had traveled down our very first day, and assembled there were maybe two dozen people shaking makeshift signs demanding that Oppenheimer return the elevator car and let people leave if they so chose. I squinted before we hit the tunnel and recognized some of the protesters. There was Old Man Reeves. There was Barb from HR and *The Steady-State Ecstasy of Fred Hoyle*. There was Jin, the mysterious driver-cum-pilot who had shepherded me from the StayRomp in Indianapolis all the way to the aboveground ranch on the outskirts of Los Alamos.

"Christ," I managed.

"There's still hope," Nessa said. "There's always hope."

It was difficult to believe her. How exactly had I, a mild-mannered cosmologist hailing from the hardscrabble remains of Binghamton, ended up here: witness to an underground disaster-in-waiting? Could you telegraph my present back in Alaska? What about in Wren's dorm room that night of the Battle of the Bands? What about when I won the ISC Rising Stars Challenge? I found myself dwelling on that contest, on the thick sea of balloons cascading down from the ceiling. How easier things had been back then. How black and white.

"Life was so much simpler when we were kids," I told Delbar. "Like at the ISC. You either knew your science or you didn't. The fate of the known world didn't hang in the balance. I miss that."

"The ISC Rising Stars challenge?" Nessa cocked her head. "You know about that?"

We stared at her. "You know about that?"

"Yeah, it came through Berkeley when I was twelve-years-old. I won it."

"We won it when we were twelve, too."

Nessa pushed me hard in the chest, and I almost went careening into Stefansson/Sigurdsson's coke blade. "Shut the fuck up," she shouted.

"I will not shut the fuck up."

Nessa paced. "Guys, you're totally not going to believe this, but do you remember the man who hosted the ISC? The British scientist? Guys, that was my dad!"

"What?" Delbar asked.

"You heard me." The train was grinding to a halt now in front of The Control Center. "This is crazy, just crazy. What are the odds that all three of us would win some weirdo science competition hosted by my dad and then be reunited underground by Oppenheimer, my father's mentor? This can't be a coincidence. It can't." Nessa grabbed Delbar by the shoulders. "Have you ever even Googled the ISC? Do you even know what it stands for?"

Del shook her head no.

"The International Scientific Community. That's what my dad told me. I always took it at face value, but I Googled it after he died." Her eyes widened. "There's nothing. Not a trace of it on the internet. Nothing."

"How's that possible?" I asked. "The ISC had enough cash to fund a worldwide science competition for children, not to mention scholarships that didn't pay out for nearly a decade later. Who could have done all that and then made it disappear?"

The train doors pulled apart, and The Control Center was revealed. On the top floor, we could see Oppenheimer puttering around, smoking up a storm, his straw hat set low. We didn't even have to acknowledge our next step. Our trio hurried past the throng of scientists and up the stairs to confront the Hologram of Dr. J. Robert Oppenheimer. He didn't even look at us. He was busy altering the algorithm for whatever parallel world Nessa and I were slated to visit that day, and he looked as nonplussed by the deteriorating morale of Perro Caliente as a child by the slumping enthusiasm of an anthill.

"Oppenheimer." Nessa bent low so they were eye-to-eye. "Did you know all three of us won the ISC Rising Stars Challenge as children?"

Oppie didn't look away from his computer screen. "What?"

"I said, 'Did you know all three of us won the ISC Rising Stars Challenge as children?'"

He rubbed at his eyes. He looked exhausted. "Of course I did, weirdos. Your father ran the competition. How could I not know?"

"Well, what does it mean?"

"What do you mean, 'what does it mean?'"

"Don't you think it's a little strange we all won my father's competition and ended up here? There's nothing about it anywhere on the internet. How's that possible?"

Oppenheimer rose from the computer terminal and crumpled his hat in his hands. "Balderdash! Poppycock! What's so strange about any of that? Elgin was always interested in kids. There were hundreds of winners all across the world. Winning the ISC signified you were one of the best and brightest minds in science. Doesn't it make sense that the best ISC alumni would find their way to me? I don't know what happened to the ISC. It probably lost funding like a trillion other programs. You kids want to make everything into a gd conspiracy." He pointed through the window at The God Laser. "You want to sleuth out a mystery? Put your minds to work on The God Laser. The world is going to end. We're running out of time, and you three are running around like that mystery solving pooch and his gaggle of cartoon hippies."

"Scooby Doo?" I asked.

Everyone stared at me.

"Now," Oppenheimer continued, "can you please get to work? We'll be ready to power up The God Laser in just a few minutes. The algorithm we're working on will send you to a world where Nixon never won the presidency. Given all the excitement yesterday, we never decided where to send you. Any thoughts?"

"The University of Alaska," I blurted.

Even I was surprised by how quickly I decided, how quickly the mystery of the Rising Stars was swept away by the larger conundrum of our dying planet. Oppenheimer always let us choose where we'd physically materialize within the parallel worlds, and I usually let Nessa pick. She oscillated between the comforting—UC Berkeley's campus—and exotic wish fulfillment—Miami Beach turned New Berlin City during our romp in the Neo-Nazi universe. But that morning, I desperately wanted something that reminded me of home in an age of the fantastic. I wanted to see Alaska again because it provided me refuge during a difficult period in my life, and I hoped that perhaps this parallel version might provide similar comforts even as the walls of our endeavor crumbled upon us.

"The University of Alaska it is," Oppenheimer said. "Good luck." His voice turned sorrowful and even somewhat pathetic. "We all need some right now."

#

I had no idea how deleting Nixon's presidency might affect society-at-large. If pressed on the subject before we left, I would've predicted that maybe Vietnam would have turned out differently, and since Dr. Fenton's veggie pizza had such radical consequences—an event surely less "important" in the grand design of human history—then removing Nixon's presidency might have an even larger effect. Even I, however, was stunned when we materialized in that Nixon-less world. We appeared outside Rasmuson Library, one of my favorite U of A buildings because it wasn't a boxy cube like so many other academic architectural throwbacks. Instead, the Rasmuson looked like an undulating algorithm of windows that curved into a cone-shaped brick entrance. It was neat, futuristic, and that's partly why it was so troubling to see it reduced to rubble upon our arrival in this strange new world.

Every academic building of the once prestigious U of A had been pulverized into the charred remains of the scrap heap. The rolling greens had shriveled up into patches of crab grass. The sky above was stained the neon red of Oppenheimer's SimuSun during twilight. Even the mountains in the distance had been altered. No longer were they capped with little cones of snow. Now they were burning. Tall, bright tentacles of orange reaching for the doomed sky above. Everything stank of burned onions.

I moved closer to Nessa, and she put her arm around my shoulder. Any lingering awkwardness from our romantic failure-to-launch was wiped away by the destruction of Alaska. "In this world, the apocalypse's already happened, hasn't it?" I asked.

We should've realized this was always a possibility. If the Multiverse was a dense web where every human choice or outcome was represented by its own unique universe, then it only made sense that of course there existed many Earths where extinction—the very threat Oppie had constructed The God Laser to fight, the mirror image of the great kaboom my Apocalypse Pocket Watch counted down to—had already occurred. I felt Nessa's shoulder buckle and realized she was softly crying. I pulled her in for a hug and felt her convulsing against my shoulder. This was her nightmare, the deep-rooted fear of all futurists, the end of everything, unavoidable proof that the truth revealed in her mother's car crash—the terrifying knowledge that we all one day will die—would eventually come true and lay everything to waste.

We stood there like that only for a minute before Nessa snaked free from my grip and straightened the hem of her lab coat. She wiped the tears from her eyes and took three deep breaths. "This doesn't mean anything for our world," she said more to herself than to me. "We can still overcome this in our world. We still have time."

I nodded, unsure if I agreed, and retrieved my Calabi-Yau Computation Tablet. I swiped for some background information and explained to Nessa that in this world, because Nixon never became president, the Environmental Protection Agency was never founded. President McGovern never visited China behind the Iron Curtain, and relations grew worse and worse until an all-out nuclear catastrophe befell the entire planet just a few months prior to our arrival.

Nessa didn't acknowledge any of this verbally. She simply started the environmental scan, anything to get us out of there faster. But I found myself morbidly intrigued. We were only a few minutes' walk away from the Integrated Science Building, where I'd birthed The Copeland Principle. I wanted to see it. I wanted to see it destroyed. It was the impulse of a child ripping off a scab just to watch the fresh stream of pus and blood.

I explained to Nessa where I was going, and reluctantly, she followed along, clearly spooked and not even remotely curious. If it was up to her, she would've streamed *Your Romantic Star-Filled Journey* on her tablet until the environmental scan was complete. Instead, we marched across the death fields before arriving at the melted brick and support beams that had once constituted the nexus of my working life, the very place where I made my singular contribution to the field of cosmology. It was gone now, and I stared into the destruction of the Integrated Science Building and wondered if this had all been a mistake. Maybe everything since that fucking Battle of the Bands ten years earlier had been a terrible misunderstanding. Maybe I shouldn't have been trying to save Wren from death, maybe I should have been trying to prevent myself from meeting Wren.

Nessa sensed my discomfort and took my hand. "This isn't your Anchorage. Your Anchorage is fine. Everything is fine."

I didn't believe her. "I want to see my apartment."

She released my hand. "What? Why?"

"This all happened a few months back, right? That means I might still be there. I want to see for myself."

"Teddy—"

"I want to see for myself."

I set off over the charred hill behind the Integrated Science Building and went down into the cluster of dormitories and apartment buildings on the west side of campus. That area fared slightly better than the academic contingent. It was still abandoned, still blanketed by the red sky of holocaust, but at least half of the dorms and apartments still stood, flanked by craters or piles of debris reminiscent of the Rasmuson. None of the buildings had escaped totally unscathed, however. All were blackened with soot, and most sported car-sized holes in their roofs and sides. We cut through the parking lot, and I spotted my beater Saturn—purchased for a few hundred from a car lot in nearby Chugiak—squashed and flattened like a pancake. I pointed it out as we passed through the valley of crushed machines.

"That's mine," I whispered.

Nessa nodded, unsure how to react.

We marched past the dorms and into the Templewood Apartments, a set of ten prefab homes erected quickly for the U of A's rapidly growing graduate student population. Like the dorms, some of these buildings had been destroyed in the fallout, but mine had not been wholly wrecked in whatever Chinese/American misadventures had led to the eradication of the planet. It was merely charred, and my complex had remained intact. Even though I fully understood that no good could come from this exploration, I stepped around Nessa and opened the swinging door that led inside. It fell off the hinges as soon as I touched it.

"I lived here," I said.

"Teddy, I don't think we should do this. Why don't we just wait here until the scan's done?"

I didn't reply. Instead, I entered the hallway that fed into each individual unit. My loafers left behind footprints in the ash, and when I reached my front door, all I had to do was gingerly push it to send it knocking forward into the living room, the mausoleum of my old life. The inside of my apartment was relatively preserved. The living room wasn't charred, wasn't wholly blanketed in ash, and instead, my dumpy futon, wooden entertainment system, and the piles and piles of boxes and old plates and yogurt containers were layered in a coat of dust even more prominent than the one I'd left behind when I'd abandoned this apartment's counterpart for the ASA and eventually Perro Caliente. The furniture had been knocked around, and the television and framed photographs of my family at graduation had fallen and cracked on the floor, but otherwise it was recognizable. The Teddy Copeland who'd lived here was surely a facsimile of me, a friendly, sympathetic doppelgänger.

I walked toward the kitchen, but before I could cross the threshold, Nessa entered the apartment and called out to me. "Teddy. Seriously. Let's go. This is a mistake." I knew she was unsettled because she didn't even comment on how messy everything was.

I entered the kitchen. How vividly I remembered the many awkward endeavors staged there, the many torched fish, the many ruined slabs of pork, how often I would descend upon the junk drawer and its grand collection of takeout menus, how often I would end up eating from those cartons of gunk over the sink, crumbs fluttering like waves in the wake of a jet ski. The drawers had tumbled free, and knives and forks littered the hideous linoleum. The refrigerator was ruptured on its side, emitting an odor that can only be described as sour testicle sweat. I committed this image to memory. It all seemed very important, a warning perhaps, a harbinger of all that was to come.

The bedroom door was shut, and I feared whatever nightmare I might find lurking inside. I knew I could still turn back, that Nessa lingered on the edge of the kitchen calling for me to return, to leave this quixotic quest behind once and for all. But still I persisted, urged on by the same mysterious itch that had led me to The Wren Algorithm and accursed Eastern Market and Baltimore. I had to know even if I understood that knowledge might harm me more than my own ignorance.

I opened the door and discovered the bedroom in far worse disarray than even the rest of my apartment. My dresser had toppled over and the contents of the closet had spilled out over the garish linoleum, carpeting the bedroom in a dense layer of dress shirts and cardigans. Even my safe had come loose, cracked apart, and although I didn't immediately find the picture of Wren or my wedding ring, I knew they were there somewhere, hidden amongst the wreckage, proof that this Teddy Copeland had also shouldered my collegiate burden. But the true shock was the hole in the roof directly over my bed, the exposed shaft of red light that filled my tiny bedroom. I squinted in the dust and saw that a support beam had fallen from above and pierced the bed. It was only then that I realized this long plank of broken wood had struck more than mere mattress. There was a shape on the bed, something that might have once been human beneath the sheets. Nessa was behind me now, and surely she too figured it out.

"Teddy, don't. Teddy, don't."

But it was far too late to turn back now. The revelation was plain as day, just waiting for me to pull back the covers. None of this could be undone. I climbed onto the pile of clothes, crawled over the decimated dresser, and stood alongside the destroyed bed. The sheet felt brittle in my hand, like sandpaper, and when I ripped it free, all my fears were confirmed. I stood face-to-face with my own corpse, a support beam lodged in his chest, his face already blackened in the early stages of decomposition. I reached for my mouth, but before my hands could even rise an inch, I was gagging and then retching onto the clothes and floor. Nessa didn't dare move from the doorway. At last I had come in direct contact with the image I had so feared in the years after Wren's death: my youthful potential forever snuffed out, my existence washed away as nothing more than a mere moment in the grand overture of coldly indifferent time. I died alone. I vomited onto this other me's clothes, and when I was finished, my body sweating and panting, Nessa crawled across the dresser and debris and draped an arm over my shoulder.

"It's going to be ok, Teddy. Come on, let's get out of here."

I recoiled from her touch. "Please, I just want to be left alone."

She nodded. She patted me on the shoulder. Then she crouch-walked away over the pile of clothes and left the bedroom and then the apartment of this other, dead me. I was left alone with my corpse, with nothing to do but sit cross-legged on the clothes and stare into the black sockets where my eyes had once been. For twenty-five minutes, I barely blinked, barely thought, and when that time at last ended, Nessa called out to me from the living room, "The scan's done, Teddy. Let's go home." What else could I do? I moved the sheet back over the other me's face and joined Nessa outside. What I no longer could deny was that I was changing. For better or worse, I did not know, but I was changing, the proof as obvious as the dead skies overhead.

When we returned to The God Laser and the pallid, fluorescent lights of The Control Center, I didn't utter a word. I let Nessa explain what had happened, and she mercifully omitted our jaunt to the Templewood Apartments. I said nothing to the other scientists, not to Delbar or Oppenheimer or even Nessa. Instead, I parked myself in front of my workspace terminal and began toying with The Wren Algorithm right there in front of everyone. It didn't matter.

They couldn't decipher the insidious intent behind the plethora of numbers on my screen any more than they could deduce that removing Nixon from the presidency would somehow lead to my corpse in Anchorage decades later. And besides, The Wren Algorithm was complete, the five remaining Wren-worlds waiting for me like ripened fruit on a branch. I recalled the sense of failure and disgust I'd felt upon my encounter with Wren in Baltimore, but coming face-to-face with my corpse rekindled my morbid desire to see this through. I was loathsome and vile. Perhaps we were all loathsome and vile. And the remaining five Wren-worlds represented the terminal velocity of my ascent into monstrosity. I waited for each and every last scientist to leave, even Nessa who said nothing to me on her way out. And when they were gone, when I was at last alone among the humming computers and silent God Laser beyond, I keyed up The Wren Algorithm and awaited the birth of the wormhole egg between its pointed lasers.

I would continue my work, global consequences be damned.

From outside, the Espionage Lounge looked like it had once been a factory. It had all the right details: the familiar brick, extraordinarily tall windows, multiple garage doors, and even a row of rusted smokestacks jutting from the roof. The key difference was the line of bespectacled hipsters in chest-hugging tees and worn denim snaking out from the front entrance all the way around the corner. I'd read about it on my Calabi-Yau, how in this reality where I spun a three instead of a one, Wren and the Femme Furies had stayed together after college—Ithaca in this world—and had actually cut a few LPs on an indie label in Omaha that garnered high praise everywhere from *Pitchfork* to *Spin*, publications I never read but understood held a certain cultural panache for contemporaries more interested in EPs than isotopes. But it wasn't until I stood across the street from their homecoming show in Omaha that I truly believed in this world. The Espionage Lounge pulsated with the up-tempo guitars and bass kicks I recognized from my days as a Susquehanna student head-over-heels obsessed. Wren Wells and the other Furies awaited me inside. All I had to do was get in line and enter.

An hour later—their set almost completed—I finally made it in. The interior of the Espionage Lounge was what I'd come to expect from years of punk and ska shows with Wren. Merch table in the back, a long pit flush with a hundred fist pumping, skanking fans, and a tiny stage that hung over the audience. Then the band. Only this time it wasn't Child of Rib Fest or Monopoly Junior or even the subpar Rad McPooch. This time it was the Femme Furies. Some members I recognized. Some I didn't. But there, unmistakably in the center, was Wren Wells as charismatic and dangerous as the first day I'd met her at that seemingly mythical Battle of the Bands.

A cut-up Nebraska volleyball shirt hung limply from her shoulders. Long-dead Tamagotchis dangled from her neck and wrists. She clutched the mic with both hands and held it directly to her lips, screaming, "Riot grrrl 2.0! Riot grrrl 2.0! Smash your patriarchal disco show!" I watched stunned as she whipped her fans into a frenzy, how they skanked together in a massive circle that revved faster and faster like the electromagnets of The God Laser. This venue was so much bigger than any I'd ever seen the Femme Furies perform in, and I was so heartbreakingly happy for Wren, that in this life she'd gotten exactly what she always wanted. How easy it would be to hang around after the show, to wait near the vans outside, to catch Wren and the Furies and approach them just as I had as a fresh-faced teenager after the Battle of the Bands back at Susquehanna. But watching her undulate across the stage, I decided against it. It wasn't right. It wasn't fair for me to disturb this modest fantasy life Wren had carved out for herself in this better, truer world. I would not pierce her tranquil bubble, but I could not resist wading out into the crowd and making my way toward the stage, toward holy Wren. It had been so long since I'd heard her sing.

Finally, and not without a new bruise or two, I made it to the front of the stage. They'd just finished an upbeat song about cats, and Wren put her back to the crowd as she communicated with the other Furies. She was near the edge of the stage, and if I really wanted to, I could reach out and touch her skin. A slow drumbeat began as Wren turned around and crouched low, her eyes scanning the audience, and for one glorious moment she paused on mine, so near, so far. I wondered if she recognized anything. I rationally understood that in this universe Wren had never met my counterpart, but I wondered and sadly hoped that perhaps our love was so powerful that it transcended The Copeland Principle and The Many Worlds Interpretation of Quantum Mechanics and even The Theory of Almost Everything and anything else ordained thinkers might dream up in the past, present, or future. I wanted so desperately to believe that Wren had been wrong that day on the shores of the Atlantic, that we were destined to be together, that our love was real and legendary and eternal. But Wren recognized nothing.

She swept over my gaze like any other fan in the Espionage Lounge, another unwashed troglodyte who just wanted a piece of the artistic goddess summoned before him.

Wren unhooked the microphone from the stand and paced back and forth on the stage. "All right, maniacs. Got time for one more song. One more song, then it's back to debauchery and whatever else the corporate news doesn't want us to be doing. This one's not about love, it's about lust. You probably know it as 'I Choose You (Pikachu).'"

This song was slower, more downbeat. It was a tactic I recognized from so many shows over the years, how bands would say they were ending with a mood-killing song just so they could return for an encore and blow everyone away with an up-tempo classic. But "I Choose You (Pikachu)" seemed to speak directly to me. Or maybe I just assigned it special relevance like so many other mundane happenings in my mildly tragic life. Wren and the back-up Furies sang of old flames they thought they loved, but in reality, it was just obsession. The song's protagonist wished those men well but understood her life's outcome was not tied up in the fate of her partners, that she and her collection of choices would accumulate into something so much more. It was an anti-Disney princess feminist anthem, and it made me question exactly what I hoped to find in these various Wren-worlds. I pushed my way back from the stage and exited the club. Across the street, I found a secluded space in a park where I could teleport away. But why? What good would it do? According to Oppenheimer, we had five-to-ten years before the end of human existence, and he wanted me to shepherd Perro Caliente through the calamity of said end times. I should've been prepping, but the moment I retrieved my Calabi-Yau, I knew where I was going. I loaded up the fourth world embedded within The Wren Algorithm. "I'm not hurting anyone," I told myself. "I'm not hurting anyone." Anyone but myself.

#

The next target was Pittsburgh, a neighborhood called Squirrel Hill. A hilly cross section of cobblestone streets, beaucoup ethnic restaurants, and a synagogue or friendly looking bar on every single corner. I walked downhill from the boutiques and artisan coffee shops towards my true goal: the residence of one Wren Wells, her husband Michael Bishop, and their child, Genevieve Bishop-Wells.

Even though it was late spring encroaching on summer, a chill had fallen across this world's Squirrel Hill. What the Calabi-Yau had explained to me was this: in this world, Wren had gone to Oberlin and, after graduating with a master's degree in library science, taken a job in Pittsburgh. There, she met a local doofus, Michael Bishop, and together they courted and married a year prior. The phantom nymph Genevieve was barely two months old.

I turned onto their street with its middle-class, urbane houses complete with fenced-in yards and front porches. I could not bring myself to accept the fact that there existed realities where Wren Wells had already conceived a child. I could understand and rationalize The God Laser or even the fact that said technological marvel had been ushered into existence by the hologram of the man who had perpetrated the atom bomb, the same man whose decaying brain lurked underneath all of Perro Caliente's scientific endeavors. But I could not bring myself to rationalize this simple human truth, that the majority of humans end up copulating and procreating, that this would be the outcome of most Wren-worlds: Wren happy and sated, never the wiser that she had missed out on me, on us! Truly this was science fiction. Wren Wells was a mother!

Their home was fantastically predictable and mundane. Brick. Two stories. A compact car in the driveway. Here was the raw detritus of everyday human life not punctured by apocalypse or leukemia. I shivered on the sidewalk still unsure why I had lingered in this world, why I hadn't immediately teleported to the next—only three possible *Explorers of Verenzetti Island!* spins remained—the moment I realized this Wren was married and any meaningful reunion would be impossible. But standing there, I understood why. I wanted to bear witness with my own eyes. I wanted to bear witness to Wren's perfectly average joy.

I snuck into the bushes beneath their picture window. Light burst from inside, and I had to adjust my eyes as I rose just enough to have myself a peek. What I saw was and forever will be burned into my memory. There in a quaint living room filled with books were the happy newlyweds splayed out on the carpet, limbs akimbo, angelic babe cooing serenely between. At first, I could not glimpse the phantom child's body, but Wren and the accursed Michael Bishop were unmistakable. Wren was heavier here, her flesh ripened with the fruit of childbirth. She smiled wider than I'd ever seen in my presence, one hand on the prized offspring, the other stroking the hair of her beloved. Michael Bishop was basically what I expected. I was the prototype for her future lovers, or maybe I was just a faint echo of this future husband, a pebble tossed in a shallow lake. Bishop was tall and lanky, his hair messy and unkempt, a pair of totally out-of-style wire frames obscuring his face. This inter-dimensional goon kissed Wren on the cheek, then raised his daughter to the sky like an ancient sacrament. I once believed that all babies essentially looked the same, but one glimpse at this child forever altered my understanding. I cannot bring myself to describe the young babe Genevieve. That image is mine and mine alone, not fit for public consumption. All I will say is that her appearance pierced something hard in my chest, some outer layer I hadn't realized calcified even before Wren's death, maybe from the very first moment she told me she'd been diagnosed. Genevieve Wells-Bishop. Oh, how I longed to snap a photo, to take her with me, to do anything to maintain some sense of her when I returned to my own Wren-less world. This could've been my life, I thought. This could've been my life.

I staggered into the yard, and that was the movement that triggered Wren and Michael's attention. They stood, baby-less now, outlined in the picture window like a Rockwell painting, two doting parents with good-natured confusion on their faces. Maybe they hadn't experienced loss the way I had and didn't automatically expect that dour outcome from the everyday events of the world. Maybe I was just projecting.

Wren whispered something in Michael's ear, and by the time he emerged on the lawn, I had the Calabi-Yau brandished like a weapon.

"Hey," he called. "Hey, are you ok?"

I swiped a button and teleported away from that world, that family, that man who had stolen what was rightfully mine. I teleported away. One more I told myself. One more. One more maudlin parade into memory and possibility and then I would retire for the evening. One more.

#

I had never been to Japan before, never envisioned myself suddenly appearing in the land of the rising sun. I stood on the edge of the Peace Park, mildly stunned to discover that Hiroshima had actually been rebuilt into a city just like Oppenheimer foretold. The park was green and pristine, surrounded on all sides by tiny, straight rivers and a towering shopping district. I don't know what I was expecting exactly. Oppenheimer's gadget incinerated the city more than seventy years ago, but for some reason, whenever I imagined present-day Hiroshima, I always envisioned a crater, not this thriving city flush with a smiling citizenry enjoying weekday strolls.

I had teleported to Hiroshima because, according to the Calabi-Yau, in this world Wren was at that very moment exploring the Atomic Peace Park. I retrieved my tablet and swiped around for additional information. According to the search, Wren had moved to Hiroshima from the US to teach English to the middle schoolers of the city's elite. She brought the children to the park and its various memorials to provide glimpses into the lives of their World War II counterparts, the majority of whom had died in nearby rivers immediately after the bomb or from radiation sickness weeks or months or even years later. I scrolled and nearly dropped the tablet to the ground. There was one more vital piece of information. In this world, Wren Wells had attended Susquehanna. So had this world's version of Teddy Copeland. She'd dated my doppelganger all through college before breaking things off to move to Japan seven years earlier. I chewed at my thumbs and sat on the sidewalk that hugged the park. In this world, Wren would recognize me as her ex. In this world, our love had withered even though she'd never contracted that accursed disease.

It would be so strange to find a Wren who knew me here of all places, in the hypocenter of Oppenheimer's destruction. I passed a structure called the Genbaku Dome, an old observatory and the only downtown building that had withstood the bombing. It was mostly ruins now, reduced to an open skeleton. How could a man dream of utopia when this had been his most significant achievement in the scientific world: death and destruction? The Genbaku Dome was fenced in, and I was surprised by the dozens of tourists, the huddled mass of families snapping photos while explaining to children exactly what it represented. It brought the effects of the bomb home to me in a way pictures never had before. In history books, all I'd ever seen were aerial shots of that mushroom cloud above a brief snippet of text listing the unimaginable death count. Watching an old man bend to one knee and explain the bomb to a small girl—probably his granddaughter—was a thousand times more chilling. He was old enough to be a survivor.

I dug my hands in my pockets and hurried over a bridge to the next memorial. There were signs everywhere guiding you along the paths, and as I turned a corner, I heard a group of children singing a song not unlike the Japanese choir music Oppenheimer played. I saw a marble statue of a young girl holding up a giant paper crane, and behind it were massive glass displays of thousands upon thousands of neon origami straight out of the Nessa Newmar anxiety playbook. Twenty students stood in front of the statue, holding printed out lyrics and singing in the completely uninhibited way only children are capable of. I scanned the crowd for their teacher and at last spotted Wren Wells singing as unabashedly as her students. In this world she wore dark pants and a bulky denim dress shirt, her hair cropped short and jagged, probably because she cut it herself. I stood on the edge of the memorial unsure what to do next. I wanted to talk with her and determine why exactly we'd broken up if no specter of leukemia had torn us apart. I wanted closure in the very worst way, but I also didn't want to disturb the scene and those sweet singing children. I lingered on the periphery long enough for the students to finish, long enough for Wren to herd them in a neatly packed line, long enough for Wren to start toward the dome and finally see me. She stopped midstride. Our eyes met, and I was at last given what I had wanted so very badly. Recognition. This Wren Wells knew me, or at the very least, this world's iteration of Teddy Copeland. But it wasn't exactly the tender reunion I'd craved. Her face flashed a series of quick and wide-ranging emotions. First surprise, then irritation. She spoke in Japanese to her children, then hurried over alone to greet me.

"What the hell are you doing here?" she asked.

"I was just passing through."

"You were just passing through Hiroshima, Japan?"

"I'm on vacation. Hey, do you want to grab food?"

Her eyes widened in disbelief. "Teddy, I'm teaching. Those are my students."

"When you're done?"

She sighed the longest, most annoyed sigh in the vast history of women dealing with boys. "Fine. Go one block up and meet me at the ramen house on the right in an hour. It's the only one where you have to climb stairs."

Wren hurried off, and the students made cooing noises as she led them to the Genbaku Dome. I fully understood that Wren was far from thrilled to see me, but I still felt a happy eagerness surging behind my chest. I'd spoken to my wife.

I'd spoken to my wife!

#

I found the ramen house in an outdoor mall along the edge of the Peace Park. Everything was neon and loud, the storefronts adorned with boxy televisions blaring out incomprehensible commercials promising fantastic robot figurines or even just discount socks. The hour passed slowly, but finally Wren turned the corner. She saw me but didn't wave, the same look of confusion on her face as before. I think she might have convinced herself she'd imagined my presence earlier, that my appearance was nothing more than a strange apparition. But on the stoop I sat. I had traveled the Multiverse for this reunion, and I would not be deterred.

"Hi, Wren," I said.

"Hi, Teddy."

I followed her up the stairs into a lobby barely bigger than a bathroom. There was a vending machine, but instead of pictures of soda, there were drawings of various food items over a dozen coin slots. One was for ramen with pork, another for beer, another for a hard-boiled egg. Wren slid in a coin beneath a picture of noodles with veggies, and a tiny, paper slip emerged from the machine.

"This is crazy," I said.

She looked me up and down. "This is nothing. Your being here is crazy. This is just ramen."

I realized I had no yen. "Can I borrow some money?"

Another sigh. "You haven't changed at all."

I paid for ramen and an egg and followed Wren through a beaded curtain into a hallway with one curtained doorway after another. I squinted through the beads and saw people on wooden benches slurping great big bowls of noodles. Wren chose a tiny room in back, and we sat on a bench facing a bamboo—probably faux bamboo—partition. We couldn't really look at each other, and I was about to complain about this when the partition slid open revealing the torso of a waitress. She said nothing and stuck out her hand. Wren handed her the slip, and I did the same.

"Japan is awesome," I said.

Wren futzed with the chopstick dispenser and handed me a set. "How long have you been here?"

"Not long. A few days. A routine vacation, you know? Just a vacation. Ha ha. What about you? How's Hiroshima? Those were your students?"

Finally Wren divulged the details of her life. She told me what it was like to teach Japanese middle schoolers and how much she'd come to enjoy Japanese culture and cuisine. When asked about her music, she said she sang in an all women band with some rad ladies she'd met at a place called the Hiroshima Highball Club. In fact, they'd recently taken the JR Train to Tokyo for a set at Frenzy. I watched Wren as she spoke. It'd been seven years since we'd had a conversation that was more than just her screaming at me in Baltimore, and although I assumed I'd committed her very essence to memory, it turned out I'd been wrong. Her forehead was slightly different than I remembered, an inch or two more pronounced. Her lips were fuller, their pink shade deeper. She spoke with an accent I didn't recall, a modest Pennsylvania twang in which the nonexistent h was stressed in the word water; the word mine was pronounced with two syllables like Mayan. None of these individual aspects were positive or negative, they were just different from the Wren who had persisted in my memories the past seven years, and I once again faced the possibility that perhaps I was not obsessed with the human Wren Wells, but with the ghost queen I had conjured from my widower's grief. The truth was I didn't feel much energy beneath the surface of our conversation. It felt like running into a best friend from kindergarten twenty years later. You understand there's supposed to be something between you, some craggy history that hints at some crucial understanding, but it's almost impossible to recreate or even approach that bond. I didn't feel any of the color I'd experienced with her as an undergraduate and felt as black-and-white as ever. I listened to Wren, and the conversation was pleasant if uneventful, but I was stunned to discover I wished I was with Nessa instead. She would've loved that restaurant.

Our waitress delivered our food, and the broth was so hearty, so untainted by boatloads of salt that I could scarcely believe it. But even as I savored each and every morsel, I noticed the effect the food had on our conversation: it stalled. I finished my hard-boiled egg and decided to be brave. I had risked everything for closure, and closure I would attain.

"So, Wren. Do you ever think about what would've happened if we stayed together?"

She set her chopsticks in her bowl and looked at me hard. We were late-twenties ex-lovers separated by the swaying velvet curtains of the Multiverse. We would have our dénouement a mere fifty yards away from where the atomic bomb had exploded. It was difficult to conceive. "What do you mean?" she asked.

"If you hadn't gone to Japan after graduation? If we tried to make things work after Susquehanna?" If. If. If. The defining principle of my life.

"Teddy," she said, her voice turning soft the first time since I'd found her, "we didn't break up because I moved to Japan. We broke up because we didn't work as a couple.

Come on." She socked me on the shoulder. "Are you serious? We were just kids. We met ten years ago."

"I am serious." I didn't want to sound huffy, but I sounded huffy. "Why didn't we work as a couple? Explain it to me then."

"It was so long ago, I barely even think about it."

"Then think about it."

Her eyes narrowed. "Ok. This. Right now is part of the reason why we didn't work. You're so pushy. You have your views on how life and the universe are supposed to work. At 18, you knew you wanted to major in physics, and then it was graduate school, and then we'd get married and you'd work in a lab on the east coast, and I'd push out 2.5 kids, and that'd be the end of me. You can't just let things happen. Everything has to be part of some grand multi-step plan. You never live in the moment, and everything's black-and-white. You always act like the universe owes you something because you've been told your whole life you're just so special at science." She shook her head. "You knew exactly what you wanted to be at 18. I still don't. I want to bum around Japan and make music, and if tomorrow some crazy opportunity opens up where I have to go to India or Thailand, I'm taking it. That's not you. You're neurotic and goofy, and I really did love you when we were teenagers, but we don't fit together as adults."

"I could change," I managed.

"No you can't, and neither of us would want you to."

I balled my napkin beneath the table. The room felt too small, and for a second I feared I might puke all over Wren and the faux-bamboo partition. I clamped down on my knees and dug crescent-moon slivers into my skin.

"What the hell is all this about anyway?" Wren asked. "You just showing up out of the blue here of all places? You knew I was here. You could have vacationed anywhere.

Almost everybody goes to Tokyo or Kyoto instead. I thought you were engaged."

"What?"

"Yeah, I saw it online. What's her name? Sloan Smith? I saw pictures of you two. You looked happy. I was happy for you."

I broke skin and struck blood. I hadn't even considered that in this world—where Wren never got sick, where Wren had simply dumped me—my counterpart Teddy Copeland would still be capable of happy normalcy. It was a punch to the gut. This other me had accepted that he and Wren didn't belong together and moved on. I felt dizzy. I felt disgusting. "I need to go to the bathroom," I said.

I staggered out of our booth and into the men's room down the hall. I gripped the sink as hard as I could, staring into my face, my eyes, the ever enlarged pores on my nose, trying to see down to my very core, the blood and neurons and flesh that made Teddy Copeland whole. Who was I? What was I doing? Was I as valid as this world's more well-adjusted Teddy Copeland? Was he in some subtle way more Teddy Copeland-ish than me, or did I represent the purest form of Teddy Copeland? Perhaps that honor belonged to Teddy Copeland Prime, that nightmarish brute I'd encountered in Eastern Market during my first foray into a wretched Wren-world. I turned on the faucet and splashed cold water over my face. There was nothing for me here. I'd say goodbye to Wren, then find a secluded spot where I could teleport home. I was a clown lobbing jokes at no one.

But when I returned to our booth, I found Wren Wells white-faced, as pale as if she'd seen a ghost. I stood at the entrance and asked, "What's the matter?"

She held up her smartphone. “What the fuck is this? Can you please explain what the fuck this is?”

I bent for a better angle. On her phone was a status update from none other than this world’s Teddy Copeland, the one she’d actually dated. He’d posted a picture of himself, a more boisterous looking me, grinning over a plate of poached eggs and salmon in some terribly trendy brunch spot, his arm locked around a woman I could only assume was Sloan Smith. She was pretty in an unconventional way, boxy and short, her hair a mess, large glasses sliding to the tip of her nose. Her face was olive-skinned and beautiful, and their wide smiles made it clear that these two human beings had found each other amid a world of billions. They had beaten the odds of The Soul Mate Formula. They were happy. They were some other next-level emotion beyond happiness that I could not even imagine. It was more stunning than learning about The God Laser or the fact that the human race might only have five-to-ten years to live. I was capable of loving someone not named Wren Wells. This doppelgänger revealed the truth.

But that didn’t explain the sick look on Wren’s face. I leaned in closer and finally understood what had her so spooked. The image was timestamped. The other Teddy Copeland had posted it on the internet only seconds earlier. Wren Wells had undeniable proof that at this present moment two Teddy Copelands stalked her earth. I had become a ghost.

“Who the fuck are you?” Wren asked.

I acted on instinct and ran. Out into the hallway I went, then into the lobby and down the staircase to the blinking neon of the outdoor mall. The moment I did so, a figure lurking behind a shoe display across the way bolted north, deeper into the mall and away from the Peace Park. I didn’t get a good look at his face, but the lab coat swinging behind gave him away. Surely, this was the mysterious scientist I'd caught spying on me in Baltimore. I was positive. The other universe hopper had followed me all the way to Japan!

"Wait!" I screamed.

I ran after the hooligan dashing between loose clusters of shoppers and was only twenty yards back when he tripped face first into the pavement. For the first time, I was given a solid glimpse of my nemesis. Tight pants and a lab coat. A mop of messy brown hair. His face hidden against the pavement. I called out to him again, but before I could reach him, he pulled out his Calabi-Yau and, in a flash, teleported away to Earths unknown. I came to a stop at the precise spot in the street where he'd disappeared, and I stood there clutching my knees, catching my breath. Who was this villain? Why was he tracking me throughout the various Wren-worlds? And if I continued exploring these Wren-worlds—there were only two to go—would he at last reveal himself? I couldn't say. I knelt there panting, surrounded by a yelping crowd shocked by the man's sudden disappearance. I looked back to see if Wren had followed me, and when it was clear she hadn't, I retrieved my Calabi-Yau and left that Earth forever.

I expected to find The God Laser empty when I returned home. I'd left for the Omaha Wren-world immediately after everyone left for the day, and it was already midnight. I wanted nothing more than to return to my apartment and reflect on what I had learned, what I had done, how I had so selfishly altered Hiroshima Wren's life. But those desires were dashed the moment I materialized in front of The God Laser. Waiting for me on the stone walkway was none other than Delbar Javari chomping a Cuban, her arms folded across her chest.

"Oh, hi, Del," I said sheepishly.

"Where the hell have you been, dummy?" she asked.

"Oh, me? Just now? I was just doing a little extracurricular parallel world exploring. You know, for extra environmental scans."

Delbar gave me the fakest smile I'd ever seen. I remembered what she'd endured to escape Iran, the burden of her missing family, and didn't doubt that she could grind me to dust beneath her mighty heels. "Why are you lying, Dr. Copeland? I came back after everybody left to work on my own secret project and saw that somebody else was already using The God Laser. You didn't send any scan transmissions."

"Secret project?"

She came closer. "We'll get to that, buddy, don't you worry. I unlocked your workstation to see what changes you made to The Theory of Almost Everything. Something called The Wren Algorithm? All you changed was the occurrence rate of leukemia in women and some random board game spin from over a decade ago. Why? Tell me. I deserve that much." She was so close I could smell the perfumey scent of her hair, one part citrus, another artificial toxicant, the scent of doomsday. "Come on. Out with it," she said. "You show me yours, and I'll show you mine."

It was clear the jig was finally up. The people of Perro Caliente were protesting. The God Laser project was possibly doomed. And we only had five-to-ten years to live according to the steady rhythm of the Apocalypse Pocket Watch tucked safely in my pocket. I had no choice but to tell Del the truth. She caught me red-handed.

"I'm a widower. My wife died when she was twenty-two of leukemia. I've been searching for her in worlds where she didn't die."

I waited for some show of sympathy, some acknowledgment that Delbar now understood I was a sensitive, emotionally wounded young man. Quite the opposite happened. Delbar's eyes widened and she pushed me as hard as she could. I fell smack on my ass, and she towered over me. It took all my restraint not to shield myself in case she really did curb stomp me with her heels.

"Are you serious?" she yelled. "Really? That's what you've been using The God Laser for?"

"Yeah. So what? What have you been using it for?"

She threw her cigar off the edge of the walkway. "Copeland, do you realize you've been given access to a trillion dollar piece of equipment intended to save the world, and you've been using it to spy on your dead wife like a teenage Peeping Tom? We all have losses in our past we could've corrected with The God Laser. What about my family? What about my fucking family, Copeland? The militia probably did god knows what to my sister and mother and even my father, and did I once think about using this technology to see what my life would be like if they'd survived? No. Because I'm not that fucking selfish, you little prick. Nessa's mom died in a car crash. But she never went back to try and 'fix' things. Ugh. You're gross. Do you realize that if you lost your Calabi-Yau in one of those worlds you would've been trapped there? Do you know what a privilege it is to be able to explore parallel worlds? Do you know how jealous I've been? I'm the seventh smartest person in the world. I'm the lead engineer on this project, but Oppenheimer chose you to go in my place just because you wrote The Copeland Principle, and you're an oblivious privileged white dude just like him. You think we don't know about your dumb little horse rides with him? He brags about them in the break room all the time. We know he's giving you special treatment." She shook her head. "You want to know about my secret project? Fine. I'm sure you've noticed all the times when either Nessa or I have been too busy to go to Trinity or whatever. That's because one of us was here working. That's right. Nessa's in on it too. But we haven't been building some little fantasy life. We've been applying the early prediction work she was peddling at the ASA to The God Laser. We're trying to build an early warning system that can tell us when anything negative is about to happen in the world. Murder. Viral outbreak. Famine. War. Then we can send that information to the correct authorities." She was breathing hard through her nose now. "I can't believe you were gawking at your dead wife when we were trying to save the world. Do you have anything to say for yourself, Dr. Copeland?"

I put my hands over my eyes. I couldn't look at her anymore. Over the last few weeks, I'd considered the fact that I was misusing The God Laser and possibly intruding on the privacy of the various Wrens of the many Wren-worlds I entered. But never before was it made so abundantly clear how I had failed not only my deceased bride, but also the trust of Nessa and Delbar and Oppenheimer and the entire world itself. I had failed each and every one of them and had assumed that my life's catastrophes somehow outweighed everyone else's. And yet, there were still two more Wren-worlds to explore. Like an addict who realizes they have a problem only to understand they aren't strong enough to stop, I could scarcely envision a scenario where I didn't take the plunge into those final unlived fantasies. I pinched the skin around my eyes and whispered, "I'm sorry. I'm so, so sorry."

"You're an idiot, Teddy Copeland. By the way, the final results on The God Laser project will be ready tomorrow. Remember that? The thing you should actually be focused on?" She shook her head. "You're just a sad sack asshole."

I held my head in my hands as Dr. Delbar Javari left The Control Center. I was twenty-eight-years-old. In less than ten years, everyone I'd ever known would be dead, myself included.

SAUL ON THE ROAD TO DAMASCUS

The results of The God Laser project were finally completed, and I received a text from Oppenheimer instructing me to come to his cabin immediately. It was the morning after my romp in Hiroshima, and Oppie's simplistic prose betrayed nothing. On one hand, I was frightened to discover the truth, the stark possibility that The God Laser would not shield us from impending doom. On the other, I was extremely nervous to see Delbar and Nessa after my inter-dimensional hijinks the night before. While they'd been engineering something meant to combat the many injustices and tragedies occurring in real time across our planet, I'd used the near mythical power of The God Laser to pick at the lingering wound of Wren Wells. I rode the elevator from my apartment down to the street and hoped that maybe Del hadn't told Nessa just yet. I wanted to be the one to do it, to explain myself, to atone. I wanted a bagel. It was a strange and confusing time.

Old Man Reeves' bodega was boarded up across the street. A woman in the third floor of Housing Unit Six rolled down her window and screamed, "We're all going to die! We're all going to fucking die!" Then she dumped the contents of her trash can onto the street. A fire truck siren wailed in the distance, and I wondered if people had actually started burning things to protest Oppenheimer dismantling the main entrance elevator car. What would they do if the results showed that The God Laser project had been worthless? How far might they be pushed if they discovered they only had five-to-ten years to live, not sixty-to-seventy as Oppenheimer's Apocalypse Hypothesis promised? Was I prepared to accept the Directorship of Perro Caliente when our once utopian research lab had been pushed off the ledge into the blisteringly bright canyon of madness? I tried not to dwell as I climbed the monorail platform, and waiting there was Nessa and Delbar clutching cups of coffee. They were red-eyed and sullen, but from the way Nessa waved, I could tell Del hadn't told her about what she'd seen the night before maybe in some misguided attempt to spare Nessa's feelings. The Iranian engineer glared at me from behind Nessa's back, and I couldn't imagine what it might take to earn their forgiveness.

We stood there silently, a far cry from those early underground days whiled away at The Trinity Tavern when we'd been loud and excited and boisterous, when Nessa and Delbar had convinced me of the phoenix-like powers of friendship and working toward a singular well-intentioned goal. So much had happened in the interim, and try as I might, I could not find a way to articulate my many feelings before our train arrived. It was empty save for an arm strap and used needle abandoned on the floor.

"Shit got real fast," Nessa said.

"Yup," Del agreed.

From high above the streets of the Mezzanine, we were granted a more cumulative view of Perro Caliente's unrest. The siren I'd heard moments earlier was no impotent warning. A trio of fires blazed in the southwest region of the Mezzanine, just between the Nightlife District and the tunnel that fed into the horse experiments. Screams rang out from back alley confrontations between enraged scientists arguing over the Kaluza-Klein Theory. I reached for Nessa's hand, and to my utter astonishment, she didn't swat me away like an unwanted mosquito at a July cookout. She squeezed it, physical proof that there was still goodness in the world, that our resident futurist had not given up on saving everyone.

"This only happened because Oppenheimer dismantled the elevator," she said. "Let the people who want to leave go."

"Would you leave?" I asked. "If you knew we only had a few years left and The God Laser was doomed?"

Nessa and Delbar looked at me like I was the biggest dunce on a planet full of them, and it was difficult to disagree. "Of course not," Nessa said. "There's always another way. We'll figure something out. Science always overcomes adversity." She pointed at the isolated pockets of looters below. "But you can't force it on people who want to be with their families."

We saw the long, clear shaft of the elevator ahead, and it was almost comical to realize this was the source of their discontent, this elevator that from a distance looked like a harmless pipe, something a plumber might tinker with on a lazy Saturday afternoon. But as we drew closer, we spotted crowds of shouting masses gathered at the base, fist pumping to the incantations of some unseen speaker. Nessa pointed at the makeshift stage and three people shouting over megaphones.

"What do you think's going on down there?"

I turned away from the window. "What do you think? Looters. Riots."

Delbar shook her head. "No, those people are organized." She reached for the grab handle. "I'm going to check it out."

"Me too," Nessa said.

"Guys. Oppenheimer's waiting for us."

Delbar shot me a withering look, and I once again feared she might plunge her heel through my abdomen. "This whole place is going to shit, and you're worried that Oppenheimer's going to be upset because we're a few minutes late to his melodramatic tea party? Relax, kid."

The monorail ground to a stop a block away from the protest, and we heard their chants the moment we disembarked. "Let us out! Let us out!" Nessa held my hand again, and together we pushed toward that mixed crowd of lay people and scientists, bottles of cheap whiskey in hand, some pumping torches. I squinted and recognized the trio atop the makeshift stage. This little soirée had been cooked up by Barb from HR, Old Man Reeves, and driver/pilot Jin, a funhouse reflection of our own friendly trio. Barb was by far the more animated of the three, chicken strutting across the stage as she yelled, "Let us out!" into her megaphone over and over to the delight of the incensed crowd. Jin and Old Man Reeves hung back, their beefy arms locked across their chests, looking more like bouncers than any brand of political revolutionaries.

“We only came underground because Oppenheimer promised us we could save the world,” Barb shouted. “What if he was lying? What if his Apocalypse Hypothesis or whatever is totally wrong? Being a hologram has turned him insane! We haven’t wasted years of our life without the sun only to learn The God Laser is completely worthless! He has to let us be with our families!”

The crowd shouted back in agreement.

“Tell them, Old Man Reeves. Tell them,” she said.

Barb handed him the megaphone, and he reluctantly began. “I’ve been down here ten years,” he mumbled. “I only came because my daughter needed money for college. I thought it was my duty to protect her, and this was the only way I could help stop the apocalypse: serving you all bodega stuff. Do you realize how much time I’ve missed with Kelly? If that was all for nothing—I can’t even imagine what I’ll do.”

Jin grabbed the microphone. “Burn it down. We’ll burn this motherfucker right to the fucking ground!”

The protesters cheered and thrust their torches and bottles into the air. Our trio lingered on the edge, but from the way Nessa leaned forward, it was clear she wanted to wade into the masses and make amends.

“What are you doing?” I asked.

“I want to talk to them. If we can just explain what’s happening, why what we’re doing here is still important, they might choose to stay. Then Oppenheimer might reinstate elevator service.”

I reached for her arm. “Nessa, don’t.”

“Ugh, I can’t believe I’m agreeing with sock tie here, but I am.” Del grabbed Nessa’s other arm. “There’s nothing we can do right now.”

Before Nessa could rush in and make amends with the crowd, we heard a mighty chorus of boos on our left. We turned and saw Thomas Arm, loyal bartender of The Trinity Tavern. He cupped his hands around his lips and screamed at Old Man Reeves to shut up and return to his bodega.

"Thomas Arm!" I shouted. "What are you doing here?"

He ceased booing and squeezed through the crowd in our direction. "Oh, hey, guys. I'm just protesting the protest."

Del cocked her head. "You're happy Oppenheimer shut down the elevator?"

"No, of course not. But that doesn't mean I want to burn this place to the ground. These people are taking things way too far. What we're doing down here is important. I'm not returning to the surface if we're all going to die. I want to stay and fight."

"Us too, Thomas," Nessa said. "Us too."

He nodded. "Well, we're not the only ones. We might be a minority, but we're not the only ones."

Del shook his hand. "Thomas, you're all right. We're on our way to Oppenheimer's. Maybe we can convince him to reinstate the elevators."

We left Thomas Arm to struggle against the crowd and didn't speak the rest of the way to the replica ranch. We didn't need to. We were all thinking the same thing in spite of Thomas Arm's meta-protest: Oppenheimer's dream was dangerously close to flat-lining.

#

It didn't take a trio of ambitious prodigies to guess which way the results had shaken. We entered the replica ranch and discovered Oppenheimer slumped in his armchair gripping a bottle of bourbon by the stem. He smelled drunk, and it was obvious he wasn't drinking to celebrate. We lingered in the doorway, unwilling to cross the threshold between knowledge and un-knowledge.

"Eighty-nine years," he whispered. "The final estimate is that at our current rate of exploration it'll take eighty-nine years to figure out a solution to human extinction via parallel worlds and The God Laser. By that time, we'll all be dead." He spat on the hardwood. "It would take a hundred God Lasers running 24/7 to find a solution in time."

It was Delbar who stepped forward, Delbar who refused to show even the slightest sympathy for Dr. Oppenheimer, the genesis behind Hiroshima, Nagasaki, the man who'd trapped thousands of his followers underground. "Oppie," she said sternly, "you have to open up the elevators."

"Then everyone will leave me."

"Not everyone."

"Enough will."

Nessa joined her on the other side of the doorway. "There are people here who still believe we can figure this out. But you have to let the people who want to be with their families leave."

Oppenheimer hurled the bottle at the wall a mere foot from Nessa's face. I instinctively pulled her back and recalled the trepidation I'd felt upon meeting the father of the atomic bomb, the understanding that there was an underlying darkness to this man we could scarcely begin to understand, this hologram we'd entrusted our futures to.

"Fuck them and their families! Fuck them! They failed me. You failed me. You saccharine ignoramuses running around with your 'save everyone' attitudes. Fuck you too." He grabbed another bottle from his liquor cart and took a mighty swig, rye dribbling down his translucent chin. "The God Laser is a failure. Now you'll all burn with me underground when the apocalypse comes. An under-the-surface Hiroshima. It's fitting really." Another swig. "Only two groups on earth are responsible for United Nations sanctioned negative world heritage sites: the Nazis for Auschwitz and me for Hiroshima. I probably deserve this." He looked up from his bottle. "I did the best I could, you little twats. You know my mother had a congenitally unformed right hand? She was always wearing this fucking glove. That really did a number on me, children."

"Let's go," Delbar said quietly. "Let's get the hell out of here."

We followed Dr. Javari outside and across the SimuDesert, and none of us spoke until we were back onboard the monorail en route to—well, nowhere really. I had no grand designs, and it was clear they didn't either. We just sat there amid the darkness of the tunnels until finally Nessa Newmar, ever the futurist, spoke.

"We'll redouble our efforts," she said. "We'll figure out a way to reassemble the elevator, and then we'll assess who stays and goes from there. This doesn't change anything. Our generation, we didn't cause any of these problems. We inherited them, and now we're going to solve them on our own. Oppenheimer's Apocalypse Hypothesis says we have sixty-to-seventy years before the human race is extinct, right? That's a lot of time. We can still figure out another solution."

There was nowhere left to hide, and I could scarcely imagine how things could get any worse. I'd put off revealing the truth about the Apocalypse Pocket Watch for far too long, and if Nessa and Delbar really wanted to spend the rest of their lives underground toiling away against the inevitable, they had the right to know what they were really up against, the monolith specter of dwindling time. I dug out the pocket watch and dangled it in front of their faces.

"Oppenheimer gave me this last week. He calls it his Apocalypse Pocket Watch. It predicts how much time we have left before human extinction."

They squinted. "That says five-to-ten years not sixty-to-seventy."

"He lied to us. He didn't think anyone would come down here if they thought they only had five years to live. He only told me because he wants me to take over Perro Caliente so he can die. That's why he brought us here. It was a three-way competition, and you two were deemed too optimistic. Oppenheimer doesn't trust optimists. For whatever it's worth, I disagree with that assessment."

The monorail rattled into the Mezzanine proper, and Nessa and Delbar were silent. We passed stop after stop, until finally Delbar said, "He picked you? Talk about boys' club, am I right?"

Nessa groaned. "Five years. Seventy years. We have to keep working. Five years is still a long time. We can figure something out. We can't let everyone die."

"Everyone dies." Even I was surprised I'd said it. I'd spent the last seven years of my life fighting this very truth. But maybe I was finally ready to admit it: everyone dies. Everyone dies.

"Ugh. You're such a self-indulgent, self-important downer," Del said. "Look. First things first. We have to tell people the truth. Let's go to The Communications Center and make an announcement. These people have the right to know they only have five years left, not seventy."

I stood. I sat. I stood again. I can't articulate exactly what I was expecting—perhaps Nessa and Del would plan some type of breakout and the three of us would ride out the wave of apocalypse at halcyon Google—but this wasn't it. Revealing the truth to everyone felt like a path toward madness and full-scale revolt. I pointed at the billowing flames below. "Really? You want to tell these people that not only has Oppenheimer trapped them underground, but he did so under false pretenses and they're all going to die in less than a decade?"

"They deserve the truth," Nessa said.

"We can't betray Oppenheimer like this."

"'Betray Oppenheimer?' He's a loony toon!" Delbar said. "Besides, Nessa and I can't just sit on a lie this big. We're not you, Dr. Copeland."

I closed the Apocalypse Pocket Watch, unable to look either of them in the eye. They weren't me. I thanked Einstein above they were so much better. When the monorail stopped at The Communications Center, I watched from my seat as Nessa and Delbar hurried up the metal stairs so they could broadcast the news to the thousands of already enraged employees. The train jolted forward, and I sincerely hoped that it would just shuttle me away, beyond Perro Caliente, beyond the earth, beyond time. I let Nessa and Delbar down. I let everyone down. And I couldn't for the life of me see any way out of this mess that didn't involve the deaths of everyone trapped underground. I held my head in my hands and thought of the ASA. I should have listened to those dour panelists and taken a cushy job teaching in the friendly Midwest. I thought of my parents. I hadn't called them in weeks. Just a clipped e-mail explaining that I'd taken a new job and wouldn't be able to call for awhile. What would they think if I never returned? I dug my fingernails into my knees and when I at last opened my eyes, I was faced with The God Laser. The train had delivered me to The Control Center and Oppenheimer's all-powerful particle accelerator. I remembered the final two Wren-worlds. I knew I should stay and somehow assist Nessa and Delbar, somehow convince the people of Perro Caliente that our mission was worthwhile and good. But I just couldn't figure out how to do that, how best to capitalize on my abilities, and I told myself I just needed thirty seconds with Wren—less than half-a-minute—and then I'd be able to deduce a solution. Thirty seconds as my best possible self, and then I could solve everything. Just thirty seconds.

I left the train and sprinted to my workspace terminal. Nobody was stupid enough to show up for work when half the facility was in revolt. I keyed up the sixth world of The Wren Algorithm, and The God Laser spun to life birthing its familiar black egg wormhole. But before I could even enter the wormhole, the loudspeakers chimed on, and I heard the voice of Nessa Newmar, that woman who had moved me so much during *The Steady-State Ecstasy of Sir Fred Hoyle*.

"You think it's on, Del? Am I on?" She cleared her throat. "Citizens of Perro Caliente! My name is Dr. Nessa Newmar. I'm a mathematician on The God Laser project, and I know you're all upset, but I have some troubling news. I don't know exactly how to tell you all this, but we've just learned that we don't have sixty-to-seventy years to live. According to Oppenheimer, it's five-to-ten. I know this is terrifying, but please hear me out. We can still fix things. We can redouble our efforts and keep trying to beat back the apocalypse. Help us. We'll try and reinstate the elevators. We're trying. We have to keep trying!"

I told myself I was trying. I told myself that in Wren's presence I would find the solution like Isaac Newtown stumbling on gravity in the form of a Red Delicious. But even from The God Laser, I could hear the wail of protesters back in the Mezzanine, the great, big wave of righteous anger that would no doubt wash away everything Oppenheimer had been striving for these past twenty-five years. I closed my eyes and ran at the wormhole.

I would return.

An hour later, I stood outside the Visitor's Center of St. Anthony's Cemetery in Wilkes-Barre with a crude photocopied map in my hands. I hadn't even known that cemeteries had visitor centers, but then again, I hadn't actually stepped foot inside one—excluding Oppenheimer's—since my grandmother died when I was seventeen. The friendly administrative assistant inside had circled the grave on my map, and I struck off in that direction even though it was snowing, even though I was woefully underdressed in my khakis and lab coat, my Italian loafers and silk knit tie that provided shockingly little warmth.

This was the penultimate Wren-world, and there were two major differences from all the others: 1) global warming had already advanced to the point where winter claimed ownership of the northeast for ten months of the year, and 2) despite the lowered leukemia rate for women, Wren Wells had still contracted the disease and subsequently died at the tender age of twenty-two. It didn't matter that I had birthed thousands of minute modifications within The Theory of Almost Everything. She still died, and again I'd been powerless to save her. Maybe that was the point. There was nothing I or anyone else could do to protect her. Maybe there was no point, and my life and its grand accumulation of experiences was just one of many sent adrift across the sea of meaningless infinity.

I can't explain why exactly when I read this information on my Calabi-Yau—proof that there would be no Wren-reunion in this Wren-world—I hadn't immediately returned home or continued on to the final Wren-filled universe. But what I'd felt was a calming wave of acceptance, the knowledge that Wren was gone, that there was nothing I could do, that she existed in other universes and that had to be enough for me, that according to her counterpart in Hiroshima we wouldn't have wound up together anyway and I had to move on. I remembered how I'd avoided her funeral, her grave, had never once made that pilgrimage in the seven years since her death. I felt that mistake had to be rectified even if this Wren was not my Wren, that in this perpetually frozen world, my counterpart had attended Penn State instead of Susquehanna, that those star-crossed lovers had never met. Even in the face of doomsday, I would repent.

I at last came upon the row of graves the admin had circled for me. She told me Wren's was third from the left. An older woman, she'd scrunched her eyebrows as she dug through her files and came across Wren's record and date-of-birth/ date-of-death. She looked sympathetic and had asked, even though she knew, "She was young, wasn't she?"

"Very."

"How did you know her?"

What a question! Maybe I'd been trying to answer that riddle ever since I first met her, ever since I found her singing above me on that Susquehanna stage a decade earlier. I stared at the administrative assistant and found myself speechless. How could I explain any of it, not just what happened between me and Wren, but what happened between everyone: the sticky, wet fuel of life itself? "We met," I tried. "We met—I—" I looked into her eyes. "I wish I'd died instead of her."

I'd never been able to articulate that before, and the admin rose from her chair and hugged me. It was so nice. So sweet. And I couldn't remember the last time a stranger held me. Maybe never. She opened the candy jar on her desk and handed me a Hershey kiss. Then she turned to the window and the fantastically whipping snow. "Who knows how long any of us have left considering the state of things? Stay warm out there, son."

I counted graves. One. Two. Three. But the third wasn't Wren's, it was the tombstone of an Italian man who'd lived seventy years, a prince's ransom compared to what Wren siphoned away from this fleeting earth. But there was a particularly large space between graves two and three, and that's when I noticed equally large spaces between many of the gravestones littered throughout St. Anthony's. Perhaps those spaces hinted at ground markers beneath the hard snow, stony reminders of those who couldn't afford the flashy headstones of the middle-class and wealthy. Perhaps in this world Wren's hospital bills had driven her family into financial ruin. I hoped this wasn't the case even as I dropped to my knees in the snow—how my nose hairs froze, how my fingers burned, how I yearned for a winter jacket and gloves instead of my wrinkled lab coat—and dug out where I believed Wren's marker would be with my bare hands.

I dug and scraped, dug and scraped, and just when I thought my hands were about to fall off the bone, I hit stone and uncovered Wren's name, the date of her death. She was only twenty-two-years-old. Twenty-two! I crouched in the snow, and for the first time in a very long time, openly wept. Only this time, I was not weeping for what I had lost, the life I imagined had been crossed out by leukemia, but I cried for Wren and what she had lost, that unlived life

I now understood wouldn't have involved me in any way. I wept for Wren and only Wren. I had to let my childish delusions go once and for all. And finally, the full weight of the transgressions I'd committed underground caught up to me like a bullet train. I had not just been selfish or childish when I'd used The God Laser for my own personal curiosity. I had been monstrous. I had been a monster. I was putting not only my own life on the line by using The God Laser for anything other than its noble intent, I was risking the lives of Nessa, Delbar, every single person on earth, and perhaps, every single person living amongst fading earths in the vast tapestry of the Multiverse. I didn't want to be the kind of person I'd been in Alaska anymore, an isolated misanthrope sealed off from other humans. I wanted to rejoin the whole, be part of the many.

I remembered Oppie's words to me when he'd first explained why he founded Perro Caliente. It was penance for the three hundred thousand people he had murdered in the name of cavalier astro-science. Surely I was as terrible if not worse. I had risked the lives of an infinite amount of people to peep the fantasy of a weak-willed teenage boy. Wren could not force me to become a better person, a person who lived in color instead of black-and-white. Neither could Nessa. That was my task and mine alone. But what penance could ever balance what I had done? How could I possibly make up for something so utterly terrible?

I stood up from Wren's grave. My knees almost buckled, and I realized just how long I'd been exposed to the raw snow and cold of a Pennsylvania terrorized by an apocalyptic winter. I couldn't feel my legs or arms and fell facedown over Wren's grave. But before I lost consciousness, I had a thought, a holy vision not unlike my father's beloved Saul on the road to Damascus. I recalled how the resurrected Christ appeared to Saul and asked him to abandon his nefarious ways and transform into Paul, an apostle, a legitimate force for good in a world tipped toward chaos. I remembered Oppenheimer's request alongside his atrophied brain: that I take over Perro Caliente, that I remain forever underground. Surely exiling myself underground and striving for a tunnel out of apocalypse was an adequate penance, but was I truly worthy enough to become the Director of Perro Caliente? And what about Nessa and Delbar? Weren't they equally qualified? Weren't they much more qualified? Weren't they the kind of global saviors this crazy age really needed?

My body went numb as I passed out in the falling snow. The last thing I heard was the steady ticking of the Apocalypse Pocket Watch, the clockwork machinery that told me over and over that I would one day die, that I would one day die, that I would one day die.

EXILE

Pale, yellow light. The steady beeps and bloops of machines I did not recognize, the shuffling of sneakers across a linoleum floor not unlike the sounds I'd awoken to as a postdoc in Templewood Apartments. But this was no Templewood Apartment. I opened my eyes and found myself atop a stiff hospital bed that overlooked the rugged coal-rich hills of Wilkes-Barre, birthplace of Wren Wells in this doomed world and my own. My bony tucchus was exposed in a hospital gown, but I could feel and move all of my extremities, a happy revelation indeed. I felt loopy, but no worse for wear than if I'd contracted the flu, a malady I encountered at least once a school year as a postdoc exposed to too many students and their germ-riddled flesh, hulking across the snowy Alaskan campus like carrier polar bears.

A nurse entered and made a large production out of seeing me awake. He was young and bubbly and reminded me of the chipper attitudes of all those scientists in Perro Caliente before the results came back negative, before Oppenheimer's deception was at last revealed.

"How long have I been out?" I asked.

He checked my vitals on a complex web of screens near my head. I've always been ashamed by how little I know of the medical universe and was relieved that he didn't know I was a man of science. "Three days," he said. "You had a nasty case of frostbite, but you'll be fine. You're lucky someone at the cemetery saw you and called in an ambulance. Things could have been worse if you were out there much longer. You know the national regulations about being outside in the dark during severe wind chill."

"Yeah," I deadpanned, pretending to understand, "but three days? I was really out for three days?"

"Three days," he repeated.

Three days! Who knew what might have transpired in Perro Caliente over the course of three days? The entire facility might have already been engulfed in flames.

"So," the nurse said, "we actually have some questions for you. We were able to track down your medical coverage based on your driver's license, but this morning we got a call from a man claiming to be you on the other side of the state. He received all the claim information and said he lives in Erie and has never been to Wilkes-Barre a day in his life. We're assuming this guy is some kind of nut job, but do you have any idea what's going on?"

The nut job in question was no doubt this universe's iteration of Teddy Copeland, stunned and mystified by why his insurance company was paying for another Teddy Copeland struck down by frostbite on the opposite edge of

Pennsylvania. “No,” I said softly. “I don’t know about any of that. Look, I’m really tired. You think I could get some sleep?

The nurse smiled. “Sure, I’ll check up with you in a few.”

As soon he shut the door, I ripped the IV cords from my body and tore through the dresser on the lookout for my clothes, and more importantly, the Calabi-Yau and Apocalypse Pocket Watch. Luckily, the folks of Wilkes-Barre were as trusting as they were friendly, and everything I’d had on my person when I passed out in the cemetery was bundled together in the top drawer. I felt overwhelmingly weak, but none of that mattered. The only thing that mattered was teleporting back to Perro Caliente. The only thing that mattered was apologizing to my friends and somehow making up for the myriad ways in which I had betrayed them. It was time for Saul to at last become Paul.

I materialized beneath the dual electromagnets of The God Laser. Three days had passed, yet I could still hear the wailing sirens and screaming scientists all the way from my perch atop the stone walkway. Clearly, conditions had deteriorated even further. I started down the walkway when I spotted a familiar figure in the top floor of The Control Center. It was Nessa Newmar, hopeful genius Nessa Newmar, her hair a tangled mess, her lab coat collar half-popped. An unmistakable expression of relief flashed across her face when she saw me, and she rushed down the stairs to meet me at the base of the laser. She smiled in a shy, confused way. I’d been in another universe for three full days. She’d caught me, and I understood there was no more hiding the truth. I could no longer deny exactly what I’d been up to in the various Wren-worlds of the Multiverse.

"I thought you were dead," Nessa said. "I thought you jumped into another universe and got yourself killed."

"This fella? Never. I got frostbite. I was unconscious in a hospital for three days."

She frowned. "What the hell were you doing? We needed you. This whole place is going to shit."

I remembered her prophecy in Indianapolis. *Nostalgia is nihilism*. Perhaps there was still time to right the ship. "Can you tell me what's happening here first?"

She looked at her Forces. "The protesters got serious when Del and I made our announcement. They started burning buildings en masse. Word on the street is they're building scaffolding around the elevator and gathering explosives. I think they're going to blow a hole in the SimuSky and climb their way up to the surface. Oppenheimer's missing. People went to his ranch to force him to return the elevator car, but he's gone."

"Where's Del?" I asked. "What are you doing here?"

"Del's trying to organize the people who want to stay underground and keep them safe until everyone else has escaped. Me?" She looked at me like I was the stupidest human being on the earth, and maybe I was. Maybe my PhD and early accomplishments were a front, and I was the dumbest Neanderthal to ever stalk across the Multiverse, a doomed misanthrope. "I was here looking for you. You weren't in your room, and your Calabi-Yau was missing. I assumed you were out there somewhere." She nodded toward The God Laser and the infinite universes vibrating invisibly behind it. "Where were you? What was so important that you left us to deal with this alone?"

I looked Nessa in the eyes and found myself dwelling on our marathon sessions of *Your Romantic Star-Filled Journey*.

How sweet life had been then. How much I wanted to return to that safe space. She didn't deserve what was about to happen, and I certainly didn't deserve her stabilizing presence in my life. *I won't compete with a ghost.* I hoped that somehow, someway she might be able to forgive me. "I modified The Theory of Almost Everything to create seven parallel worlds where my wife was still alive. I've been stalking her."

She didn't grow angry like I expected. She looked hurt. And believe it or not that made it so much worse. I could imagine the neurons firing in her brain, how she no doubt linked my awkward reluctance outside her apartment to my continued obsession with my dead wife. She surely connected my quixotic desire to see Wren again to her father who had ignored her in favor of his deluded notions that he might use Perro Caliente to revive Nessa's mother. The world was coming to an end, and I had chosen to bury my head in the sands of the past. Nessa stood very straight, reminding me of how strong and confrontational she had appeared when Oppenheimer first goaded her about the whereabouts of her father. Dr. Nessa Newmar, I remembered, was not someone to be trifled with.

"You're going to die bitter and alone, Dr. Copeland, and I truly, utterly pity you. Enjoy the apocalypse."

She started toward the monorail platform, and I tried to call out to her, tried to reach out for her, but she froze mid-step, a single hand raised in my direction. "Don't you dare. Don't you fucking dare."

I watched her leave and put my head in my hands. I readied myself for a bout of mental self-flagellation the likes of which the world had never seen. Over and over again I replayed the events of my time underground, and I longed not for an alternate universe where I might see Wren Wells again, but one where I'd never bothered with The Wren Algorithm in the first place and instead had utterly and completely given myself up to the holy work at hand. Would things be any different? Would my increased effort impact the destinies of billions? I sat there pondering all of these questions, when I heard a curious sound coming from The Control Center, the slow clap of a James Bond villain about to explain his totally outlandish, yet somehow predictable, world domination scheme. It was none other than the Hologram of Dr. J. Robert Oppenheimer. Nessa and I had not been alone, and old Oppie had been hiding in plain sight, right in The Control Center, perhaps beneath us in his chamber of servers.

"You really screwed the pooch this time, eh, Copeland, old sport?"

The father of the atomic bomb stood in the doorway, a silver flask clutched tightly in his paw. I didn't dare move away from The God Laser. There was something new and unsettling behind Oppie's translucent blue eyes, something even more unhinged than usual, something that went far beyond the fact that he was a century-old hologram, and I found myself recalling Katasumi swallowing the powdered bones of her mother.

He strutted up the walkway until we were face-to-face. "Do you know how much of my fortune I've invested in The God Laser over the years?" he asked with a smile.

"No," I said.

"Take a guess. Come on, Mr. Fancy PhD Cosmologist. You owe me a guess, don't you?"

I stared at him.

"74.2 trillion," he answered, "the overwhelming majority of Perro Caliente's operating budget. You all think it'll be so easy to move onto the next solution, the next big thing. But here's the problem, Dr. Copeland, we're running low on funds. It's kind of difficult these days to absorb the financial hit from a one hundred mile particle accelerator." He returned his flask to his jacket. "74.2 trillion dollars, and what have you been using it for again? Can you explain it to me one more time? Go on. Just like you did for your little buddy, Dr. Newmar. Don't think we haven't all noticed your little will-they-or-won't-they shenanigans. It's all been quite charming that you've been focused on wetting your member when the gd world is ending. Very professional."

I couldn't meet his eyes. I wanted to melt into a puddle and be swept down a sewer.

"Out with it!" Oppenheimer yelled, his voice echoing.

"I just wanted to see what would've happened to my wife if she lived."

"Oh! You just wanted to see what would've happened to your wife if she lived! That sounds like a totally appropriate way to use a piece of scientific equipment designed to save the world that cost 74.2 trillion dollars. Because no one else in Perro Caliente has ever experienced loss before, right? Your wife's death stands alone as the single worst and most unique tragedy in the history of mankind? Is that about right, Copeland? Let's not stop the holocaust. Let's see about your precious little wife!" Oppenheimer took another step closer, and I could almost taste the bourbon on his breath. "You know, I coded a world out of egotistical wish fulfillment too. One where I was never involved with The Manhattan Project. I was curious if it would still lead to the destruction of Hiroshima and Nagasaki, my black listing, the death of my family, and so on and so forth. But do you know what happened?" When I didn't respond, he poked me hard in the chest. "I said, 'Do you know what happened?' You give me an answer, boy."

"I don't know what happened."

"I didn't go fucking through with it, you chowder head, because even I don't think my own personal failures are more important than the fate of the entire Multiverse." He clenched and unclenched his fists. "You've been nothing but a disappointment. Nothing. I gave you the Apocalypse Pocket Watch over two weeks ago, and you still haven't given me a decision. Why?"

"I'm really interested in the position," I squeaked. "But I think Nessa and Delbar are equally qualified. I'm having a tough time figuring out who's the most qualified."

"Do you know why I chose you over them, Copeland? Because I recognized something in you, a hardness, an inherent cynicism. You don't trust other people. You've cut yourself off from them, you're separate. Newmar and Javari are very much part of this world. You're not. That division is what allowed me to oversee the atomic bomb project. A scientific leader needs that quality." He shook his head. "Not that any of it even matters anymore. Perro Caliente's in ruins, no thanks to you. This place is done for. Done for!"

I dropped to my knees. I knew it was unbecoming for a scientist, and I'd never groveled for anything in my life, but surely if there was ever a time for outright begging, this was it. "Dr. Oppenheimer," I pleaded, "I know I've made terrible mistakes. Huge ones. But that's all behind me now. I don't need to go back into the Multiverse. I know I've failed you, but I really believe in this place and what it stands for. Gathering the best minds in the world to operate free from interference from the world's governments. I know one of us can run it.

Either me or Nessa or Del. I'm just not sure which one yet. I need a little more time."

"Let me think about it," Oppie deadpanned. "Nope. Not going to happen. Not a chance, Copeland. No chance in hell."

Then something strange happened, an image even more unbelievable and crazier than anything I'd seen up until that point underground, Neo-Nazis and living Wrens included. Dr. Oppenheimer reached inside his lab coat and retrieved not a flask but a small, olde timey pistol. He pointed it straight at my brain and cocked the revolver.

"Perro Caliente's on fire. There's nothing left to be in charge of, Dr. Copeland. Now stand up, and give me your Calabi-Yau."

I handed it over, my fingers trembling.

"Now get ready, Copeland. We don't have much time for my final experiment."

My mind buzzed, a radio station tuned to static. Was Dr. Oppenheimer really going to kill me? Was he even capable of killing? Of course he was. It was his handiwork at Los Alamos that had directly led to the incineration of three hundred thousand people in Japan. What was one more person? Jesus Christ. Was this how my life ended: unredeemed and gunned down by the father of the atomic bomb in an underground laboratory? Oppenheimer swiped in a command on my Calabi-Yau and the quadrupole lasers roared to life, spinning and spinning, bolts of electricity cackling between.

"What do you say to one last voyage into the great beyond, eh, Dr. Copeland?"

He tossed my Calabi-Yau over the edge, and we heard it smash into a million little pieces. The black egg of the wormhole grew behind me, and I suddenly understood

Oppenheimer's punishment: he was exiling me to a parallel universe forever.

"Dr. Oppenheimer," I pleaded. "Oppie. Please. Don't do this."

He shook his pistol and told me to march. "It's much too late for that, Dr. Copeland. Perro Caliente's in shambles, and someone has to pay. Looks like that someone's you. Think of it this way: I'm giving you exactly what you always wanted. You wanted to explore worlds where your wife still lived? No problem! That's where I'm sending you to: the seventh and final world of your so-called Wren Algorithm. I've already loaded it up. You'll be trapped there forever, but I'm not wholly un-benevolent. I'll give you a head start. Right at this very moment in space-time, your beloved's in a bar. Double Daughter's it's called. I'm sending you a mere ten feet away from the entrance. I'm not without compassion. You wanted your wife? Go get her."

The wormhole spun faster and faster and with each step backwards, I could feel my bones shaking, feel myself edging closer to being sucked inside, forever closed off from the world of my birth. "Oppie, please. I don't want this anymore. I made a mistake."

"Well, I'll tell you what, great cosmologist, Dr. Theodore Copeland. If, through some scientific miracle, you're able to escape your exile and return to this world, I'll let you choose who'll rule the ruins of Perro Caliente. You game, old chap?"

"You know that's impossible."

"Nothing's impossible! I built an atom bomb out of spit and paperclips! Now march, dingbat!"

Dr. Oppenheimer waved his gun, so I took another step and was sucked into the wormhole and my permanent exile. My final image before I blinked out of existence was Oppenheimer cackling like a deranged hyena.

PERRO CALIENTE PRIME

I materialized at a bus stop on an empty city street. Darkness had fallen, and wherever I'd been sentenced had long ago turned cold. Gray snow had been shoveled into small hills every few feet where they completely solidified. I was more than cold in my khakis and dress shirt, as I rubbed my arms and tried to get a handle on the situation. Dr. Oppenheimer had banished me to this final Wren-world with no Calabi-Yau. Not only did that mean I couldn't teleport home whenever I wanted, but also that I was unable to research my new surroundings. I didn't know which city I'd appeared in or how this parallel world diverged from my own. All I knew was what the tall wooden sign for Double Daughter's across the street signified: that the final Wren Wells awaited me inside. That was it. That was all the information I had to go on. Not how she differed from my Wren, or more importantly, how I might outthink Oppenheimer and scheme my way back home. Surely there existed a way. Surely I might return and somehow contribute to Nessa and Delbar's goal of saving everyone. Surely Oppenheimer, cruel but still a man of science, had not dangled the opportunity of selecting a new director without there existing at least some modicum of hope. Regardless, my first step toward glorious homecoming meant that unlike my previous foray into the Multiverse, I had to avoid frostbite. That meant venturing inside Double Daughter's to warm up and construct a hypothesis.

Double Daughter's reminded me of the lone trendy club my PhD cohort and I once visited in Anchorage. Pointed red booths lined the right side of DD's, and a long bar stretched across the left, its stools crimson and made to resemble dripping wax candles. The walls were brick, the floors hardwood, and in the back stood a small glowing stage, huge lights pulsating not to music, but the voices of the few people gathered there, tallboy PBRs in hand. Everyone looked hip. Tight pants. Tight shirts. Perfectly sculpted facial hair. Goofy glasses. I guessed I was in an American city, a bar too cool for the rust belt or plains. Some place urbane and young and hip. As I sidled up to the bar to ask the nose-studded bartender some probing questions about our location, I spotted a living Wren Wells just like Dr. Oppenheimer predicted.

She sat three empty stools away, hunched over a bourbon on the rocks, a smug look across her wry face. She'd deviated from the uniform of Double Daughter's, opting instead for a white tank top and black vest, her jeans self-consciously pre-ripped. I tried to ignore my resurrected wife for the moment and, instead, caught the attention of the bartender with a quick wave of my hand.

"What'll it be?" she asked.

"Hi! Yes. Hello. Can you tell me if you're going to play the big game tonight?"

She frowned. "Yeah, we don't really show sports in here, bruh."

"Yeah, but let's say you did show sports, which team would you show?"

The bartender's face turned grim. "You wanna drink or what?"

I shrugged. "Yeah, give me a bourbon. You got Eagle Rare?"

For the first time since my arrival in that final Wren-world, I considered the possibility that perhaps I really was trapped. Perhaps there was no method for me to scrape back home and somehow find a way to fix Perro Caliente. Perhaps this was simply my life now: alone in a mysterious world where I knew no one, where I possessed no birth certificate, no home, no clothes, just the wrinkled Andrew Jackson in my wallet. The only person I knew was Wren, but of course, she didn't know me.

I cradled my drink and sat next to her. My options were thin. Wren was my only lifeline in this unknown universe, and if she paid for her drink and left, then what? I extended my hand. "Name's Cope."

Her face remained neutral. "Wren." Her reaction signaled that in this universe she'd never met me or, at the very least, my counterpart hadn't made a striking impression.

"I just moved here," I tried.

Her eyes perked up. Everyone liked to have some knowledge over someone else, to be able to pontificate about subjects well known. "Yeah? What brings you to ol' Denver?"

Denver, Colorado! Land of snow and weed and ski lodges! A variable uncovered! "I'm here for work."

"What do you do?"

"Uh, I'm a cosmologist. Actually, I'm between jobs at the moment. That's why I moved to Denver really. Looking for work."

She raised her bourbon in toast, and we clinked glasses. "Well, cheers to finding work, Cope." Wren drank in a series of long gulps. I followed suit, and we placed our empties on the bar. "Buy me another round?" Wren asked, and what else could I do? Would you not buy your resurrected wife a bourbon if you ran into her in a bar? Did you not owe her those few precious ounces?

The bartender returned with new drinks, and I suddenly remembered that I hadn't eaten all day, that the last time I'd consumed food was the morning before Nessa, Delbar, and I ran into the barking protestors at the Mezzanine. Surely I'd been pumped full of nutrients during my stay in the Wilkes-Barre hospital, but either way my stomach was empty, and I could already feel the alcohol flooding up to my brain. How sweet and peculiar the world seemed now. Here was Wren Wells, and unlike the other Wrens I'd encountered in the Multiverse, this one seemed almost relieved to speak with me, her eyes watery with a bodacious buzz flirting with drunkenness.

"What do you do?" I asked.

Wren shrugged. "I adjunct at a bunch of community colleges all over town. I teach basic writing. Got my MFA in poetry from Colorado State."

"That sounds really fulfilling."

She laughed before downing her second bourbon and signaling for another. "It's not. I'd make more working at Walmart. CSU should put that on the brochure. Come focus on your writing for three years, then make less than the minimum wage!"

I ordered a third even though I knew I shouldn't. I already felt loosened, adrift in the bourbon-rich ocean of Double Daughter's. "Is that why you're drinking so much?" I blurted.

"You're one to talk."

"I'm sorry."

She reached out and touched my shoulder. It was the first time any of the Wrens showed me any affection or kindness whatsoever, and I almost dropped my drink and fell to the ground. "The job situation isn't why I'm drinking. At least not tonight anyway."

"So why then?"

She pushed her hair away from her forehead. "I don't even know you."

"But you feel like you do, don't you?" I was buzzed. I hadn't consumed solid food in days. I had been banished to another universe by the father of the atomic bomb. I was at the very least owed this dumb, sappy moment. The Multiverse owed me something! "You feel like you know me, don't you?"

She didn't break my gaze. The noise of the bar pulsed stupidly around us, but in that moment, it fell away until it was just the two of us in Double Daughter's, the two of us in Denver, the two of us on earth, the two of us against the entire Multiverse. "Yeah," she said. "I do."

"Then why are you drinking so heavily?"

"I broke up with my boyfriend today. We've been dating for over a year."

"Why?"

Wren kept her eyes trained on mine. "We were talking about moving in together. He's a great guy. A documentary filmmaker. I respect him. He respects me. And he started saying how ridiculous it was that we were talking about moving in, but we'd never actually said we loved each other.

Then he just said it. Just like that. Out of nowhere when we were on the couch watching reality TV like a couple of goons. He just said it."

I thumbed the edge of my glass. I reached across that immeasurably vast space between our bodies and held Wren's hand. She did not back away. "Then what happened?"

"I freaked out and broke things off. I'm ashamed of myself."

I remembered that night in Housing Unit Seven when Nessa asked me to come inside. "I understand that completely."

"Then you're just as fucked up as I am, Cope." Wren looked at me, her eyes rimmed with tears. "Hey," she said in her self-destructive-cum-seductive way. "Do you want to get out of here? Do you want to go back to my place? I have a record player and some records. I'm a cool person. I'm not a murderer or anything."

Every internal organ went dead inside my body, and I felt rooted to my barstool like a hundred-year-old oak. "Ok," I squeaked. "That sounds cool."

She slid two twenties across the bar and hopped off her stool. She leaned in near my ear and said, "I'm going to hit the bathroom," and then she was gone, vanished in the growing crowd of Double Daughter's like the ghost she truly was.

I clung to the bar and weighed my options. On one hand, I could go back to Wren's apartment, and perhaps the two of us might resume the lives we'd left behind at 22, finally transforming into the golden couple I'd always imagined us becoming amongst the farmland of idyllic Susquehanna. On the other hand, I could slip out of Double Daughter's right that very moment. I could leave Wren to her filmmaker boyfriend and the ensuing realization that she was capable and truly deserving of love, that she didn't have to annihilate her opportunities at happiness. I could leave her to the people who rightfully belonged to this universe, but what of me then? What would happen to me? Was the final fate of one Dr. Teddy Copeland becoming a wandering nomad, a nameless, homeless creature doomed to wander a parallel reality for all eternity? I couldn't say in the moment of the decision exactly what the future held, but I knew that road did not lead through Wren's apartment and whatever mistakes we might make there. Down that path lay only the past, and I understood it was finally time to move on from the specter of Wren's death and into the future. I turned to the bartender and said, "When that woman comes back, if she's looking for me, can you tell her I'm really sorry, and she's fantastic, but I just couldn't?"

The bartender pinched her nose. "Ugh, dude. Tell her yourself, you sanctimonious asshole." Her voice was raised now. "Wren's one of our regulars. Who are you anyway? I hate guys like you."

I deserved that—much more than that when you got down to it—and began my slow sulk away from the bar. But before I could make it outside, I noticed something, or more accurately, someone, out of the corner of my eye. I saw a man duck behind a booth on the opposite side of Double Daughter's. I could only make out his mop of brown hair, but I sensed the moment I spotted him that he'd been watching me, the curious, dangling thread of déjà vu. I paused at the doorway and, perhaps it took me longer because I was buzzed, realized that this man might be the mysterious stranger who'd been tailing me in so many of the Wren-worlds. I spun around to finally confront my arch-villain, but he was already upon me, pushing me out the front door and onto the frozen sidewalk outside. I shielded my face with my arms as my nemesis landed body blow after body blow while shouting,

"You bastard! You fucking bastard!" I'd never actually been in a fight before, and how exhilarating it was even as his fey little fists hammered my rib cage. I tensed up, drew my right arm back, and struck him as hard as I could across the jaw. The villain staggered backwards, and finally I was able to stand. Snow was falling, but even through the thick, white flakes and somber darkness of nightfall, I at last recognized the face of my attacker. He rubbed his chin before charging me again, and this time his identity was unmistakable.

It was me.

I'd been pursued through infinity by another Teddy Copeland.

"You sniveling little shit," he yelled as he struck me across my jaw, a duplicate punch of my own. "I can't believe you were going to sleep with her. I can't believe you were going to interfere with her life like that! You're not god!"

I put up both hands and shouted, "Jesus Christ! Can you stop hitting me for one goddamn second?" I nodded toward the window of Double Daughter's now filled with hip patrons eager for a glimpse at our rough-and-tumble fisticuffs. "We can't let Wren see this."

He groaned, but this other me knew I was right. He grabbed me by the neck, kicked my shins, and together we moseyed down the snowy streets of Denver like a couple of conjoined twins in a potato sack race.

"What the hell is your problem anyway?" he asked.

"My problem? You stalked me all across the Multiverse and have the nerve to ask what my problem is? I wasn't going back with her. I thought about it, sure, but I wasn't going through with it."

"Fine. Whatever. We're both done then. This is the final Wren-world. Let's just go home and forget any of this ever happened."

I was shivering now and big flakes of snow caught on my eyelashes. "I can't," I said, and for the first time all evening it dawned on me how truly fucked I was. "Oppenheimer banished me here."

"Oppenheimer?" the other me asked. He released me from his grip and pointed to a well-lit diner across the street. "Come on. I want an explanation."

#

Over two identical bowls of soup—of course we ordered chicken dumpling, of course we ordered water-no-lemon-black-coffee—I explained my sad tale of woe culminating in my banishment to this final Wren-world. For his part, the other me nodded and slurped. We sported duplicate bruises on our faces, and to the passerby of snowy Denver, we must have looked like the burliest pair of fighting twins this side of the Rockies. The other me had yet to divulge his own story of scientific sorrows that had led him to this diner, and I waited with bated breath as he leaned in on his elbows and asked, "When you were a kid, did you play *Explorers of Verenzetti Island!* with your dad just one time?"

"Yes."

"And it ended with you spinning a one when you needed a seven?"

"Yes."

"And that's the modification you made to The Theory of Almost Everything? First you modified the leukemia occurrence rate for women, and that led you to Washington, DC and that whole mob of Teddy Copelands, and then you modified the outcome of that board game in the hopes that none of the other Teddys had that specific game of *Explorers of Verenzetti Island!* in their pasts?"

"Yes."

"Me too. We might be the only Teddy Copelands in the entire Multiverse who played that game, remembered it, lost Wren to cancer, and ended up working on The God Laser in Perro Caliente."

I slurped my chicken broth. "You were there in DC when all those Teddy Copelands appeared outside the coffee shop?"

"I was the one who got everybody to leave."

"Teddy Copeland Prime!" I shouted. How ludicrous and ironic and oh-so-perfect that the man who'd been stalking me across the Multiverse was none other than Teddy Copeland Prime, the stronger, kinder, better version of myself I'd glimpsed outside that Eastern Market café. "I call you Teddy Copeland Prime."

He sipped his coffee. "Interesting. I call you Teddy Copeland-X of Earth 2."

"Why am I Earth 2? Why aren't you Earth 2? I'm clearly Earth 1."

"Obviously, I'm Earth 1," Teddy Copeland Prime said matter-of-factly. "My story's the real story. Yours is just a side story."

"Uh, I highly doubt that, Teddy Copeland Prime."

We stared at each other. We had arrived at a stalemate and quickly agreed never again to bring up the lingering question of which Teddy Copeland was the more important, truer Teddy Copeland, the not-so-noble protagonist of our respective narratives.

"Imagine my surprise," Teddy Copeland continued, "when I teleported to that bus stop in Baltimore and found you waiting."

We both went for the pepper and almost knocked hands. "You were there right from the start?"

"Right from the start. With backgrounds as similar as ours, I assumed that whenever I thought about exploring another Wren-world, you'd be in your universe having the exact same thought. That way, neither of us could ever really be alone with Wren. There'd always be this doppelgänger in hiding. I even boarded that bus in Baltimore right behind you. I bet you didn't notice that. You were too busy gawking at Wren."

I narrowed my eyes. I was not about to be condemned by myself.

"When I saw you staring at her on the bus, I realized how pathetic I was. What was I really searching for? What good would a reunion do? Hadn't she made it abundantly clear she didn't see herself growing old with me/us anyway? I decided right then and there I would no longer explore these worlds to reconnect with Wren. Instead, I would try to prevent you from doing something irreversible. I remembered all those Teddy Copelands outside that café in Eastern Market. What would've happened if I wasn't there? If that hulking mass actually made it inside? I didn't know your intentions, but I had to find out." He paused. "Teddy Copeland-X, I followed you every step of the way."

"Every Wren-world? Not just the ones I saw you in?"

"I was at her concert in Omaha and across the street from her home in Pittsburgh. Who do you think called the ambulance in Wilkes-Barre when you passed out? I started to believe you were mostly innocent, and that like me, you'd soon realize that what happened in the past had to stay in the past, that it wasn't fair to all the Wrens across infinity to subject them to our selfish, not to mention childish, desires. But when I overheard her ask you back to her apartment at Double Daughter's, that's when I had to make my presence known. It wouldn't be fair to her."

"I know that. That's why I was leaving. I came to the same realization at her grave. Like I said, the only reason I'm even here is because Oppenheimer banished me."

Teddy Copeland Prime asked for two bags of frozen peas from the waitress. She returned, and we held them to our respective bruises. An elderly man in suspenders fed a stack of quarters into the jukebox and "A Teenager in Love" warbled out from the dusty speakers.

Teddy Copeland Prime smiled. "Gee, I wonder how we'll get you home."

I knew this was rhetorical, because if I'd figured out the solution fifteen minutes into our dinner, surely Teddy Copeland Prime had as well. "You use the Calabi-Yau to teleport us both to your world and God Laser," I said. "Then we tweak your Theory of Almost Everything to open a gateway back to my world. Our lives have been almost identical with the exception of how we both acted in the Wren-worlds. It won't take long."

Teddy Copeland Prime shook his index finger and grinned. "Don't be so quick to assume, Teddy Copeland-X. There's at least one other significant difference between our two worlds. In mine, Dr. J. Robert Oppenheimer is dead."

#

Perro Caliente Prime was nearly identical to my Perro Caliente with the exception of two extremely important distinctions: 1) this world's Perro Caliente had not fallen into the anarchy of disrepair mine had following the revelations about Oppenheimer's Apocalypse Pocket Watch, and 2) the existence of a towering granite statue of Dr. Oppenheimer erected in the middle of the underground cemetery. Teddy Copeland Prime and I stood in front of the statue, admiring its likeness to the sometimes mentoring, sometimes sadistic founder of Perro Caliente. I ran my fingers across the inscription on its base. *Now I am become Death, the destroyer of worlds.*

"He truly had a deranged sense of humor, didn't he?" I asked.

"He sure did."

We'd arrived an hour earlier. Teddy Copeland Prime had used his Calabi-Yau to lock onto my physical properties the same way Nessa had during our many adventures throughout the Multiverse. Then we reappeared beneath the squeaky clean God Laser of Perro Caliente Prime, a mere monorail jaunt away from the fabled Dr. Oppenheimer's grave.

"How'd he die?" I asked.

"You've seen his brain, no doubt?"

I remembered that unholy antechamber hidden beneath his replica cabin. I remembered the vat of liquid and shriveled up gray wad of gum inside, what remained of Oppenheimer's once legendary mind. Some things could never be unseen. "I have."

"He asked us to shut it down, to let him die."

"When?"

"After we agreed on his replacement."

And so, we finally hit upon the chief difference between Teddy Copeland Prime's world and mine, the reason his Perro Caliente was spotless and clean, and mine had tipped into chaos. This Perro Caliente had already transitioned into a new regime. "Are you the Director?" I asked.

"I didn't say that. But I figured out the solution once I returned from our encounter in Baltimore. I knew I had to change."

If not him/me, then who? "Do you know a Nessa Newmar or Delbar Javari in this universe?"

He grinned. "Absolutely. They're going to help me send you home, X."

"Did Nessa take it over?"

"No."

"Del?"

"No."

"Old Man Reeves? Barb? Jin? Was it Thomas Arm the Momofuku bartender?

He sighed and planted a hand on my shoulder. "You need to figure this out on your own. I don't want to deny you the pleasure. Now come on, let's head to The Control Center. I've already asked them to work on sending you back."

"Who?" I asked even though I knew.

"Nessa and Delbar."

Nessa and Delbar Prime!

#

I met them on the top floor of The Control Center, in front of the same workplace terminal where I'd spent the previous month and a half toiling away in pursuit of an escape route from extinction. In many ways, Nessa and Delbar Prime were very much like the Nessa and Delbar of my own universe. Sure, Nessa Prime opted for green Air Force Ones over red, and Delbar Prime smoked Italian cigars instead of Cubans, but they otherwise resembled the two sterling gems of chaos math and engineering I had come to know and respect and admire. The biggest difference was how they greeted me.

Nessa Prime wasn't horribly disappointed in me like her inter-dimensional counterpart. And Delbar Prime didn't look ready to throttle me on account of my many failings. They both waved and smiled. Nessa Prime even hugged me. I was not a flawed asshole to these women, but a respected partner, friend, a good person, and I longed to live up to the gauntlet thrown down by this other, better me. I longed to return to my own universe and make it up to my Nessa and Delbar even if we were all doomed to burn underground.

"This is so weird," Nessa Prime said. "I've never seen two versions of the same person before. Just so cool. So cool." She took me by the shoulders. "I wonder if you and our Teddy share exactly the same memories or if there are tiny divergences along the way? What about your DNA? It'd be so cool if we could scan both of your DNA codes and see if there are any differences. What if your universe has some kind of mutation that ours doesn't or vice versa? Two Teddys. So neat."

Del Prime cleared her throat. "Nice to meet you, X. We've already coded an algorithm that'll take you home. Our universes are pretty closely linked."

Teddy Copeland Prime bent low over the control panel and threw a lever. We listened to The God Laser thunder to life, and it was still so very beautiful. The crackling blades of electricity. The isolated bands of wind. The slowly forming egg of the wormhole itself. All this time, and I still could scarcely believe The Copeland Principle had been right.

"Come on," Teddy Copeland Prime said. "We'll walk you out."

I followed them downstairs. They were whispering, and I so desperately wanted to know what scientific solutions they were cooking up next, what marvels they hoped to unleash upon their dying earth and Multiverse beyond. They talked and talked, and at last I understood how things worked there. I understood who ran Perro Caliente Prime in the wake of Oppenheimer's death. It wasn't Teddy Prime, nor Nessa Prime, or Delbar Prime, not even Thomas Arm. They ran it together. A triumvirate of ambitious prodigies. I smacked my forehead. The futurist, the tough-as-nails savior, and the cynical nostalgic. We balanced each other. And because of that, we could push Perro Caliente so much further than Oppenheimer who'd remained separated from other people. I couldn't believe how obvious the solution was. It'd been staring me in the face since our very first night sharing drinks at the Trinity. Maybe I wasn't emotionally capable of running Perro Caliente all by myself. But with Nessa and Delbar? I could finally chart a future.

"You run this place together, don't you?" I asked. "All three of you?"

Nessa turned and grinned. "That's our Teddy."

"Fuck," I said.

We lined up at the base of the walkway. It was time to return to my own world where maybe I could convince my versions of Nessa and Del that we could run Perro Caliente together. It was a longshot after the way I'd behaved, but I finally had hope. It was the best I could do.

"I want to thank you for everything, Teddy Copeland Prime."

"No problem, Teddy Copeland-X."

We were awkward then. In any other circumstance, a goodbye hug would've been totally appropriate. But embracing a parallel version of myself? It felt oddly shallow, the sentimental equivalent of masturbation.

"I guess this is goodbye then," he said.

I rubbed at the back of my neck. "Not necessarily. You have the algorithm for my world now, right? So you can enter at any time. I was thinking maybe you could come catch up with me in a week or so."

He blinked, and a split second later, I recognized it. The slight widening of the eyes, the upward tug of the lips. He'd reached the same conclusion I had about the neon potential of multiple Teddy/Nessa/Delbar triumvirates working in tandem. "Oh, I get it. You're a clever one, Teddy Copeland-X."

"See you in a week then, Teddy Copeland Prime," I said.

"See you in a week."

I walked toward the wormhole, but before I ran inside, I turned back for one final glimpse at my parallel friends. I saw something noteworthy just before I was sucked back home. I saw Nessa reach out for Teddy's hand. They smiled at each other, not like friends, but something more. It was a tender moment, something I realized I truly wanted for myself after my long exile from other people. But I couldn't dwell on that picturesque image. There were still so many more obstacles ahead, and I finally had to return home and face the music.

It was finally time to confront the Hologram of Dr. J. Robert Oppenheimer.

RISING STARS

My homecoming was greeted with a curious silence. I materialized beneath The God Laser, and this time there was no reassuring Nessa Newmar in The Control Center above, no gun-wielding Oppenheimer hiding in the proverbial bushes, no cries of protesters burning Perro Caliente to the ground. There was nothing but a silence as deafening as anything I could imagine, a black wave reverberating between the great walls of our facilities. There was no denying it. I had found myself alone.

I walked through The Control Center, but there were no trains waiting for me at the monorail platform. For a brief, nauseating moment, I feared I was already too late, that Perro Caliente had been purged of all human souls, that Oppenheimer had descended into his secret chamber and pulled the plug on his much-maligned brain. But before I was totally consumed by these many doubts, a train covered in graffiti emerged from the tunnel and rolled to a stop at my platform. The metal doors peeled apart, and I literally gasped at who I saw inside. It was the seventh smartest person on earth herself, Dr. Delbar Javari, a rolling cooler of bottled water at her feet, a megaphone clutched in her hands, a thick Cuban protruding precariously from her lips. She tapped her heels against the floor when she saw me. "Where the hell have you been, donkey? I thought you left for the surface."

I wrapped Del tight in my arms, and she went stiff in my embrace. Never before had we hugged, but I clung to her then, so genuinely overjoyed at coming across a friendly face from my own native universe.

"Delbar," I said into her hair, "I know I've let you down. I know I've let everyone down. But I want you to know how sorry I am, how I'll never let it happen again. From here on out, I'm dedicated to the cause. You've been such a good friend to me, and if you give me a chance, I'll make it up to you. I promise."

Del pushed me away. "Jeez, calm down with all the feels." It suddenly occurred to me that maybe Delbar was even worse at talking about her emotions than I was. Or maybe I was just projecting. Maybe Del was the most well-adjusted of all of us. Maybe she always had been. "I'll think about maybe forgiving you, ok?" she said. "Everyone, with the exception of yours truly makes mistakes. I understand that. What matters is you're here now."

I gestured toward the cooler and megaphone. "What happened?"

The monorail shot through the southbound tunnel. "The rioters blew a hole in the SimuSky where the elevator used to be. They set up a giant pulley, and everyone who wanted to leave left." She clicked her tongue. "But they turned the

Mezzanine upside down in the process. So many buildings burned to the ground. They mostly left the scientific sites alone, but we're going to need to rebuild."

"Who's left?"

"Maybe a hundred of us gathered at the Trinity, mostly scientists, a few lay people. Thomas Arm's grilling burgers." She kicked at the cooler. "I'm looking for more survivors, but you're the only one I've found."

"Where's Nessa? There's something I have to talk to you both about."

Del raised an eyebrow. "She went looking for survivors this morning. I haven't seen her since. Said she was going where the apartments used to be. Said she was looking for you."

Before I could dwell on what exactly "where the apartments used to be" meant, our train entered the Mezzanine and I at last bore witness to the fate that had befallen our once glorious Perro Caliente. As Delbar had warned, the rioters had torn through our home. A quarter of the buildings had been burned to the ground, and oh, how chilling it was to sail along the monorail high above the smoking ashes. We zoomed past a train line that had been blown up in the ensuing melee, and even the buildings that had survived had not gone undamaged. Windows were blown out, front doors torn down by looters no doubt looking for electronics or other valuables before returning to the surface and the five-to-ten years remaining to them on planet Earth. But the most terrifying difference in this strange, new Perro Caliente was the jagged hole blown into the now blinking SimuSky. The blue sky and orange sun blinked black and red, a rickety-looking pulley system swinging beneath the hole. All of this was on account of Oppenheimer's stubbornness and refusal to trust anyone but himself or those precious few he deemed worthy, deluded misanthropes like me and Nessa's father, men who only realized their stupidity when it was too late.

Del put a reassuring hand on my shoulder. "We'll rebuild. But I need to know what happened to you. I haven't seen you since Oppenheimer told us the results. I need to know if I can trust you again."

I explained my sorry tale, everything from finding Wren's grave in Wilkes-Barre to Teddy Copeland Prime sending me home. I only excluded the bit about the Prime Triumvirate, a pivotal revelation I wanted to save until our trio of ambitious prodigies was at last reunited. Delbar played the role of a good friend to a tee, chastising me when I did something foolish, urging me on when I accomplished something promising. She no doubt had been the emotional rock of our weird little underground trio, and I told her so and emphasized how much I appreciated her.

"I know," she said. "I'm bodacious."

The monorail shuddered to a stop, and we arrived at the metal platform for the apartment buildings. It's difficult to put into words exactly how I felt as I followed Delbar down the steps. Most of the buildings were gone, burned to ashes. Even Old Man Reeves' bodega had been toppled, and I was keenly reminded of that annihilated Alaska where I had stumbled across my own corpse. How strange it was to strut through the wreckage of my life. Only this time, it was no parallel world. It was home, a grim omen of what was lurking for us in less than a decade's time. Del called out on her megaphone for any survivors, for any Perro Caliente faithful that had barricaded themselves indoors at the first sounds of frenzy and destruction, and I tried not to acknowledge how unlikely it would be to find someone in this mess. How did people like Delbar and Nessa even exist? How were they able to remain hopeful no matter the circumstances they found themselves in? It didn't matter if their family was murdered by militia or killed in a random car crash. It didn't matter if they found themselves trapped in an underground apocalypse. They strove forward, perennially casting light on solutions. It was a quality I wanted to duplicate, a reaffirming nectar that might at last render me worthy of this place. We walked and we walked and we walked, and finally we came across the last known whereabouts of Dr. Nessa Newmar: Housing Unit Seven. It too had been burned to the ground in a fit of petulance. All that remained was a scrap heap, mounds of rubble and the shattered bones of support beams. A strange thought occurred to me. What if she'd been inside when the building went down? What if she died searching for me?

"Nessa!" I ran to the edge of the debris and heaved a hunk of metal out of the way. "Nessa!"

I could scarcely imagine what would happen to me if I lost Nessa too, if I became newly burdened not just with the weight of one untimely death, but two. Delbar joined me, and together we dug, dug, dug until our hands bled, and I felt that familiar wave of guilty bile rise from my stomach into my throat. Perhaps this was the true essence of one Teddy Copeland, doomed to forever fail those he most cared about, doomed to outlast everyone and drag their sorry tales into the unblinking maw of the end times. I shoved a shattered support beam out of our way, then another, then another, and not once did we come across anything that might signal we were getting close, that there was even a modicum of hope we might find Nessa unharmed in the debris. But Delbar and I persisted like Katasumi, her fingers bleeding as she dug out the powder of her mother's bones. I thought of her then, caught in her own apocalypse, yet another doomsday brought on by our glorious leader.

I can't say how much time passed exactly. All I could focus on was the realization that while I was sharing drinks with Wren Wells at Double Daughter's, Nessa might have been buried alive searching for stupid Teddy Copeland. I dug out a tattered couch cushion with my fingernails and remembered that awkward evening when Nessa invited me back to her room, tangible proof of my many failings. And then, when it felt like even Delbar's eternal hope had been extinguished like a melted candle, we heard her voice calling out to us from the other side of the rubble, the delicate song of a mourning dove.

"Did you find something neat?" she called. "Did you find something awesome?"

We looked up, and there was Nessa Newmar carefully climbing across the top of the debris, her cheeks smudged with dirt but clearly no worse for wear. It was obvious she hadn't been buried in the riots, and I collapsed on the ground at the sight of her. I was exhausted but so utterly relieved that Nessa Newmar was fine.

"Where the hell were you?" Delbar shouted.

Nessa climbed down, shrugging as she did so. "I started looking for our pal Copeland over there, but while I was digging around, I found this strange little weed growing beneath the cracked foundation. Can you imagine weeds growing this far beneath the surface of the earth? It was really neat, you guys. We should send it for analysis."

We stared at her.

"What happened to you?" Nessa asked me.

"Oppenheimer banished me to a parallel world, and I found my way back." I shook my head and laughed. How strange life was. How peculiar. I reached out for a handful of ash, and it suddenly occurred to me that all three of our apartments had been destroyed. Obviously, I'd understood that the moment I saw the heap of ashes, but I hadn't fully teased out the ramifications while digging for Nessa. This meant my clothes were gone, my computer, everything. And then I realized my wedding band and final photo of Wren must have been destroyed too. They were lost to me now, and all I was left with was memory, weak and malleable, fleeting flickers, ghost whispers. A younger, less nuanced Teddy Copeland would have dove headfirst into the ashes, content to bury himself for the flimsy hope that perhaps that mythical safe had not been melted clean by flame. But I knew those trinkets didn't really matter. Unlike Alaska, my underground apartment was Spartan, devoid of trash, practically empty. I understood this was because of how little time I spent there compared to Alaska, how often I was among friends at the Trinity, among other people. I had finally managed to rejoin the world. My feelings for Wren Wells had been purged, and what I'd truly fallen in love with in the fever dream of my own mourning was tumbling down the rabbit hole of needy obsession. That was over for me now. I was twenty-eight-years-old on the precipice of global destruction. It was finally time to march into adulthood.

I grabbed my knees and stood up. I had to tell them my bright, shiny idea delivered from across the Multiverse. "I met another version of us. Another me, another Nessa, another Del. They helped me come home, and they helped me realize something else."

Nessa snatched a bottle of water from Delbar's cooler and chugged. "You met another me? Wow. Lucky you. Was she the coolest?"

I put my arm around her shoulder. "In their universe, Oppenheimer was dead. The three of them took over Perro Caliente together as a triumvirate. I know you guys have basically been running things the past few days, but maybe, maybe you could let me help you? Could we run this place together?"

Cue dual expressions of disbelief.

"Hear me out. We balance each other. Nessa's the futurist. Delbar's the tough-as-nails savior. I'm the cynical nostalgic. We'll keep each other in line and spur each other on. Oppenheimer never maximized the resources of this place because he never trusted anyone. Some skepticism is good, necessary. That's where I'll come in. But we have to be more open, more forward-thinking. We need to at least try to save everyone even if that is admittedly idealistic and maybe impossible. We can toy with The God Laser while still working on your secret prediction project that'll better the world for everyone. Look. You guys have helped me become someone better. Can you imagine what we could accomplish if we ran this place together?"

For once, I was the one playing the role of the optimist. Both Nessa and Del glanced around the wreckage and the gaping wound left behind in the SimuSky.

"There's a hundred of us left, right?" I asked. "And most of the scientific sites are untouched. We can rebuild, recruit, and redouble our efforts toward preventing the end of the world. Come on. What else are we going to do? Can we really leave this place and return to our regular lives knowing the apocalypse is coming in less than a decade? We have to band together." I grabbed both of their shoulders. I couldn't explain why exactly, but I felt on the verge of tears, the way a caterpillar must feel in its final moments trapped in its cocoon. I so desperately wanted to rebuke Oppenheimer's call for isolation in the digital mountains behind his cabin. I wanted to be part of the whole. I wanted to be on the front lines with Nessa and Delbar and every other messy, amazing human being. "Even if the world is ending, we have to keep trying to be better people. We have to keep trying to fix this. Even if it's impossible. We have to. That's all we can do. That's the best we can hope for. Come on. Come on. The alternative is giving up, and I refuse." I was shaking. "Please don't make me endure this alone."

Nessa wiped the tears from my eyes. "Ok, Teddy. I'm in."

Del shrugged. "I'll do it if you quit with the waterworks. My god." She handed me a tissue from her lab coat. "Here's the real issue though. Oppenheimer just forced you at gunpoint into a parallel world, right? So what makes you think he's going to let us take this place over?"

I blew my nose and turned stone-faced. It was difficult to be badass after tearing up and blowing bright streams of snot onto your pal's tissue, but I was trying, and wasn't that half the battle anyway? "Then we force him. He wants to die anyway. He wants to turn this place over. Let's let him off the hook."

Nessa looked longingly in the direction of her weeds. "Here we go again."

"Nobody's seen him in hours," Del said. "We should check his cabin, but he shut off the train line that runs there yesterday."

"Then we'll walk."

"We can't walk," Nessa said. "It's like twelve miles without the monorail."

"Wait a second," Del said. "Do you guys remember the episode of *Your Romantic Star-Filled Journey* where Kim and

Park—God rest their souls—got stranded in the Desert Dome with those professional wrestlers from Glamarama 17?"

"Of course," Nessa said breathlessly.

"They found horses and rode to the escape hatch. Oppenheimer's horses are wandering around here somewhere. The scientists who worked with them bolted during the purge and let them loose. I think I saw some by the sushi place a few blocks over."

And so, we marched off to find those sushi-enthusiast horses.

#

It took an hour of wandering around the ravaged buildings of Perro Caliente before we came upon the ruins of The Fish Dies at Midnight and, more importantly, three of Oppenheimer's majestic steeds. The horses loitered by a shattered fire hydrant, licking at the sputtering puddle left behind in its wake. I inched closer to the beasts, but they seemed not to recognize me away from Oppenheimer's SimuDesert. I raised both arms in the gentle supplication of a woodland elf and shouted, "Nice ponies! Nice ponies!" They stopped drinking and stared at me like high school cheerleaders stunned when approached by a nerd at a party, a look I knew all too well. I patted the horse I usually rode and whispered sweetly into his coat. I held fast to the saddle and, after a great deal of struggling, pulled myself atop the creature, reins clutched tightly between my fists. I turned to Nessa and Delbar and shouted, "See? That wasn't so hard."

"Can we name the horses?" Nessa asked as she approached the second animal. "I'll call mine Li'l Ada Lovelace."

Del removed her heels. “Then this one’s Li’l Anita Borg. She’s a little boss bitch, isn’t she? Aren’t you a little boss bitch, Li’l Anita Borg?”

We accustomed ourselves to our beasts, and I pointed in the direction of the monorail tunnel. I kicked at my horse’s underbelly just like I’d seen John Wayne do a thousand times on cable television, and just like that, our trio was off, racing toward Oppenheimer’s replica cabin and our greater destiny beyond.

#

We shot out the other side of the monorail tunnel like a gaggle of triumphant heroes, all with the exception of Delbar who clutched her heels tightly to her chest and spat a litany of Iranian curses at mighty boss bitch Li’l Anita Borg. Nothing stood between us and the replica ranch save for the yellow sand of Oppenheimer’s SimuDesert, and we crossed that obstacle on horseback like it was nothing, just one more step toward the inevitability of our assent to the Perro Caliente throne.

I unhooked my loafers from the saddle strap and disembarked from my loyal steed. “Horses,” I said, “if we manage to leave this replica cabin alive, I promise we’ll return for you and provide a feast the likes of which you’ve never seen.”

My horse’s stupid face was unchanged, but I felt a peculiar kinship with our animals. They sauntered away, and we did the same, ambling toward Oppenheimer’s ranch like Old West gunslingers minus the guns. In my heart of hearts, I didn’t believe Oppenheimer would actually murder us, but I never would’ve guessed he was capable of banishing me to another universe or trapping us underground. I remembered the Genbaku Dome in Hiroshima and steeled myself for whatever was to come.

"Are we ready?" I asked.

They answered with their faces, more solemn and determined than I'd even imagined when I first glimpsed the possibility of assembling our triumvirate in Perro Caliente Prime. We were ready, but that overconfident swagger withered to dust the moment we climbed Oppenheimer's porch and saw his screen door eerily ajar. What if he wasn't there? What if, like Old Man Reeves and Barb and Jin and all the other protesters, Oppenheimer had fled to the surface? What if some drunken protester had made the same journey we had and shot him dead where he stood? Could holograms even be killed that way? And what if at the very moment Oppenheimer was in the chamber that held his brain punching in some secret self-destruct code that would kill us all?

Nessa squeezed my shoulder in a show of solidarity. "Let's get this motherfucker."

I went in first, Nessa and Delbar tight behind. We found the Hologram of Dr. J. Robert Oppenheimer where we always did: in his armchair in front of the fireplace, an almost empty glass of bourbon clutched tightly in his fist. He looked defeated and pitiful. His hat sat limply at his feet, and for the first time we saw his craggy head exposed and his few wisps of translucent blue hair. His wrists trembled ever so slightly, and I was surprised by how thin they were, more bone than flesh. He appeared so utterly beaten, and I could barely reconcile this ghoul with the atomic titan who had first introduced the world to Fat Man and Little Boy, the man who banished me at gunpoint. I actually pitied him.

Oppenheimer looked up from his bourbon with the same disinterest as a cat prodded by a too anxious master. But then he recognized me, the scapegoat, the one he'd exiled to the edges of the Multiverse, and his eyes went wide with alarm.

"How is this possible?"

We surrounded him. I knew he was asking how I'd returned from the final world of The Wren Algorithm without a Calabi-Yau, but the question felt so much larger like asking how Perro Caliente itself was possible or how he'd come to be intimidated by his trio of ambitious prodigies or even when he'd become so ancient.

"I met another me. He took me to his Perro Caliente, and he and his versions of Nessa and Delbar sent me home."

This piqued his interest. "You went to another Perro Caliente?"

"Yes."

"And where was I?"

"Dead."

Dr. Oppenheimer nodded and finished his drink. He was still wearing his lab coat, and I was half-afraid he might produce his pistol. "And who ran Perro Caliente in this other world?"

Dr. Delbar Javari stepped forward. "We did."

Then Nessa. "The three of us. Together."

Oppenheimer had to smile at that. He refilled his glass and bent to retrieve his hat. "Let me guess. Now you three have delusions of grandeur and think you can actually take this place over and run it effectively, is that right?"

"You got it," I said.

He laughed through gritted teeth. "And may I ask why exactly? I've seen the damage. My dream is dead. Perro Caliente is ash. Go home. Why would you want to run a mausoleum?"

I felt like the answer had been accumulating in my bones ever since Perro Caliente Prime, since seeing Wren's grave firsthand, since that missed opportunity outside Nessa's apartment, since encountering infinite Teddy Copelands in Eastern Market, since meeting Delbar and Nessa, since writing The Copeland Principle, since Wren's death, our wedding, her leukemia announcement, her screaming voice washing over me at the battle of the bands, ever since the big bang and the very origins of the Multiverse itself. It had been building up inside of me, a pure beam of light that proved I was slowly becoming a better, kinder Teddy. Proof that I one day would be whole again, that my life could move beyond the damage done at twenty-one, that I would not recede into Oppenheimer's isolation. I had endured. "Everything ends," I said. "You either accept it and become a positive force for good, or you wallow in your own despair." I threw the Apocalypse Pocket Watch at his feet. "I'm done wallowing, Oppenheimer. I'm not going to end up like you."

Oppenheimer stared at the watch for a long time, the very symbol of the inevitability that would one day befall everything and everyone. He spoke directly to Nessa. "Do you remember on your first day when I took you to your father's grave and told you he spearheaded a second project in addition to The God Laser? It was Rising Stars."

Nessa slammed her palm like a hammy Sherlock Holmes. "I knew it."

"Rising Stars," Oppenheimer continued, "was launched as a global campaign to find my successor. The ISC was merely a front. Two hundred and fifty adolescents won the competition, the best young minds in the world, you three included, and Elgin and I tracked all of your careers. Only one hundred and ninety-seven of the winners actually went into the sciences. Only eighty-four went on for their PhDs. Before Elgin died, I told him I selected you three as the finalists and wanted to bring you here for the last stage of the competition, an on-site interview where I could survey how you dealt with The God Laser project up close and personal before picking my successor. He agreed to Copeland and Javari, but not his daughter. He was terrified of Nessa becoming like him, an underground husk obsessed with the past."

With great difficulty, Oppenheimer hoisted himself to his feet. He lit a clove and went over to the screen door to gaze upon his SimuDesert and the SimuStars so high above.

"I told Elgin that when the time was right, I'd let Copeland pick our chaos mathematician from a list of twelve Rising Stars who specialized in it, including Nessa. If Copeland chose her too, so be it. And, as you kiddos know, Copeland agreed with me."

We couldn't help but exchange excited glances. It was really going to happen. We were going to run an underground research laboratory complete with the most powerful particle accelerator on earth! Surely, that's where Oppenheimer's speech was headed.

"You're probably excited, aren't you? Don't be." His expression turned cold.

"As far as I'm concerned, none of you won this final stage of Rising Stars." He pointed at Nessa and Delbar. "Too naively hopeful." Then he directed his ire at me. "Too obsessed with your poor, dead wife." Oppenheimer tossed his clove through the open door. He returned to his chair and glared. "I don't believe in any of you. I've lost touch with the people. I'm tired. I'm exhausted. I want out. There's nothing that can be done to stop the end of everything. You're right, Copeland. Everything dies, and nothing you can do will change that.

You're all going to die. Every Earth throughout the Multiverse is going to die." He was practically snarling. "You want the constant burden of this monkey house, the incessant life-or-death choices? You think it's so easy to be the ones in charge, the elder statesmen? You got it. Congratulations, children. Perro Caliente is yours." He looked at each of us, his eyes on the verge of tears. "I'm beaten. I'm through. I've failed."

#

The Hologram of Dr. J. Robert Oppenheimer agreed to turn over the Directorship of Perro Caliente to our triumvirate but only on the condition that we accompanied him beneath his replica ranch and were present for his death. We set his makeshift funeral for a week's time, and in that period a kind of strained stability returned to Perro Caliente. The monorail came back online, albeit on a reduced schedule, and the hundred scientists and laypeople who remained underground were steadfast in their belief that we would press on under new leadership, that even in the face of Armageddon we would strive toward scientific understanding and hope. We all relocated to Housing Unit Twelve, one of the few apartment buildings left standing post-riot, and as I showered in preparation for Oppenheimer's funeral, I couldn't help but feel cautiously optimistic. The future beckoned.

I'd agreed to meet Nessa and Delbar in the common room, but only Nessa was ready when I arrived. She looked the same as ever—still sported her t-shirt and lab coat, jeans and Forces despite the fact we were funeral-bound—but there was no mistaking how much things had changed since those fortunate drinks shared in Indianapolis so long ago. I waved shyly at her, and to her credit, Nessa waved back. She did not run screaming in the opposite direction, a cruel fate I probably deserved. I coughed into my fist and couldn't help remember that other common room, that night in Housing Unit Seven when Nessa invited me to her bedroom. I wouldn't make the same mistake twice. I'd appeared ten minutes early on purpose. Delbar was always on time for everything. Nessa was always early. We smiled at each other, and it finally felt like I'd discovered the off-the-beaten-path life I'd so yearned for in Indianapolis.

"Hey," I said.

"Hey," she said.

"You have a minute?"

She rolled her eyes and tapped her watch. "Ten."

I squeezed my fists so hard my knuckles turned white. Facing down atomic holograms was one thing, but Nessa Newmar was another matter entirely. But I understood what I had to do, the final steps necessary to end the self-exile I'd set out upon since flying to Anchorage. "I want to apologize for all that stuff with Wren," I said, "about that night outside your apartment. It wasn't fair to you. It was inconsiderate. I've been a selfish, petty person these last few years, but I'm really trying to change. I understand now that no one can fix me or transform me into the best possible version of myself. It has to start with me, and there are no grand, sweeping transformations. It's an everyday thing. I just want you to know I think you're amazing, and I admire the hell out of you, and I so deeply regret how badly I messed things up. All I can do is keep trying to be better. Is there any way you could forgive me?"

She waited a beat, let me stew a moment before saying, "Yeah. I guess I could maybe forgive you."

I breathed a sigh of relief. "Holy crap. Wow. That's awesome. If you weren't capable of forgiving me, man, that would make working together really awkward, am I right?" I put my hands in my pockets. "Hey. Would you want to grab dinner sometime? You like food, right? Food's pretty cool. You want to go on a date sometime, Dr. Nessa Newmar? A date involving food of some kind?"

She shook her head in disbelief. And for a moment, I thought that would be the end of things, that I'd been kindly rebuffed by our resident optimist. But then she did something very un-Nessa like. She grabbed my tie and pulled me close. Nessa kissed me slowly, sweetly, a terribly charming moment. I held her waist and prayed to whatever higher power who still might listen to me—God, Einstein, Darwin, anyone—that we wouldn't fail each other. Nessa's kiss was an act of faith in an age of fantastic desperation. It was all we had.

Delbar emerged in the hallway, her eyebrows arched knowingly. For once, she didn't rattle off a sarcastic remark, and we followed her solemnly down the stairwell and into the monorail. We were ready for the task at hand. It was time to send Dr. J. Robert Oppenheimer into the great unknown voyage of death.

He greeted us silently at his cabin, still looking as resigned and defeated as he had the week before. We said nothing, just a quick series of nods that seemed to signify so much more than they ever really could, before Oppenheimer led us to the fireplace and pulled back the choker. The bookshelf slid to the right, and the elevator that would take us to his submerged brain was again revealed.

For the very first time, Nessa and Delbar saw the abomination of Oppenheimer's brain trapped in that vat of swirling blue liquid. I could tell Nessa was disturbed but trying to hide it from the way she fiddled with the hem of her t-shirt, and I reached out for her. Oppenheimer, the physical manifestation of all our scientific elders, was leaving earth for good. If we sought comfort and solutions, we had to find them in each other and our contemporaries. No longer could we look toward the guidance of titans and generations past. The elevator touched the floor, and we followed Oppenheimer to the cylindrical control panel layered in dust and levers. He popped open the glass compartment that protected the red ABORT button, the grand kill switch.

"Well," he said, turning to face us, "I guess this is it. I'm not going to lie to you and tell you I think you're going to succeed. You're not. The only inevitability if your goal is to save everyone is that you're going to fail in spectacular, disheartening ways. I'll leave you with what General Groves told me when he hired me to run Los Alamos. 'Don't fuck it up, kid.'"

Oppenheimer slammed the button before we could reply. There was no fanfare. The blue waters of the cryo-chamber turned red, and his brain sank to the bottom of the tube amid a flurry of bubbles. His hologram simply faded out the way a flickering television signal disappeared in the age before cable and satellite, in the age of antennas and radio waves, when we knew there were Technicolor worlds vibrating out there beyond our grasp, knowledge that we only needed the right equipment to reach them.

J. Robert Oppenheimer was gone, and we were on our own.

Nessa was captivated by Oppenheimer's dead brain. "What now?"

"I've got an idea," I said.

EPILOGUE: THE INFINITY COUNCIL

The appointed hour finally arrived, and Drs. Nessa Newmar, Delbar Javari, and I stood outside the meeting room in Conference Center Four, a building we'd ordered emptied in preparation for the day's significant festivities. For the special occasion, I'd donned my very best tailored suit, shined-up Italian loafers, and a rather fetching knit tie if I do say so myself. Delbar sported her prototypical skirt suit and heels, and Nessa, my Nessa, showed up wearing jeans and a t-shirt. I wouldn't have had it any other way.

"How do I look?" I asked her.

Nessa frowned. "Do you have to dress up for everything? You make me feel guilty for not dressing up. And man, I do not want to dress up. You look ok. Not terrible. I'm not embarrassed to stand next to you is what I'm saying."

"Thanks for the boost of confidence, Dr. Newmar."

"No problem whatsoever, Dr. Copeland." She tightened my knot.

Delbar groaned. "Ugh, you two are the absolute worst. Is it going to be like this all the time? Am I going to have to deal with you two making googly eyes at each other every day for the rest of my life?"

"Not every day," I said.

"The worst. The absolute worst ever."

Delbar entered the conference room and Nessa and I followed like a pair of yukking teenagers. Just like we requested, the room was devoid of all pomp and circumstance. All we needed was something large enough to house a circular conference table and thirty chairs, and we stressed to the folks in Scheduling that no one should feel more or less important than anyone else in this particular meeting. It was key to the entire enterprise. I placed a hand on one of the chairs and checked my watch. It was time.

We heard the familiar churning of Calabi-Yau Teleportations, but it wasn't just one human materializing in our world, it was twenty-seven. They appeared around the table. Doppelgangers of Nessa, clones of Delbar, alternate versions of me. They wore similar clothes and nearly identical faces. Ten versions of our Perro Caliente Triumvirate gathered around a conference table miles beneath the surface of the earth. The future was now.

"Everyone, welcome." I outstretched my arms. "I'm so glad you could join us today, but before we get started, can we go around the room and state our names to avoid any confusion? And please, please sit down." We sat. "As you've no doubt already guessed, I'm Teddy Copeland-X. Thank you for meeting in our universe this week."

"Teddy Copeland Prime," Teddy Copeland Prime said.

"Nessa Newmar of Earth I."

"Delbar Javari Omega."

"Teddy Copeland of Universe A"

"Ultimate Nessa Newmar."

"Delbar Javari of the Mondo Universe."

Around and around they went until we came to *Theo* Copeland weakly whispering his name to the crowd. God, how we all hated *Theo* and his myriad pretentions, but if our last ditch, harebrained scheme had any hope of working, we needed that froo-froo bastard. But I could still feel the eight other like-minded Teddy Copelands resisting rolling their eyes at affected *Theo*. What a name!

Nessa cleared her throat. "Last time we met, we agreed that we would each go out and recruit nine other Triumvirates in charge of nine other Perro Calientes with access to nine other God Lasers. I'm assuming everyone met their objectives, right?"

There was a murmur of agreement throughout the room.

"Perfect," Delbar said. "That means we have an army of one hundred Triumvirates running one hundred God Lasers all across the Multiverse united under a single, noble purpose."

"Infinity Council," I said, "I'm not sure if this is going to work. But as you know, there really is a chance that if we pool our resources and findings and personnel, we might be able to find a solution for extinction before the Apocalypse Pocket Watch ticks down to zero. We've been behind the proverbial eight ball since before we were even born, and I know Oppenheimer didn't believe this would work, but I want to thank all of you for joining us. It doesn't matter if

it'll work or not. Nobody's coming to save us, but we're still going to try." My hands were as steady as rock. "We're trying. That has to count for something."

ACKNOWLEDGMENTS

First, thanks always to my wife, the curious, the thoughtful, the intelligent, the beautiful Theresa J. Beckhusen. When everything feels overwhelmingly dark, you give me strength, and I hope I provide the same for you.

Thanks also to my parents for always supporting whatever weird interest or subculture I momentarily find myself obsessed with—everything from pro wrestling to *Goodfellas* to Richard Yates to *Skyrim*.

Thanks to Katie Coyle and Eric Kroczek for reading very early versions of this manuscript and providing essential feedback.

And a very special thanks to Jeffrey Condran, Robert Peluso, and everyone at Braddock Avenue Books for championing my writing for the past six years and counting. I can't express enough how much your work has meant to me.

Salvatore Pane is the author of the novel *Last Call in the City of Bridges* in addition to the nonfiction *Mega Man 3*. His work has appeared in *American Short Fiction*, *Indiana Review*, *Hobart*, and many other venues. He holds an MFA in Creative Writing from the University of Pittsburgh and teaches English at the University of St. Thomas. He was born and raised in Scranton, Pennsylvania and can be reached at www.salvatore-pane.com.

Photo credit: Josh DeHonney.

CPSIA information can be obtained
at www.ICGtesting.com
Printed in the USA
FFHW020951070119
50086539-54928FF